PRAISE FOR KATHE

Seven Sisters
(Australian title for *Kill Yours, Kill Mine*)

SHORTLISTED FOR BEST CRIME FICTION IN THE 2023 NED KELLY AWARDS

"[This] taut, morally ambiguous thriller measures out a precise cocktail of parable and revenge fantasy."

—*Sydney Morning Herald*

"A love letter to Hitchcock and Highsmith, fueled by women's rage. Once you start, you won't be able to stop."

—Hayley Scrivenor, bestselling author

"An intense, page-turning psychological thriller that grips the reader with two-handed fury. Perfect for fans of Patricia Highsmith, Candice Fox, and Jacqueline Bublitz, *Seven Sisters* will have you questioning your idea of justice and how far you would go to help others—including taking an eye for an eye."

—*Books+Publishing*

"A cracking thriller that I could not put down for a second... This is a chilling, compelling, and completely addictive descent down the rabbit hole."

—Dinuka McKenzie, author of the Detective Kate Miles crime fiction series

"Compelling reading! *Seven Sisters* is the ultimate fight-back novel."

—Vikki Petraitis, award-winning true crime author

Just Murdered: A Ms. Fisher's Modern Murder Mystery

"A sprightly pace, amusing characters, and a vividly rendered Melbourne bode well for the sequel. Fans of Kerry Greenwood's Phryne Fisher series will want to check out this one."

—*Publishers Weekly*

"A splendid read, with an authentic '60s flavour. I recommend it unreservedly."

—Kerry Greenwood

"Based on the hit TV sequel, this has all the pizzazz of the Phryne Fisher novels updated for a younger generation."

—*Kirkus Reviews*

"A fun, fast-paced read, *Just Murdered* also has a great heroine. Peregrine is intelligent and independent, and her jack-of-all-trades background allows her to cleverly unspool the threads of the mystery."

—*BookPage*

Also by Katherine Kovacic

Ms. Fisher's Modern Murder Mysteries
Just Murdered

True Crime
The Schoolgirl Strangler

The Alex Clayton Art Mysteries
The Shifting Landscape
Painting in the Shadows
The Portrait of Molly Dean

KILL YOURS, KILL MINE

KILL YOURS, KILL MINE

KATHERINE KOVACIC

Cover design by Nicole Lecht
Cover photo © VladimirFLoyd/iStockPhoto

Published by Poisoned Pen Press, an imprint of Sourcebooks
P.O. Box 4410, Naperville, Illinois 60567-4410
(630) 961-3900
sourcebooks.com

Originally published as *Seven Sisters* in 2023 in Australia by *HarperCollinsPublishers* Australia Pty Limited, Sydney, NSW 2000, Australia.

Cataloging-in-Publication Data is on file with the Library of Congress.

Printed and bound in the United States of America.
VP 10 9 8 7 6 5 4 3 2 1

For all the strong women in my life.
Different battles, same inspirational grit.

PROLOGUE

The handle of the carving knife was slippery in her palm. She couldn't tear her gaze away from the body.

Suddenly, his eyes flew open. His chest rose. Blood bubbled at his lips, and he made a wet, sucking sound.

She looked at the knife in her hand, back at the man on her lounge. When he pulled in another breath, she could see the effort it cost him.

Seconds passed, or was it minutes? She became aware of sirens in the distance, getting louder. Leaning close, she watched as he registered her face. Then she raised the knife and plunged it in a second time, feeling it glance off bone before finding the softness between two ribs.

His eyes widened, his body arching. She yanked out the knife and flung it aside.

Behind her, a floorboard creaked.

ONE

"I should go." Naomi pushed her hands back across her head, pressing hard. Her eyes felt gritty, but there were no tears—not anymore.

"We still have five minutes," said Mia. "But if you need to go..."

Naomi bent to pick up her handbag. She paused, staring down, looking at nothing, thinking about everything. She took a deep breath and peered at Mia from beneath her too-long fringe.

Mia cocked her head. "What is it, Naomi?"

"The name of your practice. The Pleiades. Stars." Naomi left her bag on the carpet and sank back into her chair. "When I arrived for our first appointment, I didn't know what to expect; the New Age bullshit name didn't match with anything I'd read about you. I figured it was worth a try, but I was prepared to leave as soon as you pulled out the crystals." Naomi smiled crookedly. "I'm glad I was wrong. And I've been meaning to ask—why The Pleiades?"

Mia smoothed her black hair, the impact of its old-Hollywood cut enhanced by a white-streaked fringe and Mia's own pale skin. Her style always impressed Naomi, so different from that of every other therapist she'd ever seen. Different, in fact, from that of most women.

She fixed Naomi with an appraising stare. "Do you know the story of the Pleiades? I mean, beyond the astronomical side of things, do you know the Greek mythology?"

Naomi laughed. "Shit, you're kidding me." She held up her hands and wiggled her fingers. "Deep down you are all woo-woo. I almost fell for it."

"Hear me out." Mia waved Naomi's teasing aside. "The Pleiades are—were—women, and there are two versions of the myth that matter to me. In one they take their own lives out of grief over the loss of the Hyades, who were their sisters. In the other, they get transformed into stars by Zeus to escape the unwanted attentions of the giant Orion, but that bastard keeps chasing them across the sky. You can see why that's relevant to what I do."

"I guess so."

"What struck me about those myths was that they're rubbish." Naomi sat up straighter, hearing the fire in Mia's voice.

"My professional goal is to subvert them. I don't want there to be women who are forced to run for their lives or whose only escape from an abuser is death—I want to help women to be strong, to fight. To face down the demons and win." Mia stood abruptly and strode across to the window. For a moment she stared out at the sun-drenched garden, shoulders tense, then she turned back to Naomi, her face set and determined. She folded her arms and focused on her client.

Naomi exhaled a long breath, opened her mouth to speak, closed it again. "When you say 'face down the demons,' you mean metaphorically, right?"

Mia cast a quick glance at the antique French carriage clock, picked a stray white hair from her sleeve. "Let me ask you a question."

Naomi sighed. "C'mon, Mia! Don't start the psychobabble and flip the questions back on the client. I've done all this."

"But here you are." Mia spread her hands, a magician with nothing to hide. "So tell me, what do you hope to get out of this? Long term, where do you hope to end up? Reconciled? Healed? Forgiving? Or just less angry than you are?"

Naomi stared into Mia's deep blue eyes, then jerked away; there were still some things she had no desire to reveal. She looked at the inoffensive watercolour on the opposite wall, the jacaranda tree outside the window, the French provincial desk in the corner, and then down at her own hands, now idle in her lap. "I don't know," she said.

"I think you do."

Silence, except for the almost imperceptible tick of the brass clock. Mia seemed relaxed, one shoulder propped against the wall, but Naomi could feel the scrutiny.

Finally, she mumbled a reply.

"I didn't quite catch that." Mia left her place by the window, returning to her chair.

"Free," Naomi said, loud this time, firm. She raised her chin.

"Free how?"

Naomi looked at the ceiling and blinked hard, struggling not to let a single tear escape. "Content . . . no, not content. Satisfied."

"That's good. And why will you feel that way?"

Naomi paused. There was little Mia didn't already know, so why not this? "I haven't told you, but I have this recurring dream. Sometimes the details change a little, but the end is always the same. He's there, standing right in front of me, smirking. Often there are figures, like shadows in the background, cowering or. . .worse, people—women—he could hurt. And every time, in every dream, I find myself with the tools to stop him. A gun, a knife, even a flame thrower or martial arts expertise."

Naomi took a breath. "And I kill him. Slow or fast, it's usually pretty graphic. But when it's done I feel…euphoric almost, but definitely new, free of anger. Because that bastard is dead. I've evened the score, delivered justice, and I'm satisfied because he can never do to another woman what he did to my sister. And when I wake up, that feeling lingers. So that's how I want to feel. The way I am after I've killed him in my dream." Naomi's chin came up as she spoke, anger and pain cracking through her words. "There. Happy now? What does your therapist training tell you about that?"

"It tells me I was right to give you my card all those months ago. It tells me we've made real progress together. And it tells me how we can move forward. I've been thinking you're a good fit for one of my group sessions, and now I'm certain. What do you say, Naomi, would you be prepared to try a small group?"

"Seriously?" Naomi's mouth twisted. "You seriously think there's a way through this? I'll give you points for optimism."

"Seriously, I do. But our time really is up now, so how about we talk about the details in group?"

After grabbing her bag, Naomi stood up and brushed down her jeans. "Fine. I'll try it. But no promises."

Mia nodded. "Thursday, seven p.m., here. The door will be locked, so hit the buzzer."

Naomi shook her head as she crossed the room and let herself out into the hall. "Don't blame me if I scare away the rest of the group."

"I never blame." Mia shut the door after her.

TWO

Naomi hadn't planned to come—she didn't do group. She'd walked out of The Pleiades on Monday thinking it might be time to find a new therapist. But some of Mia's words had remained with her, and she could picture that birdlike tilt of the head, so incongruous yet somehow so natural on the tall, curvaceous woman. Still, group—really? Naomi had spent Thursday after work distracting herself with inconsequential tasks, filling the hours until she was running very late.

At 7:25 p.m. she leaned on the buzzer. Mia opened the door so quickly Naomi wondered if she'd been standing right there, but the therapist seemed neither surprised nor overly gratified to see Naomi on the doorstep.

"Naomi." Mia smiled widely. It was either very practised or one hundred percent sincere. "I'm so glad you made it." She moved back so Naomi could enter, then closed and locked the door. "This way."

Naomi followed the older woman down the hall. Tonight, Mia was wearing a Marilyn Monroe–style fitted dress in emerald green with a pair of black patent-leather stilettos, the heels so fine that a gap between floorboards would have made a less-assured woman stuck. She walked with shoulders back, hips swaying as though she was listening to bossa nova music. Perhaps that was what had convinced Naomi to consult Mia in the first place: the almost jarring contrast between her persona as a highly qualified therapist and her 1950s movie-goddess appearance. Nothing she did was conventional—maybe this group would be the same.

Naomi was so deep in thought that when Mia stopped, she almost cannoned into her.

"Everyone else is here," Mia said without turning around. "Are you ready?"

"I'm in the building, but that's about as ready as I can be for this sort of thing."

"It all counts." Mia pushed the heavy door—one Naomi had never seen open before—and they passed into the heart of The Pleiades.

As they entered, the women already in the room stopped talking. Five pairs of eyes scrutinised Naomi, and she could see both curiosity and defensiveness in their faces. Given what she knew of Mia's style, Naomi wasn't surprised to see the group was small and the room anything but clinical; it was like a large, luxurious lounge room. The walls were painted a deep cream, almost the shade of weak coffee. Lamps were dotted here and there, bathing the space in soft light, and delicate orchids provided a touch of colour. Scattered throughout was an assortment of seating choices, from a straight-backed wooden chair to deep sofas and welcoming armchairs. And there was not a single box of tissues in sight.

"Ladies, this is Naomi." Mia stepped aside. "I won't introduce you all now—you can do it yourselves as we talk." She pointed to the back of the room where an alcove was fitted out with sleek cabinetry. "Kitchenette there. Help yourself to tea, coffee, wine, anything, then grab a spot."

Naomi looked around, a wave of uncertainty sweeping over her. She wanted to bolt.

"Come. Sit here." An East Asian woman in a business suit patted the sofa next to her.

Gratefully, Naomi did as she was told, shifting cushions behind her back, fussing unnecessarily.

"I'm Amy. Welcome." The woman lifted a jug from the coffee table. "Water?"

"Please," Naomi replied. A glass would give her something to do with her hands, and sipping was always a good way to stall when a conversation got tricky.

Mia occupied a Scandinavian-style armchair, placed so she could see everyone without dominating the room.

Naomi glanced at each of their faces: they were all staring straight back. She forced herself not to fiddle with her ponytail or grab one of the cushions and hold it defensively in front of her chest, her aching heart.

Across the room, one of the women stirred, unfolded her long, denim-clad legs and leaned forward. "Gabrielle," she said, her voice rich and smoky as though she was about to break into a Nina Simone song.

Naomi took in Gabrielle's high cheekbones and curly black hair, the flawless rich brown of her skin, and wondered if she was a model.

"Someone should probably tell you that this group might not be what you expect. We've all tried and failed with other therapists," Gabrielle said. "We've washed up on Mia's doorstep like refugees, doubting it would be any different but hoping for… something." She shrugged, a large, loose-limbed gesture, then flopped back into her chair.

"Thanks for that ringing endorsement, Gab," said Mia.

Almost imperceptibly, Naomi shook her head. These women

probably had relationship problems and issues with anxiety and self-worth: she didn't want to pollute their genteel group with her presence.

"Naomi?" Mia must have noticed the micro-gesture. "Are you okay?"

"I shouldn't be here." She swept a hand around the room, taking in everyone. "I don't belong. No offence, ladies, but I think we're not...I mean, you're not... I'm not suited to this group."

Mia leaned forward, but before she could speak, a woman in a straight-backed chair jumped in. "Why would you think that?" The voice was pleasant, the words without heat, but Naomi saw the challenge in her cool green eyes.

"Katy..." Mia cautioned.

"I'm not stirring, I just want to know." She held up a palm towards Naomi. "You think whatever brought you here is so much greater than the petty hang-ups of a bunch of whingeing—"

"That's not true!" Naomi thumped the arm of the sofa, but without conviction.

"Bull!" Katy's tone was still light. "I know what you see when you look at us, because it's exactly what I saw when I first walked into this room: a group of well-educated, well-off women. We look like we've got our shit together—careers, relationships, money—but you know what?"

Naomi took in Katy's messy red braid, the pale makeup covering freckled, slightly sun-damaged skin, and the clothes that suggested she was on her way to or from yoga. Katy had summed up exactly what Naomi was thinking.

"We're all as fucked up as you." Katy sat back, crossed one sneaker-clad ankle over the other, and folded her arms.

Naomi let out a puff of breath, half laugh, half sigh. Then she looked at Mia. "I doubt that very much. But since we're heading down this path, shall I tell you why I'm here?"

Katy opened her mouth to speak again, but Mia beat her to it. "It's entirely up to you." From the therapist's tone, they might have been discussing shades of nail polish.

"In that case… It's true I've tried and failed with other therapists—we have that in common. But the reason I need help is because my sister was murdered. Jo was in an abusive relationship with a professional rugby player. She went to the police a few times, but they never did much. Finally she got the courage to leave, but Malik came home just as she was walking out the door with her suitcase. She died of a single stab wound to the chest. He said she'd threatened him with a knife, and when he tried to take it from her, she pulled away suddenly, tripped and…" Naomi made a double-handed gesture, plunging an invisible knife into her heart. "All he got was a suspended sentence."

There was silence as the women glanced at each other.

"My beautiful, vibrant, talented, funny big sister was killed. Jo's gone! She'll never have the career she dreamed of and worked for, never be a mother or an aunt, never get laugh lines. Jo bled to death in the hallway of her own home. Meanwhile that piece of shit got away with it, and he's still out there—he can do it to another woman. And it's eating me alive." Naomi grabbed the glass of water that Amy had placed in front of her. As she took a gulp, she waited for the gasps and exclamations, the inevitable outpouring of sympathy that was really a front for curiosity.

But the room remained hushed, except for a soft clink when Gabrielle set her coffee mug down on the table.

Naomi swept her angry, defiant gaze across them all, and she realised something: this was not a shocked silence. These women were not mute with horror or embarrassment at her raw expression of emotion. Each one met her eye, and in each face there was grief and understanding and something else—a reflection of the bleakness she saw whenever she dared to look in a mirror.

"Sounds as though you fit right in," said Katy, uncrossing her legs and standing. "Anyone for a bickie? I'm starving all of a sudden, and I reckon Naomi could use a sugar hit." Katy made her way to the kitchenette and started opening and closing cupboards.

Naomi looked around at the women again, her hostility gone. "All of you?"

In a deeply padded armchair to Naomi's right, a wispy blond with dark circles under her eyes cleared her throat. "We're all sisters," she said, drawing her bony knees into the chair and hugging them to her thin chest.

"What Brooke is trying to say," Amy spoke from Naomi's other side, "is that each of us is the sister of a murdered woman—a woman killed by her partner."

Naomi raked her fingers through her hair, ripping her neat ponytail from its band. She barely noticed. "I never imagined... All of you?"

"Are you surprised to find so many of us in one room?" The speaker was probably in her thirties: fit and curvy, wearing a chic cream blouse and russet skirt, her perfectly styled blond tresses framing a tired face. "I'm Olivia, by the way. Welcome." She raised her glass of red wine.

Katy returned with two plates, each piled high with an assortment of biscuits, from plain digestives to Tim Tams and Chocolate Royals. She dumped them at either end of the coffee table and grabbed something chocolatey for herself before settling back in. "Do you need to hear our stories?" she asked. "Or do you want that sugar first?"

"Yes...no. Shit, I don't know. Sorry, I'm a bit shell-shocked.

When Mia suggested a group, I never thought it would be entirely made up of—"

"Women like you?" Katy gave her a wry smile.

"Women just like me," Naomi echoed softly. There were tears in her eyes, and she swallowed hard, her fingers digging into the edge of the sofa.

Amy put a steadying hand over Naomi's, holding it there, saying nothing, until the tension abated.

With a shuddering breath, Naomi turned to Amy, thanking her with a small nod before facing the whole group again. "I do want to hear your stories. But tonight has really caught me off guard, and I honestly don't think I can do this right now. Maybe over the next few weeks?"

"Oh, so you're coming back?" Gabrielle asked.

"I think so. I mean, I don't know if it's going to do me any good. Shit, sorry Mia."

Mia gently batted the words away.

"But even if there's no cure for me—us—it seems like I've just found my people."

Around the room, there were murmurs of agreement.

"If I may?" Mia said. "I'm glad you're planning to stay, Naomi, because I felt from our first talk that you'd be a good fit. And on that note, this group is at capacity."

"Six does feel right." Olivia eyed off the biscuits but didn't take one.

"Seven, counting our fearless leader." Katy gave Mia a mock salute.

"Lucky seven," said Gabrielle.

"It's a powerful number," said Amy. "Other than the most relevant seven—the seven sisters of the Pleiades—it's a prime number, with significance in almost every major religion."

The others stared at her.

"What?" She shrugged. "There's more to this woman than outstanding management capabilities."

Gabrielle snorted with laughter.

"As I was saying!" Mia cut in. "You're a cohesive bunch, and I believe Naomi is on the same wavelength. If that really is the case, we can soon start to talk about the other thing she mentioned."

Naomi flopped back on the sofa, struggling to remember. "What other thing?"

"The most important thing of all: the cure."

THREE

Naomi's mind was reeling, so it was a relief when talk shifted to lighter topics before the meeting broke up less than ten minutes later. She hung back while the others left, listening as Mia called out goodbyes before making her way down the hall. "So." Mia was waiting just inside the door, poised on the brink between light and shadow.

"So," Naomi echoed. "I wondered if this group would be different—no, unorthodox—but I never imagined... Why didn't you tell me?"

Mia shook her head. "I didn't want you to have any preconceived ideas, just an open mind. And I wanted to empower them to be the ones to tell you. Those women know each other intimately, and their shared experience is one of the strengths of the group. They're all aware of what the others have suffered. When you told them your story—I doubt you picked up on it, but I've seen it before when there's a newcomer—there was a tacit exchange, an agreement, to let you in. And that's when Katy revealed what lies at the heart of the group."

"I feel embarrassed now. Because I did assume my problems were bigger than anyone else's. Maybe I shouldn't—"

"Your assumption was natural," said Mia, putting her hand on Naomi's shoulder, "and not one of those women will hold it against you. They understand. Come back next week—you'll see. If you have any misgivings, we can talk about them in our private session."

Naomi tried to appear receptive, but surely Mia could feel the tension radiating through her body.

Mia gave her shoulder a final, gentle squeeze before letting her hand fall away. She stepped aside so Naomi could pass across the threshold.

The warm evening air was fragrant with night blossom, and the final bruised-purple vestiges of spring light were giving way to darkness. Naomi would go to bed, feign sleep until her husband drifted off, then lie awake most of the night with only her tormented thoughts for company. And then it would be dawn: time to put on a face and do it all again.

She murmured goodnight to Mia and stepped into the street, but made no move to go. Instead, she closed her eyes and focused on the feel of the breeze on her skin, anchoring herself. A rattle and click told her that Mia had closed and locked the door.

"Naomi."

Her eyes snapped open.

A woman stood in the deeper shadows across the road from The Pleiades, thick black curls fanning out around her shoulders.

"Gabrielle?" Naomi glanced up and down the street then crossed, joining the woman beneath a scraggly native frangipani that stretched its branches over a front fence.

"I thought you might want to talk."

Naomi scuffed a foot on the path, feeling more like she wanted to excuse herself and walk away. She didn't want to talk more about Jo tonight.

"Not about… I figured you might like to talk to someone who's been in the group from early on and knows how strange it seems at first."

"*Strange* isn't the word I would have chosen."

"As far as I know there's nothing else like it, at least not in Sydney."

"A support group specifically for the sisters of domestic violence murder victims? I'd say it was a good thing, but it's fucked up that there needs to be a group for this at all, even if there are only six of us."

"It's more than that." Gabrielle checked her watch. "Have you got a few minutes to walk and talk? Or we could sit in your car?"

"I'm heading to the train station."

Gabrielle spun around and started walking.

Naomi watched the woman for a moment, taking in her long neck and strong arms, then she threw her hands up in exasperation. "Gabrielle! The station's the other way," she called.

"I know, but my car's this way. Wherever you're going, I'll drive you. And please, call me Gab." Gabrielle kept walking, and Naomi hurried after her.

Minutes later Gabrielle pointed her key fob at a white Mazda, which beeped and flashed its lights. She slipped behind the wheel, throwing her handbag into the back.

Naomi opened the passenger door, then hesitated. She leaned into the car. "Listen, no offence, and I don't mean to be critical—it's really nice of you to offer me a ride. But you don't know where I live, we've only just met, and I'm a little weirded out right now."

Gabrielle gave her a soft, reassuring smile. "I don't blame you for feeling a bit freaked. Tell you what, let's sit here for a few minutes while I talk. Feel free to keep the door open and your feet in the gutter—believe me, I understand. Then you can either accept the ride or go to the station. Or if you just want to walk away now, I shan't be offended, and I'll see you next time at group."

"Alright." Naomi lowered herself into the passenger seat. "But if you bloody well ask me if I've found God..."

"Nuh-uh. The only time I personally look for God is when I want to ask Him what the fuck He's playing at."

"Works for me." Naomi swung her legs into the footwell and shut the door.

Gabrielle angled herself towards Naomi. "First I should tell you why I'm part of the group."

"You don't—"

"I know, but you'll hear everyone's stories eventually. I know you're reeling from everything tonight, but if it's not too much, maybe you could hear mine now. All the others know it."

Naomi's unkempt fringe was bothering her, a dark brown curtain that she wanted to puff or brush out of the way, but she stayed still. "Okay. Tell me."

"Evette..." Gabrielle's mouth turned down hard at the corners. "Evie was my baby sister. A pain in the arse sometimes, but kind. She was a nurse, an ER nurse." Her voice wobbled, and she took a deep breath.

From the corner of her eye, Naomi watched as Gabrielle dug her fingernails into her thighs. Naomi didn't react: the struggle for control was too familiar.

"Jesus! Sorry. I thought I had my emotions locked down. Anniversary coming up."

"Always harder," Naomi murmured. "The shit icing on the crap cake."

Out on the street a car swept past, its headlights arcing through the Mazda, briefly bathing the women in a halogen glow before they were plunged once more into the gloom.

"So," said Gabrielle, "Evie always wanted to take care of people. That was how she met Shane, in the ER. He came in with broken fingers and a story about a DIY job gone wrong."

Naomi nodded, but Gabrielle was staring straight ahead. "Evie found out much later that the DIY story was bullshit. His then-partner—or I should say, the woman he was abusing then—had slammed a car door on his hand as she was getting away."

Somewhere in the distance a siren wailed, the low-toned slow rise and fall identifying it as an ambulance. Gabrielle waited until the sound had faded.

"Anyway, Evie told me that when she first met Shane, he was charming and polite and funny—always interested in what she was doing, that sort of thing. It was only once she moved in with him that she realised his interest was about control." Gabrielle darted a glance at Naomi. "The first time he hit her, he immediately started blubbering, begging her to forgive him, to stay, blaming his childhood, promising never to do it again. Evie wanted to believe him, wanted to help him." Pushing the heels of her hands into her closed eyes, Gabrielle blew out a long, shuddering breath. "So she gave him one more chance, and then another. And he killed her."

Naomi waited, giving the woman space, watching for the familiar stiffness of the shoulders that signalled a stifling of emotions. Finally she asked, "What happened?"

"He strangled her. He fucking admitted to strangling Evie—forensics meant there was no way he could avoid that—but he claimed it was a sex game gone wrong. Told the police, the court, that Evie liked it rough, that it was something they often did, that *she'd said*...and *he'd thought*...and he was *devastated and heartbroken*. He pleaded guilty to involuntary manslaughter and got less than four years." Gabrielle's voice cracked.

There was no point offering condolences or commiserations, no point ranting about the inadequacies of the judicial system. They'd both said and heard it all before.

"And, of course, her skin colour meant less media coverage—apparently less reason for the majority to care, let alone be outraged."

"I remember the case," said Naomi. "I remember your sister's smile."

"That was Evie. Lit up the room! Her patients adored her—everyone did."

The atmosphere in the car changed, and Naomi felt as if she'd somehow passed a test.

Gabrielle sucked in a breath, dashed away a tear, then banged a fist on the steering wheel. "Sorry, I need a moment before I tell you more about the group. Where are we going?"

Naomi gave directions then pulled on her seat belt as Gabrielle swung the car in a U-turn. They travelled in near silence as the suburbs unfurled around them, strip shops with brightly lit restaurants, and takeaway joints dotted among the darkened doors of retailers, the occasional servo or multinational fast-food place at the larger intersections, and finally, as they moved off the main roads, the softer light and lower energy of residential streets. Every now and then Naomi gave additional instructions, but for the most part the only sounds were the engine and the tick of the indicator.

"This is my street, number four's down the other end." Naomi looked across at Gabrielle. "Normally I'd invite you in for coffee, but tonight has given me a lot to think about. Sorry, I know you wanted to talk more, but do you mind?"

"Not at all." Gabrielle slowed the Mazda as she checked the numbers, pulling up in front of a neat semidetached house. "This you? Nice."

"Rich—my husband—and I like it."

"What will you tell your husband about tonight?"

Naomi bit her lip as she thought. "Nothing. I've told him I'm seeing a therapist, but that's it. He does his best to be supportive—he's actually amazing—but…"

"But no matter how much you talk to him about everything, there's no way he can really understand what it's like?" Gabrielle pulled on the handbrake but left the car idling.

"Yeah. And I hate to get his hopes up every time I start something like this. Because I know he thinks, deep down, that I can somehow come to terms with Jo's death, or at least figure out how to cope better." She met Gabrielle's gaze and saw understanding there. "How can I explain to him that just coping is never going to be enough? Not when there was no justice for Jo. I need more."

"Our group…You should know that each of our sisters died because of a man, and none of those men got what they deserved." Gabrielle's voice was low, her words punched out, staccato, into the air between them.

"You mean…" Naomi felt her stomach roil, even as the familiar fury pressed into the back of her skull.

"I mean either a sentence so light it's an insult, or in a couple of cases not even a conviction, even though the police know who did what."

"Why am I not surprised?" Naomi kept her tone even and didn't fumble as she unclipped the seat belt, but when she faced Gabrielle, she knew the other woman would see the depth of her emotion. And she didn't care. "I should go in. Thanks for the lift, and the talk." She swung the door open, stepped into the street and tilted her face to the sky, hoping for stars but seeing only clouds. The air had cooled, and she shivered before she turned back to Gabrielle. "See you next time!" She slammed the car door, holding a palm up in farewell. But she'd only taken one step away when she heard the buzz of the passenger-side window going down. She stooped so she could see in.

Gabrielle was leaning across the centre console, one hand on the passenger seat. In the yellow glow of a nearby streetlamp, Naomi could see the intensity of her gaze. "There's one other thing you have to know about the group. Or maybe you already noticed."

"What?"

Gabrielle's hand, still resting on the seat, curled into a rigid claw. "We're all angry—really angry."

Naomi and Gabrielle stared at each other, acknowledging the commonality of their past, and Naomi felt something inside her snap into place.

She nodded and straightened up. "Alright then. See you next week."

The only answer she got was the whir of the window closing. The Mazda accelerated away, its taillights flashed briefly at the end of the street, then Naomi was alone.

FOUR

Despite what she'd said to Gabrielle, Naomi still hadn't made up her mind about returning to the group. She had been caught off guard by the fact that they shared the same trauma, but she had never been a joiner.

The following week, she surprised herself for a second time. "I knew we'd see you again," said Gabrielle as Naomi walked through the door.

"Really? Bloody hell, I didn't. I'm actually not sure how I got here." She shrugged. "One minute I was thinking about Netflix, the next I was in the car and on my way."

She surveyed the room. Gabrielle was lounging in one of the armchairs, sprawled as artfully as a rock star in a fashion shoot. Amy, with her back straight, ankles crossed, was on the same sofa as last week. She was talking to Katy, who occupied the opposite end of the three-seater. Brooke clattered around in the kitchenette, fussing with mugs and a steaming kettle, and Naomi studied her; something about her seemed familiar, but Naomi couldn't shake the thought loose.

Behind Naomi the door clicked, and she turned sharply. Olivia and Mia entered the room. Olivia looked hot and harried, flashing Naomi a distracted smile as she edged past and found a chair. Mia, on the other hand, scrutinised her closely. They hadn't talked since the last group, because Naomi had cancelled her private session. The message she'd left on Mia's voicemail had probably come across as abrupt, but it was the best Naomi could do.

"Naomi." The way Mia said her name was almost a sigh, and she waited for either a recrimination at the missed appointment or an effusive acknowledgement of her presence. Mia simply inclined her head towards the centre of the room. "Grab a spot, and a drink if you want it," she said, then moved to greet the other women.

After a moment's hesitation, Naomi settled into a wingback chair and let herself sink into the deep velvet upholstery. She felt anxious, her throat unaccountably scratchy, and the sensations made her wonder again what she was doing here. She realised she wanted a drink of water but worried that by popping out of her chair she would alert the others to her anxiety, so she stayed put. As she observed the women, she took note of their ease with each other—the quick glances and smiles, the small gestures and touches that spoke of long friendships. She wished she hadn't come.

Dropping her chin to her chest, Naomi inhaled slowly, trying to loosen the knot in her gut. When she looked up again, Mia was staring straight at her. Their eyes locked, and Naomi felt the power behind the gaze, so strong she almost gasped. Then Mia smiled, and it was gone.

"Shall we?" Mia asked the room in general. "If there's anything anyone wants to say, please feel free."

Conversations petered out, and there was a rustling as everyone made themselves more comfortable. Naomi noted that all the women seemed relaxed, with open, receptive faces; there were no folded arms, hunched shoulders, or averted gazes.

In the silence Naomi felt a soothing restfulness that perplexed her even as she was drawn to it, enjoying a sense of tranquillity that had evaded her in recent years. Her brow furrowed as she tried to analyse her feelings and figure out what she'd got herself into.

When she brought her attention back to the room, Mia was watching her again. The therapist tilted her head a fraction, questioning without demanding.

"Sorry," Naomi said, "but is everyone quiet because I'm here? I'm a bit confused."

Brooke raised a tentative hand. "You being here has nothing to do with us talking. It's great you came back. I know when I first joined, I...well, I was really scared, but we're all glad you're here."

"So..." Naomi said, "what do you usually talk about?"

"Everything and nothing," Amy said with a shrug. "We understand each other, and you never have to worry about anyone offering saccharine hugs while they are really hoping for salacious details." She stretched her arms out in front of her, laced her fingers together and, from the sound of it, managed to crack every knuckle. "Not that I put up with such treachery from anyone."

Katy gave a short bark of laughter. "I'd like to see what happens if anyone tries that with you, Ames!" She turned to Naomi. "Amy can get pretty aggro. The thing is, this group lets us be our real selves, warts and all, without all the walls we have to put up for the rest of society. You don't have to pretend you're okay, or that nothing happened. You don't have to worry that one of us will think you're a basket case if you burst into tears at the mention of your sister or, worse, turn out to be that anonymous close friend who sells your story to a gossip rag. You tell her, Olivia—you know how to call a spade a damn shovel." Katy waved languidly in Olivia's direction.

"Thanks, darl. Naomi, what they're saying is we talk about whatever the hell we want, whether it's our feelings, a rehashed story about one of our sisters in *Woman's Day,* plans for the future, or just a new lasagne recipe—or sometimes, like tonight, nothing at all. This is the only place we can just be." Olivia picked up her wineglass, but only a drop of red remained; she eyed it before placing the glass carefully on the coffee table.

Gabrielle said, "Every other place in my life is a minefield of secrets, but not here. Can you honestly say there's someone in your life, anyone, who sees all of you?"

Naomi swallowed, thinking of the many small things she did and said to convince her husband she was fine.

"For me, it's, it's…like you said. These are my people." Brooke put a bony hand to her chest. "These women get me. We all know the best and worst of each other." She paused. "It's like finding a family you never knew you had and just fitting in."

Naomi's eyes widened as she realised something. "When you said 'family'…" She stared at Brooke. "I felt there was something familiar about you, and when you said 'family' I remembered where I'd seen you before."

"It's okay, you can say it."

"I saw you on the news, standing outside the Supreme Court after Rowan Fitzpatrick was found not guilty. Your father was addressing the media, and you were beside him, supporting your mother—physically holding her up. But I could tell your own legs were about to buckle. I cried for you, with you. I couldn't imagine the depth of the grief and despair you were feeling." Naomi's voice trembled. "And then that grief became mine, too."

"That's the real guts of this group." Katy's voice was soft. "We all get it. And we are hyper-aware of stories like our own. Last week, when you told us what happened to your sister, I reckon we all remembered the case." Around her, the other women nodded. "I bet you're just the same. If each of us spoke about our sisters, you'd know their stories. And even when the media gloss over facts, I'm sure you'd see the truth beneath the spin."

Looking from face to face, Naomi felt a rush of emotion so strong that it threatened to overwhelm her.

Mia jumped in smoothly. "Let me give you some more context for this group, Naomi. I have other clients with similar issues to deal with, but their personalities—the way they're wired—mean I use other techniques in their sessions. I believe there's something in all of you that is best served by a particular approach, which is why I brought you together. I think the six of you can help each other move forward."

"So we're hand-picked?" Naomi asked.

"You could say that. No one wants to be in a group where there's that one person who, for whatever reason, upsets the energy balance."

"Pisses everyone off, you mean," Olivia muttered.

"How long have you all been meeting?" Naomi asked.

"Brooke and I are the most recent. We arrived within a couple of weeks of each other, and that was nearly two years ago. Brooke, sweetie, you were in a really bad way then." Olivia placed a hand on the younger woman's leg, giving it a comforting squeeze.

"I struggle a lot." Brooke's voice was barely audible.

Olivia moved closer to Brooke, who leaned against her. Nothing was said, but not one of the women looked away; they watched and waited, acknowledging and respecting the moment.

It was some minutes before the air in the room seemed to shift. Brooke was still pressed against Olivia but sat up straighter and reached for the small gold crucifix she wore around her neck.

"You're all very close," Naomi said.

"True," said Amy, "although it has not always been like this. I thought I hated Olivia when she first came. She seemed perfectly composed and together."

Olivia threw back her head and laughed.

"What changed?" Naomi asked.

"I said something inflammatory, and Olivia was out of her chair like lightning and in my face, returning fire in equal measure." Amy smiled ruefully. "I realised that behind her North Shore facade was the same house of cards I was hiding, one that rested on an identical foundation of grief and burning rage."

"That's exactly how I feel. Some days I don't know if I'm going to collapse in a heap or punch a fucking hole in a wall." Naomi paused, her gaze sweeping around the circle and coming to rest on Mia. "I want to be part of this."

FIVE

On New Year's Day a violent domestic murder occurred in another state, dominating the news over the following weeks. Naomi watched the coverage obsessively, analysing the way the media reported it: the softened terms because the perpetrator was a former pro footballer, the failure of authorities to act on reports of domestic abuse and coercive control, and the likely sentence the crime would attract. Because of the sport connection, a number of current affairs programs and websites drew parallels with the murder of Naomi's sister at the hands of a professional rugby player. She saw Jo's case played out again and again, narrated with varying degrees of outrage, but always with a sense that nothing ever changed. By the first week of February, and their first meeting for the year, she was desperate to get to The Pleiades and give vent to her pent-up feelings.

As soon as she walked into the room, she knew all the women were feeling the same way. Olivia sat with a wineglass in one hand and a bottle of red in the other, her flushed face indicating she was already a few glasses in. Brooke had obviously been crying, Gabrielle was pacing up and down one side of the room, and Katy, normally svelte in her yoga attire, was dressed in polyester-blend work clothes that somehow managed to appear rumpled. Amy was seated in her usual corner, her face a complete blank—only when Naomi looked more closely did she realise the woman's fists were so tightly balled, her knuckles were white.

When Mia closed the door to the meeting room, the soft clack of the latch was like the final tick of a bomb. The women all began to speak at once, voices rising as emotions heightened like an explosive blast wave. Watching them, Naomi was again reminded about the significance of their shared experience. She heard herself in their words, saw her fury and frustration reflected in every face. These women didn't just understand her, they *were* her.

Naomi dropped the last vestiges of propriety and pounded her fist into the arm of the sofa. "Why won't anyone make these fucking bastards pay?"

All activity in the room stopped, as though this was the moment before negative pressure would suck everything back to the blast epicentre in a final destructive action.

Mia's words shot into the void like bullets. "Why don't you?"

For a moment the silence was absolute, then Naomi snorted. "Is this some kind of shitty psychological trick? Whip us up into a fury then pick it apart?"

"No." Mia looked around the room. "We've all thought and said the same thing. Every woman here believes that those men deserve to die, that someone should erase them from the face of the earth." She paused, then gave a small shrug. "So why don't you?"

"What?" Naomi frowned at Mia. "What are you talking about?"

"That's what we're planning to do, Naomi. With your help."

Naomi realised everyone was watching her. "You're bloody

serious, aren't you?" Pressure bubbled in her chest, the threat of hysterical laughter.

Gabrielle, standing with her back to the window, raised her chin and took a step forward. "These men don't change. The police try—well, some of them do—but again and again the system lets women down. Someone has to take care of the problem. Why not us? For years, I've tried to advocate for better protection for women, but nothing ever really seems to change." Gabrielle shook her head. "When I came here—when I heard Mia's plan—I knew if there was a way to kill that bastard and get away with it, I'd take him out in a heartbeat. Because it's not just Evie's murder, it's what her death did to my family. It's the fact my sister's killer got a slap on the wrist, and now he's out, he could do it again." She pointed a finger and swept it around the room, taking in all of the women. "We know these men will harm someone else, kill a partner, destroy another woman's life. Mia has shown us it's in our power to take them down. So we've been planning, waiting for the right time—and the right person—to complete our group."

There were murmurs of assent as Gabrielle threw herself into an armchair with a decisive thump.

"Gab's right." Olivia caught Naomi's attention. "We'd been hoping Mia would find the right woman, and now we've had time to get to know you, well… Will you help us?"

Naomi looked for the twitch of a lip, a stifled laugh, anything to suggest this was a joke. All she saw was grim determination. She opened her mouth, a million questions crowding her mind, so many things she wanted to say, but all that came out was, "How?"

The room normally felt cosy and tranquil, regardless of the conversation, but now it seemed to crackle with electricity.

"Have you ever seen the Hitchcock film *Strangers on a Train*?" Mia asked her. "Or read the original book?"

Naomi nodded.

"The six of you can swap. Gabrielle can be sitting at a window table in a popular restaurant while Amy or Katy or Olivia takes care of Evie's killer. Then Gabrielle can help make the world safer for women by putting an end to the man who murdered Brooke's sister—while Brooke is at work. There'll be nothing to connect the killer to the crime, the sister will have an ironclad alibi if any suspicion falls that way, and between us we can come up with enough methods that all the deaths will be made to look like accidents or suicides."

"And you're all in on this—really?" Naomi could hardly believe it. They were crazy. It was crazy, and yet…

"Really," said Mia. "The only thing that connects you all is this group, and if you're like these ladies, you haven't told anyone you attend. Doesn't everyone else in your life think you're still in the office, or at yoga?" Her tone was enough to dispel any doubts. "And of course there's no money trail; that's why I asked you to donate to a women's charity instead of paying me for Thursday nights."

Naomi drew in a long breath. "Shit. I don't even know where to begin."

The other women glanced at each other, but no one moved or uttered a sound.

Then Amy leaned forward. "Let me lay it out for you. We will pool resources. We will stop meeting up here and use Mia as a coordination point only, so the rest of us have no traceable contact."

"Of course I'll continue to see my other clients, business as usual," Mia said.

"Two women for each mission," Amy continued. "One to do the job, the other there as backup. There are already a few ideas about how to solve our problems." She rapidly tapped the arm of her chair with an index finger, the burnt orange of her perfectly manicured talon flashing in the light of the lamp beside her. "Each death must differ from the others."

"Six different methods," said Katy. "For example, there's a drug I have in mind. Too obvious for me to use, given my job as a hospital pharmacist, but perfect for someone else's problem. And Brooke's IT knowledge will help us with things like communicating without leaving a digital footprint—right, Brooke?"

The blond woman jumped. "Huh?"

Olivia touched her lightly on the knee. "Katy was just explaining how your IT expertise will help us, sweetie."

Brooke nodded, reaching up to grasp her small crucifix. "Well, yeah, I guess." Her voice was uncertain. "I mean, I know my way around the net, but I'm not a hacker. I can't bring down the city's CCTV network or take control of a car or anything."

Amy arched an eyebrow. "Pity."

"But," said Olivia, "you can help us keep our computers clean and maybe find someone from their online activity, can't you?"

"Umm, yeah. Clean computers are easy. But...the thing is, a clean computer looks clean, which, y'know, may red-flag it. So it's really better not to use your own machine." Brooke frowned and paused, running her crucifix up and down its chain. "And then...umm, locating a person depends on whether he's trying to cover his trail or not, but most people are slack about things like that, so, yeah, I can probably do that."

Olivia leaned closer to Naomi, cheeks flushed, eyes bright. "It's a lot to take in, but once you see how it could work... A few months ago I put a copy of the *Strangers on a Train* movie poster on my fridge, and every time I look at it I think, as long as we're careful and work together, we can have justice."

Silence followed, and Naomi knew only she could break it. She switched her attention back to Mia, whose hands were steepled beneath her chin as she regarded the group with a small smile of satisfaction.

"This really isn't some sort of bullshit psychological exercise?" Naomi asked. "You're not about to analyse the past ten minutes, are you?"

"Naomi, I have never been more serious about anything in my life than I am about this." Mia held her gaze as she spoke.

"Why? I mean, I understand what's driving every woman in this room except you, Mia. So why are you doing this?"

"The others all know. I'm a sister too. My sister's life was also destroyed by domestic violence."

As Naomi studied Mia's face, she caught a glimpse of what lay beneath the professional veneer. She gave a decisive nod. "I'm in."

Katy slapped herself on the thigh. "I knew it. I knew you'd do it."

"Yes. Yes!" Olivia clenched her fist in triumph.

"Are…are we really going to do this?" Brooke asked. "We've talked about it for so long, I never—"

"If we can finish working out the logistics," said Amy, through gritted teeth, "I will do anything to make that bastard pay."

Naomi turned to Gabrielle. "That first night, in your car—you were bloody well checking me out."

"I did want to explain some things to you, but, partly, yes. You can understand why. We've been waiting a long time for this. As Amy said, if we can finalise the logistics, that is, how to get away with six homicides"—she smiled coldly—"if we can do that, I am ready to embark on a brief, covert career as a pest exterminator."

Naomi swallowed. What had she just agreed to?

Mia leaned back in her chair. "I think we've had quite a breakthrough this evening."

SIX

Brooke left the session with her thoughts oscillating wildly. Had her therapy group really just made the final decision to become a murder club? Maybe next week there would be laughter and reassurances, the other women embarrassed they had considered such extreme action.

But then Brooke remembered their quiet resolve. Seated in that tastefully appointed room, she had distanced herself from the discussion unfolding around her. She'd watched as mugs and glasses were pushed aside so a notepad could take centre stage on the coffee table, then listened as the others discussed burner phones, cash payments and alibis.

Now, heading home, she studied her reflection in the train window, her face sharply defined against the encroaching night. She couldn't do it. Tomorrow, she'd tell Mia she was out. Her shadowy image nodded once, decisively.

The express train thundered through a station, and the lights on the platform briefly erased her reflection. When darkness returned, it was not her own gaunt face and straight blond hair that Brooke saw: it was her sister's. Gemma had died when her abusive partner shot her in the back. Rowan later claimed he didn't know the rifle was loaded, that it was an old gun prone to misfiring, and he hadn't been pointing it at her, he had stumbled, and, besides, he had suffered psychologically from the ordeal. *And. And.* And reasonable doubt, not guilty.

Brooke had seen him immediately after the trial—backslapping, smiling, laughing. Outside the Supreme Court building, where the media pack waited, he put his head down, sunglasses on, mumbled about a tragic accident and moving on with his life, then ducked into a waiting car. Brooke was left to hold her weeping mother while she herself tried not to ugly cry in front of the cameras.

Over the following months, she had sought Rowan out, lying in wait at the places she knew he'd go—a favourite restaurant, the cricket… She watched him living his life, saw him chatting up a girl. One afternoon he noticed Brooke, and his reaction said it all. Pointing a finger at her, he mouthed, "Boom," and grinned. That night she received a text from Gemma's old number: a laughing emoji.

He'd kept her sister's phone. He had Brooke's address. Did he have her keys, the ones she'd given Gemma?

Brooke called a locksmith and researched security systems, but it wasn't enough. She moved out the same week.

Two stops before Central, she got off the train and walked the short stretch to her fifteenth-floor apartment—a far cry from the Balmain semi she had lovingly renovated, but secure, with cameras, swipe cards, and a twenty-four-hour concierge sitting in the foyer. The view was a bonus. She waved to the man at the desk as she crossed to the elevators, then rode up through the centre of the tower in blissful solitude and let herself into her apartment. She didn't turn on the lights because there was enough ambient glow from the city for her to navigate across the open-plan lounge, drop her bag on the way, and go through to the balcony. Enveloped by the warm night, she pictured the women at The Pleiades and contemplated a future that didn't include *him*. But it was her sister who occupied most of her thoughts. What would Gemma have said about the wild pact the women had made?

At first, like Naomi, Brooke had been sure Mia was goading them to discuss their feelings. Every time the idea had been raised since then, Brooke had believed it was probably just another way to let off steam. After all, Mia had kept saying they needed one more woman, the right woman, who never materialised. Until Naomi.

Now Brooke fully understood that for the others the idea was not only serious, but it was also achievable. They wanted to remove six blights from the Earth and to swap targets so there could be no trail. Targets, not victims—the only victims were the sisters, along with their families and friends living each day with the knowledge of how they had died and how little their deaths seemed to matter to everyone else.

"What would you do if it was the other way around, Gem?" Brooke asked her sister, sending the words out into the darkness. She didn't need to wait for a mystical sign, and despite her Catholicism, she'd given up on expecting a response from God. The answer was already in her gut, her heart, and her head: if Brooke had been murdered, her sister would not have let that death go unpunished, and she would never, ever have taken a chance that such a man would find another victim.

Brooke shivered and went back inside, locking the sliding door behind her—even fifteen floors up, the action was second nature. "Fuck." She clapped a hand over her mouth. The uncharacteristic expletive was loud in the double-glazed, minimally furnished apartment, ricocheting off polished concrete floors and the sharp, stainless-steel angles of the open kitchen. Brooke rested her forehead against the cool glass of the door, and for the first time she acknowledged that her life was still being controlled by the man who had killed her sister.

After kicking off her shoes, Brooke made her way past the kitchen with its overhead racks of rarely used wineglasses. Brooke didn't drink. It made her more anxious—besides, she preferred to always be on the alert. In the living area she dropped onto the sofa and nestled among a pile of cushions, hugging her knees to her chest. She'd never dreamed she was the sort of person who could kill someone. But if she had been given the opportunity, would she have killed Rowan to save her sister?

Absolutely.

Did he deserve to die? Without question.

But was it her decision?

Brooke realised she needed to speak with the one other woman in the group who would still be digesting the plan and its implications. Twisting about, Brooke spotted her bag in the middle of the floor and retrieved her mobile. She opened the encrypted messaging app that they'd all just downloaded, then sent Naomi a text.

SEVEN

It was just after midday when Naomi strode onto the ferry as though it was a luxury liner. She had mirrored sunglasses on against the summer glare, her earbuds in, and her mobile in her hand as she moved deftly through the usual lunchtime mix of tourists, retirees, and a smattering of businesspeople. She went out onto the port side and back around to the stern, hoping to avoid the sightseers. Leaning one hip against the railing, she angled her body away from the interior of the ferry and waited for it to depart.

The MV *Friendship* was quickly underway, making a graceful curve past the Opera House. Naomi took a deep breath. No matter what she was doing or feeling, a perfect day on Sydney Harbour always made her marvel at the city in all its splendour. From where she was standing, Naomi could not only see the bridge and the flamboyant Opera House receding, but she also had a beautiful view of the water as it sparkled in the ferry's wake.

Unbidden, an idea jumped to the front of her mind. She pictured herself flipping a man overboard and watching him sink into the harbour, solving a problem with no chance of fallout.

She shook her head. Things had changed so much for her since yesterday.

The ferry stopped briefly at Cremorne Point, and as it pulled away from the wharf, Naomi sensed movement to her left: Brooke. The woman was bent forward, forearms on the railing, her attention seemingly on the water below. Naomi noted Brooke was also wearing sunglasses, and that her blond hair was pulled up and concealed beneath a plain blue baseball cap. Her clothing was generic—jeans and a white T-shirt—and she wasn't wearing a watch or any jewellery other than her crucifix.

"Your message really took me by surprise, Brooke."

"Hi, Naomi. Th-thanks for meeting me." Brooke didn't look up.

"So what's going on?" Naomi asked.

"I wanted to talk to you about this...plan."

"I figured that, but why me? The others know it better, and they know you better. I don't think I—"

"B-but that's exactly it! I can't talk to them because they've already decided. You've only just heard everything. You're not so set on, on... And I need to talk to someone. Because I'm having doubts."

"I knew you were struggling with what we were talking about—what we decided—last night." Naomi's tone was gentle, her voice pitched so Brooke could hear her over the rumble of the engines and slap of water without the sound carrying too far. "And I understand, I really do. Before I say anything else, I want you to know that whatever you decide to do, you set up this meeting really bloody well—you have a flair for covert ops."

"So...you're definitely going ahead with it?"

"I've imagined it in general terms for ages, and now... It's not just about revenge. Jo's killer got off so lightly, and if someone had stopped him before he met her, she'd be alive. Removing him from the planet won't bring her back, but it will make the world a safer place. It sounds trite, but this is a way I can make a difference."

As she stared out over the water, she felt the truth of her words. She was aware of Brooke watching her and realised the woman's doubts had forced her to analyse her own willingness to proceed. And she knew now that she was committed to the plan.

Brooke pulled her cap lower. "You're not worried about… getting caught?"

"Not doing it this way. Not if we do it right."

"What about playing God? Are you worried about that?"

For the first time, Naomi turned to face Brooke properly. She kept her expression neutral, as though they didn't know each other. "If you want to talk about God in all of this, you could question where He-She-They were when my sister was being stabbed to death by the man who was supposed to love her. Or maybe God fucked up when those murderous men were born, and we're giving God an opportunity to correct that error."

"So now The Pleiades is an instrument of God?" Brooke's voice rose, and she glanced over her shoulder, even though she and Naomi were still alone in their corner of the stern.

"I'm not saying that." Naomi kept her tone mild. "I'm just saying you can look at the situation in a lot of different ways, spin it any way you like."

Brooke was quiet, and Naomi watched her, trying to gauge the other woman's thoughts. A cloud moved in front of the sun.

"Brooke, I need to ask… Are you in?"

"I…"

"It's fine if the answer is no. I'd understand, and I know the others would, too. But we also need to know that you'd keep the secret."

Another ferry approached them, heading back towards the city, and Naomi paused to watch its progress, softening her knees as the wake of its passage rocked their craft. Beside her, Brooke staggered slightly.

"Shit, sorry," Naomi said. "I should rephrase that. It's not that we don't trust you to keep quiet, but I know it's a bloody huge imposition, a massive burden for you to carry around. If you don't want to take that on, then please say so now. It's okay."

The sun emerged and the harbour sparkled again as though shot through with silver, light bouncing off the water and thousands of surrounding windows. The effect was magical, but Naomi knew all too well that the dazzling reflections made it harder to see what lay on the other side.

As the ferry began to curve towards the wharf at South Mosman, Naomi watched Brooke through her mirrored lenses, thinking that although they were very different people, this woman was one of the few to whom she could really relate. She studied the gaunt profile, its desolation somehow starker in the luminous afternoon light.

Several minutes passed before Brooke spoke. "When I messaged you asking to meet, I wanted to…question you about the plan and everything that was said last night. I wanted to tell you my doubts and fears, and I guess I hoped… Well, I hoped you'd agree with me and that would be that. But then I spent the night lying in bed, thinking about it. All of it—the how, when, where, who of it. And after hours of that, I realised there was one thing I kept coming back to, one thing that mattered to me above all else."

With a sigh, Naomi nodded slowly. Brooke's hand had gone to the cross around her neck; her religion was obviously a comfort, however small. "It's okay—"

Brooke touched Naomi lightly on the arm, then pulled back as if the contact had scalded her. "Please. Let me finish."

Naomi bit back another sigh.

"I realised there's only one question about the plan I want to ask you today."

Here it comes.

"Are you a hundred percent sure we can get away with this? Because my parents have suffered enough."

Naomi almost dropped her phone into the harbour. "Yes, I'm sure. I'm absolutely sure."

"Well then." Brooke took a deep, ragged breath. "I-I'll do it."

"Really?" Naomi straightened.

"I've decided to take my cue from the Old Testament."

"I can't tell you how bloody happy I am that you're in, but you've lost me with the Bible reference."

Brooke braced her knees against the gentle swaying of the ferry. "In Leviticus, God tells Moses that whoever takes a human life should be put to death."

"Sounds like a bloody good idea."

Naomi pulled off her sunglasses and peered intently at Brooke, seeking an affirmation beyond words. It only took a second, but she found what she was looking for in the woman's unwavering blue eyes.

Replacing the glasses, Naomi dusted down the front of her shirt and smoothed a hand across her hair, ready to disembark as the ferry approached South Mosman. The engines throttled back, the vessel bumped against the dock, and Naomi strode off through the crowd. She had enough time to call Mia and explain what had just happened before she caught the next ferry back to the city.

Naomi paused and tilted her face to the sun. Overhead, a Qantas plane cut a path through the azure sky, climbing steadily on its way to another part of the world. That was how Naomi felt, as though she was on a journey to a foreign place, with different rules and a language only half understood. She fixed her gaze on the distinctive red-and-white livery, watching until the plane disappeared into the clouds.

EIGHT

Late on Sunday afternoon, Naomi entered Centennial Park from the western end. She made her way down towards the lily pond, jogging at a medium pace, just one more Sydneysider among hundreds getting out for some exercise. The air was oppressive, and the gusting wind spoke of a coming storm, the sort that turned the sky an eerie green before blasting the Harbour City with torrential rain and a display of natural pyrotechnics.

After Naomi had told her about Brooke's decision, Mia decided they should have another meeting before their final session at The Pleiades. It would give them a chance to consolidate some details of the plan and, more importantly, for everyone to see that Brooke was fully committed.

The women agreed to meet on Sunday, but that meant they needed a different venue—Mia never ran groups at The Pleiades on Sundays, so a gathering there would seem out of place. Instead, they opted for Centennial Park. It was the ideal place to meet without attracting undue attention: it was central and with multiple points of entry, essentially no CCTV, and no chance of being overheard.

In preparation for the meeting, Naomi had spent the day in

an obsessive internet examination of the man who had stabbed her sister. Malik was a prolific poster on social media, a cocky bastard with a high opinion of his looks and physique, so it was easy for her to reacquaint herself with his life.

This wasn't the first time she'd googled him. The top hits were still about Jo's death and the court case, opinion pieces on the judicial system, reports on the memorial service and on the vigil held outside the Supreme Court—Naomi had read it all, knew it all. But this time, scrolling through pages where every hyperlink had been clicked, seeing once more the image of Malik flanked by his high-powered lawyers as he entered the court, she felt different. The grief remained, but it had hardened, forming a crust over the anger and hatred. For the first time, she felt she had control of her feelings. And there was another sensation, something entirely new.

Jogging towards the rendezvous point, she finally identified it: resolve. The women of The Pleiades could do this. They would do this.

When she probed her psyche, poking dark corners to see what hurt, Naomi had to acknowledge that the part of herself reserved for Jo, for her sister's memory, suddenly felt more like her professional self. In her role as a mining engineer, Naomi often stood in front of groups of men and told them why she was right about something: from exploration and discovery to feasibility studies and mine design. That same confidence was in her now.

She cut across the grass towards Lachlan Swamp, slowed to a stop, and began a series of stretches, taking the opportunity to look for the others as well as to scope out the area for any chance observers. She was alone except for a woman facing the other way and using a curved stick to toss a ball for her border collie. The dog seemed tireless, running out again and again, anticipating the throws. Then the woman wielded her scoop only to have the ball slip out and roll off. She turned.

Olivia.

Meeting Naomi's eye, she nodded as one might to a stranger, then went back to playing with her dog.

Naomi walked farther away from the path, moving towards the trees as she worked through a series of shoulder stretches. A movement between the trunks caught her attention; two shapes in the dappled shade that briefly resolved into Gabrielle and Amy, before the women eased into deeper shadow.

Breaking back into a jog, Naomi headed towards them. She could see that Olivia had begun to fling the ball in a different direction, and with each throw, she and the dog were drawing closer to the trees. The terrain changed from grass to leaf litter that crackled with every step. Naomi entered a small clearing where Gabrielle and Amy waited, together with Katy and Brooke. Part of the space was taken up by a racing bike, propped against a nearby tree, the helmet hanging from Gabrielle's arm proclaiming her ownership.

Before anyone could speak, Olivia appeared, her border collie now leashed.

"I didn't know you had a dog," Katy said, reaching out to pat the now-panting animal.

"I don't, darl," said Olivia. "He belongs to my neighbour—I offered to exercise him so I'd have an excuse to hang around in the park. Am I nuts? Is this cloak-and-dagger stuff complete overkill?"

Naomi was about to speak, but it was Gabrielle who answered. "Definitely not. This is good practice."

"Where's Mia?" Naomi asked, glancing around.

"I'm here." The therapist emerged from the gathering shadows, a picnic basket hanging from the crook of her arm. She hefted it slightly. "Camouflage."

There was a moment's uncertain silence, then Gabrielle

clapped her hands, the sound like a rifle shot. "Let's get down to the details, then. How are we going to divide up the jobs?"

"We're having two of us on every...job, right?" Brooke asked, and Naomi flashed a reassuring smile in her direction.

"That's the idea," said Katy. "One to do the work, the other for support and backup."

"But backup only if required," said Amy. "In each situation one woman will take the lead and execute the plan, so to speak. There should be no circumstance where one of us has to carry out a second job."

Naomi rubbed her palms down the sides of her leggings. "So, who wants to solve whose problem?"

There was another silence.

"I guess you haven't talked about that yet?"

"We thought we should wait for the final group member," said Gabrielle.

"But," said Mia, "no matter who partners with whom, you all have to trust in the group completely. So ultimately this is arbitrary, a simple decision."

"Decision-making is what I do," said Naomi, "and since I'm the last one in, I'll start." Her gaze settled on Katy. "I'll take responsibility for your problem."

Katy grabbed Naomi's arm. "Daniel," she whispered. She cleared her throat and tried again, stronger. "Daniel Pavic. The mongrel who ran my sister down. I'll give you his address and work details."

"Okay," said Naomi. "Now I need someone to second me, then I—or we—need to figure out the details and advise you, Katy, of the timing so you can be a bloody long way away and highly visible."

"Me." Brooke took a tiny step forward. "I... I'll do it." Naomi felt a flutter of uncertainty.

"Sweetie, are you sure?" Olivia was sitting on the ground with her borrowed dog, and she pulled him in close, running her fingers through his long fur.

Brooke nodded emphatically and looked from one woman to the other before finally turning to Mia. "I wasn't sure at first, but now I am, and I'm ready."

Mia held her gaze for several beats before she also nodded, slow and measured. The gesture did more to reassure Naomi than Brooke's eager declaration.

"Thanks, Brooke." Naomi hugged the younger woman. "I really appreciate it."

"Don't say that just yet." Brooke gave a nervous laugh. "Everyone else is probably relieved they're not the one stuck with me."

"We're all just glad you're here, sweetie," Olivia said quietly.

Katy exhaled a long, steady breath. She pressed her hands to her heart, one laid over the other, and closed her eyes. "I can't tell you—"

"You don't have to," Amy interrupted, not unkindly, "because we *know*."

Katy sniffed and patted her chest a few times. "I'm okay now," she said, her voice husky. "But thank you." She brushed a finger under each eye and blinked rapidly. "So, I can probably gather enough of a drug from the hospital pharmacy to take care of one problem, but I wouldn't like to take my chances with more."

"What sort of drug?" Amy asked. "I feel as though I should be taking notes. I always take notes at meetings, especially meetings this important."

"I know what you mean." Gabrielle was sitting with her back against a tree. "I've got a notebook in my bag, and I'm itching to take it out, but..." She shrugged. "Mental notes only."

"Amy," said Katy, "I can potentially get my hands on any

drug, but I have a few criteria. It has to be something that will only need a small dose, ideally something you can slip into food or a drink. And I don't want to raise any red flags, so I'll need time to accumulate enough without anyone noticing."

"I could jab a needle into one of those creeps." Gabrielle's voice was cool.

"Yes, but that would leave a mark," said Katy, sitting beside Olivia. "I mean, if you could inject it somewhere hidden, like between his toes, or if he was a drug user and one more needle mark wouldn't make any difference, that might be okay. But you've still got to do the injecting. Which is why I was thinking of oral drugs."

"Malik." Naomi spat the name out.

"What about him?" Mia's voice was soft, her question a therapist's invitation to share.

"He's a recreational user. Well, he always claimed it was recreational."

"Do you know what he uses?" asked Katy.

Naomi shrugged. "From what Jo told me, whatever he could get—cocaine, PCP, ketamine..."

"Fentanyl?" Katy leaned forward.

"Maybe. If he hasn't done it yet, he probably wants to try it. Malik is an equal opportunity user: uppers, downers, things to 'expand your mind'"—Naomi made air quotes—"things to 'shut it all off.'"

"In that case, we have options." Katy's eyes narrowed. "Leave it with me, but does this mean we should consider that drugs will be used to deal with Naomi's problem?"

The women looked at each other, nodding.

"Done," said Katy. "Obviously, I can't handle that one, so I still need a job and a 2IC."

Olivia half raised her hand. "I'll be your plus-one, darl."

"Excellent, thanks." Katy smiled. "How about we deal with Gab's piece of human sewage?" She arched her eyebrows.

Gabrielle wrinkled her nose. "The only issue is, you'll have to travel. Shane's become an opal miner. He was working a claim in South Australia—Andamooka—but last I checked, he'd moved back to New South Wales, an isolated claim out of Lightning Ridge."

"Isolated!" said Katy, slapping her hands together. "I'm up for it."

"What about your husband?" asked Gabrielle. "How will you explain the trip to him?"

"Won't have to. Emerson's taken another ten-month posting in Antarctica, so…" She shrugged. "I'm available! What do you say, Olivia? Feel like an outback road trip?"

"I'm more of a Contiki girl than a grey nomad, darl, but I am one hundred percent in." Olivia tried to match Katy's enthusiasm but didn't quite manage it.

"Trip of a lifetime!" Leaning forward, Katy gave Olivia a high five. "We'll just have to come up with a method."

Naomi was hunkered down, sitting on her heels. She'd been watching faces, both inspired and a bit stunned by the way everyone was pulling the plan together.

Now she grinned. "As for that," she said, "you remember I'm a mining engineer, right? If he's opal mining by himself, I can pretty much describe the setup he'll have at The Ridge. Which means I can also tell you exactly how you can erase that shit stain on humanity."

"Well, clearly the stars are in alignment." Gabrielle's mouth curved into a satisfied smile. "He's probably alone—he's swindled a few people, so I can't imagine anyone would want to partner with him in something like that—but I can't say for sure. At least my brother will know where he is."

"Your brother?"

"A little hothead. He would have tried to kill that bastard himself, except Mum made him promise, said she couldn't lose a second child." Gabrielle sighed heavily. "Anyway, my brother always thought there was something off about Shane, so he installed a spyware app on the bastard's phone long before..." Her voice quavered. "He's been using it to keep tabs on the man ever since, and he keeps me updated. My brother'll know if he's still up at Lightning Ridge."

Naomi pointed at her. "Find out and let me know." Then she turned to Katy. "I'll put together a plan for you. You'll need a couple of things, but nothing that would look out of place on a camping trip."

"That's my problem sorted," said Gabrielle briskly. "So which one is next? Who's going to take care of the drug addict?"

Around them the air was growing heavier and stiller, the light fading quickly. The women drew closer, talking with soft urgency. As more plans took shape, Naomi committed each partnership to memory.

Katy (and Olivia) = Shane (Gab)
Naomi (and Brooke) = Daniel (Katy)
Olivia (and Amy) = Rowan (Brooke)
Amy (and Katy) = Malik (Naomi)
Brooke (and Gabrielle) = Zac (Amy)
Gab (and Naomi) = Aaron (Olivia)

Naomi didn't know how long they'd been there when the dog whimpered, bringing all discussion to a halt.

Olivia strained to see the sky through the canopy. "We need to wrap this up for today. The storm's moving in quickly." She coiled the leash tighter around her hand.

"We still have a few details to discuss," said Katy, standing and dusting off the seat of her leggings.

"We'll discuss them on Thursday," said Mia. "Our final meeting at The Pleiades."

They quickly disbanded, leaving the shelter of the trees and heading in various directions. Naomi hunched into her jacket and hurried away. Above her, the first bolt of lightning split the sky.

NINE

Naomi arrived early on Thursday evening, eager to flesh out the details of their plan. Mia let her in, one ear pressed to a phone, and gestured towards the back room before disappearing into her office, murmuring reassurances to her caller.

The room was dim, and Naomi was reaching for the light switch when she noticed a woman standing in front of the window, facing the twilit evening. Naomi recognised the hair first, even in the gloom—a blond so naturally perfect it had to be expensive. "Olivia."

The other woman jumped and spun around, a hand to her chest.

"Sorry." Naomi left the light off and went to sit on the nearest sofa. "I didn't mean to startle you."

Olivia shook her head. "I was miles away, darl. Thinking about my sister."

Naomi nodded. "Do you want to tell me? Our doing what we're doing, it's stirred up a lot of memories for me—you too, it seems. We have time."

Naomi watched the other woman. Olivia was an outgoing and talkative member of the group—in keeping with her successful career in talent management—but she maintained it was her twin sister Vivienne who'd been the extrovert, the life of the party. And it hadn't escaped Naomi's notice that a lot of Olivia's froth and bubble was on the surface; she chatted and laughed but rarely touched on her emotions or spoke of the sister she had lost.

Now it seemed like that might change. Olivia settled herself at the other end of the sofa, sitting sideways so she was facing Naomi. "Viv and I had that twin thing, you know? When she died, it was like some sort of partial paralysis, as though half of me was dead too. It took me a long time to get through a day without falling apart, so I don't always let myself think about Viv because it opens the floodgates. But this past week I can't stop thinking about everything."

Naomi stretched out a hand, resting it on the cushion between them.

"Sometimes I think about the immediate aftermath. I steeled myself for the barrage of condolences, except…it was strange. I didn't notice at first, because I was dazed, still in shock, but instead of support, a lot of colleagues and people I thought of as friends would mumble something while their eyes slid away from my face. And when those people discovered Viv hadn't just died of something everyday and sad-but-not-shocking—a car accident or cancer—the moment they learned my sister had fallen from a cliff… Well, that was the moment I saw the shutters come down."

Naomi knew exactly what Olivia was talking about—she'd experienced the same thing—but now she kept silent.

"People were embarrassed. They assumed she'd jumped, that it was suicide, and they didn't know what to say or how to act, so they offered the bare minimum, then either carried on as usual or began to avoid me." Olivia made a sound that was half laugh, half sob, then drew a deep breath. "When it came out that police were investigating Aaron, that he had been there, that there was a history of coercive control, whispers of violence… That was when I really found out who was in my corner. People I barely knew were putting sympathetic hands on mine as they leaned in, eyes sparkling with the thrill of a scandal, and asked, 'So what really happened?' At least my daughter was only four at the time, too young to really understand. My marriage didn't survive. On the plus side, the breakup was amicable. Just as well, because I had nothing left in me to grieve for a relationship. You're married, aren't you?"

The abrupt question took Naomi by surprise. "Nine years."

Olivia nodded, but her thoughts had clearly returned to her sister. "I have to remind myself that there are still a lot of good people out there. But I find it hard to trust men. Aaron put my sister through hell, and then he killed her! I told the police Viv had always been afraid of heights, yet the bastard claimed she climbed a safety fence to take a sunrise selfie at Diamond Bay in Vaucluse, then slipped and fell from the cliff. He said he'd tried to talk her out of it, grabbed for her but failed. So it seemed like a turning point when police said a witness had come forward with a different story—a story about hearing a woman plead with someone called Aaron. I knew what he had done, and now there was proof."

"What happened?"

"Two weeks later the witness recanted, no reason given. The officer in charge apologised. They had serious doubts about Aaron's version of events, but the fall had happened at a notorious accident spot, so without the witness there wasn't enough evidence. Police dropped the investigation and declared Viv's death an accident." Olivia puffed out a soft breath. "And then he showed up at Viv's memorial. I would've thrown him out, but I didn't want to make a scene. I tried to avoid him, but he found me, right near the end. He looked around, then leaned in and whispered, 'I told your sister to watch her step.' He waited to see the expression on my face before he left. I don't know how long I stood there, feeling like I was going to vomit, wondering if the caterers had brought a carving knife and if I could stab it into Aaron's heart."

"Oh shit, Olivia." Naomi had tears in her eyes. She could feel pressure behind her breastbone, empathy for Olivia wrapping around the hard knot of her own grief.

"Soon after, I found Mia's card in my letterbox. I found this place." Olivia swung her arm out, gesturing at the room, then grabbed Naomi's hand on the sofa and held on, seeking solace, giving strength.

A snap, and the overhead light blazed to life.

"Are we talking sisters?" Amy stood in the doorway, ruffling a hand through her short spiky hair.

"Always, darl." Olivia switched back to her normal persona, but she gave Naomi's hand a final squeeze before letting go.

Naomi was transfixed by the sight of Amy in her head-to- toe leather and heavy boots, a motorbike helmet hanging from her free arm. "Bloody hell. Hi."

"My non-corporate side." Amy moved to a chair and peeled off her jacket. Naomi watched, very aware that this was the woman who would kill Malik. It still didn't quite feel real, yet Naomi was reassured by Amy's deft movements, her cool confidence.

The others arrived while Amy was arranging her things. They exchanged greetings and quickly settled around the room before focusing their attention on Mia.

"This should be the last time we're all together like this," Mia said with her customary calm. "From now on, any fine-tuning, problems, details, whatever, should come through me, especially when we're talking about timing. There can be no contact between the acting pair and the woman who most needs to be squeaky clean at that point. Right now we'll figure out a rough schedule for all the jobs and discuss some possible methods."

Naomi leaned forward. She'd been thinking about the man on the opal fields and knew what needed to be done. "I already have the method for Shane, so maybe he should be the first. It's not the sort of mining I usually deal with, but I know the country, and when summer rolls in it's too hot—a lot of the itinerants leave Lightning Ridge, and far fewer people visit. It gets down to a few locals plus the crooks and assorted pieces of shit who are trying to hide off the grid. You'll be a lot less bloody obvious if you go sometime during the real mining and tourist season, from late March through to September."

Katy nodded. "Works for me. Can't believe I'm saying this, but I'm actually keen to get cracking. I'll apply for a few days off. Olivia, will you be able to get time off from your work, say, first week of April? That will still give us several weeks to pull things together."

"Shouldn't be a problem, darl, I have plenty of time owing."

Gabrielle smoothed a hand across her hair, which she wore pulled back into a tight bun. "Even though it's summer he's definitely still up at Lightning Ridge; I have GPS coordinates for what must be his claim. The thing I don't have is a map showing the tracks that will get you to him."

"Shit," said Naomi, surprised at her own disappointment. "Those tracks can be bloody hard to spot, and they meander all over the place. It might be difficult to find the right one, and chances are you won't be able to just walk in using the coordinates—the claim might be miles from the main road. We may have to rethink this."

Katy shrugged and leaned back in her chair. "Not necessarily." She faced Gabrielle. "Does he drink?"

"Naturally."

"Then he'll come into town regularly, either to buy booze or to prop up a bar and talk bullshit with the other miners. If you have a picture, we can find him and follow him."

"But that means you'll have to be there longer," said Gabrielle.

Katy shrugged again. "As long as Olivia doesn't mind, I'm quite happy to do a bit of stalking."

"Doesn't bother me." Olivia swirled the wine in her glass. "Like I said, darl, plenty of leave accrued. And Nova will be thrilled to stay with my ex for a bit."

"Beaut," said Katy, "we'll figure out the logistics and be ready to roll by April. Naomi, do you have time tonight—after this—to take me through your proposal?"

"Sure. And it's a bloody elegant plan, if I do say so myself. You won't need to get too close, and you won't need much equipment."

"I'm intrigued!" Katy grinned. "And really grateful."

Naomi smiled back, excited to share her idea.

"So," said Katy, "if that's all sorted, who's next?"

It didn't take them long to rough out a schedule. At Mia's suggestion, they decided to aim for a minimum of eight weeks between each job. If six murderous men were eliminated in rapid succession, it would be sure to arouse suspicion no matter what. Two months seemed reasonable without putting too much mental strain on those waiting for their turn to act, or, as Katy pointed out, those waiting to see justice done. But if for any reason they had to wait longer—if they needed to let things cool down, or if the target was unreachable—then wait they would. The priorities would always be their own safety and their ability to do the job cleanly and without being caught.

Of course, should an opportunity arise before the eight-week mark, they agreed it would be foolish not to take action.

Shane the opal miner would be the most difficult to locate, but the others were closer to Sydney and much easier to find. Their lives had gone on, largely unaltered, while they continued to post photos and status updates, leaving a map of their habits, routines, and preferences all over the internet. With that in mind, the order of work was relatively easy to plan: Naomi volunteered to step up for the second job, followed by Olivia, Amy, Brooke, and, finally, Gabrielle.

Naomi found herself repeatedly glancing at Brooke, looking for signs of weakness or faltering resolve, but there was nothing to alarm her. Although the younger woman was perhaps paler than usual, her face seemed set with determination.

They all discussed how from now on, each woman would work out her own approach, only sharing the final details with her backup and Mia. The less the others knew about each operation, the more secure the setup. Should any of them be questioned by police, ignorance would be the best defence.

"Regarding methods," said Mia, "I only need to know enough to ensure there are no duplications—and of course the timing, to let each of you know when you need to have a solid alibi. Any information about the targets—addresses, habits, useful details—pass that on now. Is there anything else we need to discuss?"

"Quick question," said Naomi. "I got a couple of burners which I've brought along so we can exchange numbers tonight. But could someone just run through the burner phone details again? Brooke?"

Brooke's quiet voice was reassuringly steady when she answered. "Once you've bought a prepaid, activate it, but don't give your name and address. You should keep calls short, make them away from your home or work, and make sure you switch the phone right off when you're not using it. Then after a few calls you should remove and destroy the SIM and throw the phone away. Umm." Her brow furrowed then cleared. "Nope, that's it."

"In that case, I think it's time to exchange information." Amy stood up and crossed the room, settling next to Naomi on the sofa. "Naomi, tell me everything you can about the man I'm going to kill."

For the rest of the evening the room was filled with quiet conversation as the women moved in and out of different pairs, either exchanging phone numbers with an accomplice or settling in to learn all they could about their individual targets.

Finally, Olivia began to gather her possessions. "I guess this really is it, ladies. We won't all be in touch for a while."

"I'll keep you loosely connected," said Mia. "It's going to be an intense time, but it will be worth it. If anyone needs to talk—really talk—I walk the Bradleys Head track from Taronga Zoo Wharf every Monday morning at ten. You can lace up your sneakers and find me there."

Naomi felt as though she was vibrating, the same sort of low-intensity thrum she knew from standing on ground with a mine operating deep beneath her feet; only this time, the energy was all hers. She wanted to shout or scream, but she managed to keep her voice calm as she said, "Katy, I need to outline what I have in mind for you."

Katy nodded and crossed the room to join her on the sofa. "You guys get going." She waved a hand at the rest of the group.

"Good luck, everyone. See you on the other side! Olivia, I'll get a burner phone and message you on your current number."

Olivia raised a hand in acknowledgement and farewell before she disappeared into the hallway, the others following in her wake.

Naomi angled her body towards Katy. "This won't take long. It's a simple plan."

"Come on, then, fill me in."

TEN

Just over six weeks later, Katy and Olivia were in the far north of New South Wales, nearing the end of more than seven hundred kilometres of driving. Katy was behind the wheel for the last stretch between Coonamble and Lightning Ridge. The old Land Cruiser wasn't the most comfortable ride, but out here it was anonymous, just another dust-caked four-wheel drive, its once-white duco now yellowed and pockmarked. Despite their sense of urgency, a desire to push hard until the job was done, they'd made sure to always remain a few kilometres below the speed limit and obey every road sign; the last thing they needed was a speeding ticket. Fortunately, the Land Cruiser didn't reward a lead-footed driver: anything over about ninety-five kilometres per hour and the vibrations became almost intolerable.

"Should be just up ahead, darl." Olivia was consulting a paper map. Their throwaway phones were basic models and currently in the glove box with SIM cards out. They had decided to take no chances with GPS mapping and location tracking; they would have to interact with at least a few people in Lightning Ridge, but that didn't mean they should leave an obvious trail of their movements, especially once they had a better idea of where the target's mine camp was located.

"There." Olivia pointed to a sign on the left, and Katy flipped on the indicator.

They pulled into the isolated truck stop tucked next to the road somewhere south of Walgett, Katy easing the four-wheel drive over the rutted gravel and into the farthest corner of the spartan rest area. Engine off, they sat for a moment, listening to the tick of cooling metal, letting the dust subside before they stepped out. Katy watched Olivia stride back towards the road; for the next few minutes, she'd act as lookout. The Castlereagh Highway was hardly choked with traffic, but there was the chance a fellow motorist would see them stopped and check to make sure everything was okay. They didn't want company, and they definitely did not want to be remembered.

Katy was grateful for Olivia's people skills, especially her ability to dismiss without offending. Whether the person was a kind but too-inquisitive grey nomad or a suspiciously over-friendly trucker, somehow, Katy knew, Olivia would manage to shut them down while remaining virtually forgettable—calm voice, minimal emotion, zero information imparted.

Unsurprisingly, the highway was empty—a straight line of black asphalt that seemed to run to the ends of the earth. The silence was almost absolute, interrupted only by the occasional bird call and the gasp of a breeze teasing the leathery foliage of nearby trees. Then Katy heard a faint melody: Olivia was humming "Hey Jude" again. She had told Katy it was from her childhood, the song her mother had sung when she and her twin sister were scared. Katy's jaw tightened with irritation. She had grown up in a hardworking farm family with a toughen-up-and-get-on-with-it mentality; she hoped she wouldn't have to hear the song too often over the coming days.

Standing behind the Land Cruiser, she shook the can of spray adhesive and gave the rear licence plate a good blast, then picked up a handful of red dirt and puffed gently, blowing it onto the sticky plate, three, four times. She sat back on her heels to survey her handiwork. Satisfied, she moved to the front and repeated the procedure before looking across at Olivia, who gave a thumbs-up: still no vehicles approaching.

"Come and have a look," Katy called. "It should only take a couple of minutes to dry."

Olivia wandered over, and they both checked the effect from different angles. It was a beautiful job, the licence plate numbers obscured with streaks of soil in a way that appeared completely natural. No one would think twice about it.

Katy turned her gaze towards their destination, staring across the seemingly endless expanse of spiky grasses and low, scraggly trees, trying to picture what lay ahead. The plan was etched so deeply into her brain that she had recurring dreams about it, adding depth and colour to the details she had calculated to the nth degree. The only thing that remained inconsistent in her dreams was the backdrop, because she didn't know precisely what Shane's camp looked like. Katy had seen pictures of other opal miner's setups, enough to give her imagination something to work with, but as they drew closer, she was feeling a strong desire to fill in the gaps. She wanted the death to be perfect.

As she dusted off her hands on the seat of her jeans, she put a mental lid on the eradication plan—for now. She touched a finger to the licence plate; it was dry. "Let's make tracks," she said to Olivia.

Katy slowed the Land Cruiser as they rolled past the edge of town. Instead of the usual Rotary sign to welcome them with an estimate of the population, there was only a stark black-and-white board proclaiming, LIGHTNING RIDGE, POPULATION "?" She grinned and gave a humph of satisfaction. "Gotta love a town like this." The sign seemed like an omen: The Ridge wouldn't notice one less resident, wouldn't care.

Driving down the main drag, Katy counted four motels and a couple of pubs. It didn't matter; she'd already picked somewhere to stay for tonight. She adjusted her sunnies, then lifted the dark brown ponytail from the back of her neck, sweaty despite the breeze blowing through the open window. The unfamiliar hair colour was hideous to her, but far less likely to draw attention than her natural red.

They passed the turnoff to the Artesian Bore Baths, then the entrance to the caravan park appeared on their left, and Katy took the turn carefully, bringing them to a stop near the manager's office. Olivia kept her face angled away from the door as Katy stepped out into the lengthening shadows.

There were no other campers in the unpowered section, and they chose a spot far from everything—roads, admin, camp kitchen—and everyone. It took them less than an hour to set up the awning tent Katy had brought along. She'd explained during the long drive that she and her sister used to ride horses together, and the four-wheel drive and associated gear were relics from their eventing competition days. Katy didn't ride anymore, but she hadn't been able to bring herself to get rid of the Land Cruiser and the memories it held.

Katy had parked so that from the front of their tent they could see if anyone approached. This meant they could talk without fear of being overheard, and it would give them a chance to ready their story, should the need arise. There were a number of other people in the campground, grey nomads with mobile homes clustered together on powered sites, and backpackers bunked down in the cabins. But Katy and Olivia avoided them all, ducking in and out of the showers early and staying away from the kitchen. Lights shone from various windows as evening quickly deepened into night, but the two women had the unpowered camping area and the shadows to themselves.

They sat outside and ate a scratch dinner. Katy didn't have much of an appetite, but it wouldn't do to pass out from hunger or dehydration at the crucial moment. Their talk was of inconsequential things: politics, previous travel, even the best moisturiser for fine lines.

Over coffee, Katy broke a Mars bar in half, its form somewhat heat-affected, the sugar rush undiminished. Olivia clasped her mug, breathed in the steam, and asked, "So, what happens tomorrow?"

Katy stared into her own mug for a moment before she took a sip. "We know he's mining in the Coocoran opal fields, and that means there's only one road he can take for the last stretch back into town. I'm banking on him hitting the pub either tomorrow night or Saturday. If that doesn't happen..." She shrugged. "I don't want to have to start asking questions, but the Coocoran fields are far too big for us to just drive back and forth, checking tracks and camps."

"How long do you think it would take," said Olivia with a smile, "for word to get out about a couple of crazy women showing up on multiple claims?"

"Exactly." She shook her head. "With that sort of attention we may as well take out an ad in the local paper. At least we know from Gab what the man drives—or what he was driving last—and what he looks like. So we'll stake out the road into town from Coocoran. If he comes in before it's dark, we should be able to see his face if we pick our spot well enough. I reckon there's a good chance anyone coming into town is going to do it just before dusk. End of a long week, so he'll want plenty of time to drink and find out how everyone else's luck is running. And if it was me, I'd want to drive those roads before all the wildlife came out."

"Of course! Shows what a city girl I am—I didn't even think of that."

"Well, it's just an idea." Katy scrubbed a hand across her forehead. "And I hope it works, because it's the only one we've got, other than getting the hell out of here once the job's done."

Olivia drained the last of her coffee. "Do you mind if I turn in, darl?"

Katy shook her head. "I won't be far behind you."

After Olivia left her mug and retreated into the tent, Katy was left gazing at the sky, lost in thought. Although she'd said she wouldn't be long, the moon was well past its zenith when she finally traded the glow of a starlit outback night for the darkness of oblivion.

ELEVEN

Katy and Olivia packed up first thing, then spent the morning pottering around Lightning Ridge, doing touristy things, sunglasses and hats on at all times, polite when addressed but not initiating conversations. After lunch they drove out of town. Katy found a spot for the Land Cruiser just before the single road branched to flank the Coocoran fields. There wasn't enough scrub to completely conceal the car, but they were far enough back that no one would see anything more than a dust-covered four-wheel drive—just another blow-in scrabbling around in the dirt, hoping to stumble across a fortune. Naomi, in her thorough briefing at The Pleiades, had reassured Katy that so long as you weren't jumping a claim, there was an unwritten code of live and let live. Places like Lightning Ridge attracted all sorts: city fossickers who fancied a bit of a scrape around the tailings, serious prospectors who made a living—or tried to—out of black opal, and people looking to disappear, drop off the grid, live cash in hand with no questions asked. People like *him*.

The scrub country around The Ridge was dotted with shanty-like camps, each one signposted, *Keep out! Private! Trespassers shot!*, or with words to that effect. There were a lot of holes in the ground, and a man had to be careful where he stepped. After all, when a town proclaimed its population as a question mark, who would know if a man was still out there working a claim, if he'd given up and gone back to wherever he came from, or if he was dead? Mining accidents happened all the time.

Katy's spot gave them a good view of the road. They could afford to wait a day or so, but if he hadn't appeared by then… Well, somehow they'd have to track him down.

In the end they only had to sit tight for a few hours. Dusk was settling when a ute came from the right-hand fork of the road and rolled past, a cloud of dust rising behind it. At the point where two roads turned into one, the driver tapped the brake. The windows were down, his face clearly visible.

"It's him, isn't it?" Olivia said, holding up the photo Gabrielle had given them.

Katy lowered her binoculars and stared at the picture. "No mistake," she said. "And that ute—you could spot that a mile off." The vehicle had disappeared from view, but the DIY orange-and-white paint job, the roof-mounted spotlights, and the steer's skull attached to the bull bar were unforgettable.

If his vehicle had been the only four-by-four to head into town it would have been simple. A single set of tyre tracks in the ochre earth, leading straight to his camp. But two other vehicles, a battered van and an ex-army jeep, had also emerged from the scrub. Katy had been right about the pub. Friday night was still Friday night, even for those living beyond The Ridge. Now the night stretched ahead. They would have to wait for Shane to drive back, then covertly follow him. The pubs didn't officially close until midnight, and of course he might be out for longer; on a bender, locked up in the drunk tank, or maybe even shacked up with a woman. If he wasn't back by late morning, they'd look around town for the ute and work out what to do.

But based on what Gabrielle had said about his reputation, he probably wouldn't leave his claim unguarded for long.

Katy did a three-point turn to face the Land Cruiser the right way, then they scraped tea-tree twigs over the tyre tracks, just in case. They fired up the Primus and prepared a thermos to see them through. By eleven p.m., Katy was settled in behind the wheel, with Olivia sometimes humming "Hey Jude" softly in the seat beside her. It was irritating, but Katy knew it was a coping mechanism, so she bit her lip and kept quiet. There was nothing left for Katy to do but think—of Gabrielle's sister, Evie, and what Shane had done to her; of preventing him from killing again; and of her own sister.

Then she became aware that Olivia had stopped humming, and that silent tears were rolling down her cheeks. Katy placed soothing fingers on one of Olivia's clenched hands. "Liv?" Her voice was husky after the prolonged silence.

Olivia sucked in a shaky breath. "Sorry, darl."

"You want to talk?"

"Just thinking about Vivienne." Olivia gave a loose, helpless shrug. "About how I knew what was going on, that he was hurting her, but Viv told me to back off."

"Olivia." Katy softly rubbed her friend's hand.

"Viv reassured me that she had a plan. She was going to leave him, but there were joint accounts—assets—and Viv didn't want to lose everything. If she'd realised what he was truly capable of doing…"

In the darkness, Katy nodded. Trying to leave: the most dangerous time. Her spine straightened, just a little, where her neck met her shoulders. She would do this.

———

It was just on dawn when Katy spotted Shane's ute crawling towards them. Enough light to be extra careful about wildlife; enough light for her not to lose sight of him. And judging by the slow speed he was travelling and the way the ute drifted in and out of the ruts, enough alcohol and possibly pharmaceuticals to make it unlikely he'd register their presence.

Nonetheless, she dropped the Land Cruiser in behind him at a discreet distance and kept well back, the job of tailing him made easier by the scrub that shielded them, while affording glimpses of the faded orange duco twisting and turning on the track ahead. Luckily, he was heading into country that had a bit more coverage: most of the land around The Ridge was fairly open, with only short spindly trees dotted across the red earth. Here there were patches of denser scrub, enough to keep them hidden while Katy drove carefully, and he was inattentive, but not so much that the women couldn't spot, even from well back, the moment when he was approaching his destination.

Katy pulled their vehicle off the track and in among the sparse trees, killing the engine. They had travelled a long way to get to this point, but danger still lay ahead; they needed to make a careful reconnaissance before going the final distance. Easing themselves from the car without shutting the doors, the women crept as close to Shane's camp as they dared. The scrub became thinner, but there was still plenty of cover thanks to the detritus scattered across the area: rusting machinery, forty-four-gallon drums, and twisted shapes of wood and metal so decayed it was impossible to guess their original function.

Katy crouched behind the burnt-out chassis of a small car, Olivia close beside her. She watched as the man lurched from ute to caravan, and listened as a dog whined and an aluminium door slammed somewhere beneath the canvas shade of an enclosed awning.

"Dog," breathed Olivia.

Katy hadn't counted on that. Its presence might ruin the whole plan, but she still had to try. And whatever happened, there was no way she'd leave the dog behind. She loved dogs—her country childhood had been filled with them—and she also knew that violent men never had just one victim.

She thought about how he had been moving. In her work as a hospital pharmacist, she'd seen her fair share of people under the influence of a variety of substances. Instinct and experience measured his posture and gait, told her she wouldn't need to wait long for him to doze off. She zipped her jacket and donned the baseball cap, buffers against the frigid dawn. A few more minutes ticked past, then her gut told her it was time to go. All Katy could do was hope the dog wouldn't bark.

"Wait here," she murmured to Olivia. "Anything goes wrong, get out."

Olivia's eyes widened, and she shook her head.

Katy placed a firm hand on her shoulder. "It's what we planned." She didn't wait for a response.

As she crept around the edge of the camp, there was one excited yelp, immediately swallowed. She felt a burst of anger and pity; it seemed the dog knew there would be consequences for rousing the man from his stupor.

She kept moving slowly towards the working part of the claim. It was a fairly large area devoid of trees and scrub, populated instead with machinery for washing and sorting, for hauling up earth from below. None of that mattered to Katy—what mattered were the mine shafts.

She could see abandoned workings covered by sheets of corrugated iron weighed down with a few rocks, but the active shaft was easy to spot: it was the only one with any sort of structure around it. A low, inadequate safety fence flanked three of its sides, and the hoist, with its bucket and winch, was positioned on the fourth. She wouldn't need to use any of the equipment, only the man's lust for opal and his violent temper. According to Naomi, the current excavation always inspired the strongest reaction, because in any opal miner's mind this was where they were about to strike it rich. This was the one that would expose a fat seam of the gemstone and finance a luxurious early retirement.

Katy had done her own research. A top-quality black opal could be worth up to twenty thousand dollars a carat, four thousand dollars a gram, and there were plenty of stories of people who'd got lucky. Not this man, though; not if she could help it.

By Katy's reckoning, she still had a good half hour. Cautiously, keeping one eye on the caravan, she returned to the place where Olivia crouched. With a tilt of her head she indicated that the woman should follow her back to the Land Cruiser.

Pulling open the rear doors of the four-wheel drive, Katy began to check over her equipment.

Olivia was beside her, speaking quietly but urgently. "We can't leave the dog."

Katy stopped what she was doing but kept her eyes on the contents of the vehicle. "Oh, God, I know we can't, but how? If we take it with us, when someone eventually comes to visit or checks on him and the dog's not there, they'll know his death wasn't an accident."

"You heard it. The way it shut up. It doesn't deserve his cruelty, and it doesn't deserve to be abandoned in the bush to suit our plans."

Katy's shoulders dropped. "Of course not! We're not going to abandon the dog. Maybe we could..." She shook her head. "I'll figure it out. I don't know how long I've got, and I need to focus."

Olivia nodded, her hands twisting together.

"Now, I really have to..." Katy looked over her shoulder, towards the camp, then turned back to the Land Cruiser's interior. She grabbed the things she'd need: fine rope, a trowel, a broom head, and an iPod and speaker.

"Do you want me to...?" Olivia gestured at the truncated broom.

Katy shook her head. "That's not the way we're doing this thing. This one's mine. If anything goes wrong, get out, don't stop."

"I'm not sure if I should wish you luck," said Olivia, her voice strained.

"I don't think there's any etiquette handbook for this sort of occasion, but a little bit of luck wouldn't go astray." Katy smiled tightly then took a few backward steps, holding Olivia's gaze, before turning and retracing her steps to the camp.

She hovered at the perimeter of the scrub for a few minutes, stretching her hearing towards the caravan, feeling the tension in her scalp, in the exaggerated rise and fall of her chest. Finally, she stepped into the open, crossing quickly to the working shaft. The iPod speaker was in a small brown bag, and Katy had tied a length of fishing line to the bag's handles. Now she tied the other end tightly to one of the top rungs of the ladder that gave access to the mine. Leaving the bag on the lip of the shaft, she took a moment to properly examine the way the mining equipment was set up: it was just as Naomi had said it would be.

Katy pulled the coiled rope from her shoulder and began to lay it out, starting with a length running close in front of the edge of the shaft, the ends trailing back a couple of metres to the steel arms of the framework supporting the hoist. At those points, she ran the rope up the legs of the derrick for about forty or fifty centimetres, through a parallel pair of rivet holes and back down the other side. She had spent a good part of yesterday evening rubbing red dirt deep into the fibre of the rope, and it was all but invisible against the rusted frame.

Next, Katy played out the loose ends of rope: two straight lines leading away from the shaft, then converging at their tips. Now came the diciest part. Katy pulled the iPod from her pocket. Originally she had thought she'd be able to turn it on with its remote control, but Naomi had quickly pointed out that she'd be too far away for the device to respond. To give herself enough time to complete the next step, Katy had made a recording that began with ten minutes of silence.

She crouched next to the bag holding the speaker and was about to press play when a distant sound made her pause. Listening, she tilted her head. Had Olivia started the car for some reason?

Not Olivia—this sound had a different timbre from that of the Land Cruiser's engine, perhaps the result of a broken muffler.

Someone else was coming. *Shit.*

Hoping that Olivia and their vehicle weren't too visible, Katy snatched up her bits and pieces and sprinted away from the sound. She threw herself down behind a mullock heap just as a nondescript Toyota four-wheel drive pulled into the camp and came to a stop.

Katy cautiously lifted her face from the dirt and eased forward, sliding her body over the loose rocks, trying not to dislodge anything that would rattle down the slope behind her. She hadn't heard a door open, so she took a chance and raised herself up until she had a line of sight over the mullock heap.

A mountain of a man wearing a trucker cap emerged from the battered car. Tattoos covered both arms and every bit of skin visible around the edges of his dirt-smeared navy singlet. "Shane!" he yelled. "You here, ya bastard?"

The dog barked once, but otherwise there was no response. The man walked over to the caravan. "Shane?" Not as loud this time. He turned, heading directly towards the mine shaft where Katy had stood only moments before.

She dropped lower and kept watching, trying to breathe as quietly as possible. Her hands were braced either side of her, in case he came her way, in case she had to push herself up and run.

"Fuck," the man muttered, stopping halfway between the caravan and the mine shaft. He looked left and right, scratched his gut, pulled off his cap and ran a hand across his bald head. "Just returning your angle grinder, mate," he shouted. "I'll leave it in the tray of your ute." He paused, clearly waiting for an answer that was not forthcoming. With a shrug he returned to his car, then he retrieved the tool from the back and transferred it to the orange ute. "Thanks, mate," he called. After another short pause he got in his Toyota and drove slowly away, keeping the dust to a minimum: bush manners.

Katy pulled herself onto her hands and knees, her heart pounding as she listened to the car recede down the dirt track. He clearly hadn't spotted Olivia and the Land Cruiser on the way in, but would he see it now? She waited, expecting to hear the car stop, to hear a shout, but there was nothing other than the engine steadily fading into the distance. Now she just had to worry about Olivia holding her nerve and staying in place—that and the small matter of laying her trap before the target emerged. She studied the caravan again, surprised the shouting visitor hadn't provoked a response; she worried that behind the flimsy tin walls, the man was awake, stirring, about to emerge.

Should she get on with it, or wait another day? She didn't have too much left to do, and if he was awake enough to have heard his tattooed visitor, it could work to her advantage.

Katy carefully stood up, then made her way back to the mine

shaft. Any sound from the direction of the caravan and she would be off like a shot, with everything left there for him to find. She would lose her chance.

Once again, she took the iPod from her pocket. The bag she had tied to the ladder lay in the shadow of the hoist. Her unblinking eyes were on the caravan as she pressed play, dropped the iPod into the bag with the speaker, then grabbed the fishing line and began to lower the bag down the shaft. She kept her focus on the caravan, letting the line play out through her hand, hoping she'd allowed enough length that the bag would be lost from view but not so deep that the sound would be swallowed by the earth.

Then the line was at its full extent. From the caravan there was nothing but silence.

The clock was ticking. Katy had just under ten minutes to finish her work and get out of sight before her recording of empty air was replaced by noise.

With the trowel and broom head, she set about covering the rope she had laid out earlier, along with her footprints. She started at the shaft and worked her way back to one rope end, sprinkling loose earth, brushing away tracks. Then she repeated the process with the length of rope on the other side. By the time she was done, the entire rope was concealed, just a few more ripples in the corrugated ground.

Positioning herself where the rope ends converged behind a small pile of dirt, Katy looked at her watch and allowed herself a tiny smile. She still had a couple of minutes, and then, hopefully, the guest of honour would be making an appearance. Crouched in her hiding place, she was ready. When she checked her watch again, the ten minutes were up. Sweat trickled between her shoulder blades as she stared anxiously at the mine shaft. Why wasn't—?

Then she heard it: the sound of a pick echoing from below

the earth. Rhythmic and hypnotic, it was punctuated by occasional long silences, as though someone was peering intently at the rock face before resuming his labours.

It seemed like time slowed, but only five minutes later the door of the caravan banged back. Katy couldn't see her target from her hiding spot, but she could picture him standing there, listening in disbelief, squinting hard against the brightness of the morning.

Again, she waited. Just seconds this time.

With only birdsong for competition, the tap of the pick reverberated soft but insistent throughout the camp.

"Wha—?" He sounded wide awake. "Fuck!"

Katy risked a peek. The man snatched up a discarded shovel and strode across to the shaft, leaned over the edge. "Oi! Is that you, Moose? I heard ya before!"

The pick continued, steady, strong.

"What the fuck are ya doin', ya fuckin' claim-jumpin' mongrel!"

Silence, then the pick resumed.

"Oi!" Louder, furious, venomous. "You are fuckin' dead!"

Katy stood up, gripping the ends of the rope tightly. The target was still leaning over the shaft, so incensed at the thought of someone stealing his opal there was no chance he'd turn and see her behind him. Even if he had, it wouldn't have mattered. Pulling hard on the rope, Katy threw herself backward. The line ran taut, catching him across the shins. As it rose to pass through the rivet holes, the force yanked his feet away and up, flipping him headfirst into the shaft.

He was too surprised to yell. Katy heard the dull thump, and the drizzle of loosened gravel that followed. Then nothing.

TWELVE

Katy gathered her rope and hauled up the fishing line to retrieve the bag holding the iPod and speaker. Reaching in, she pressed stop, and the tapping pick fell silent. She carefully cut through the fishing-line knot and brushed away the last traces of her presence near the shaft. Hopefully, it would be days before anyone discovered the accident.

Then she remembered the dog. She had no idea how they'd explain it or what they would do with it, but abandoning an innocent dog out here was not something she could live with. A realisation hit her: she was worrying about the fate of a dog, but minutes ago she'd killed a man. She froze, gasping at the enormity of it, then forced herself to start moving again. It was too late for regrets, and there was no time for emotion.

At the caravan she stuck her head into the enclosed awning: no dog. The barking had been clear, unmuffled, so she knew it wasn't inside the van. She found it around the back making small, soft whines as she approached, its belly flattened to the earth, tail wagging so fast it created its own dust devil. Advancing cautiously, she wondered if the dog would turn nasty, but there was nothing but welcome in its trusting face. A heeler, it was indistinguishable from thousands of others of its breed—at least that was in their favour.

She dropped to the ground and ran her hands through dappled red fur, feeling the snag of burrs and the thick coating of desert. An idea formed, a way for the dog to vanish without raising any questions.

After making a loop with one end of her rope, she passed it over the dog's head, a makeshift collar and lead. She unbuckled and removed his thick leather collar, then refastened it and dropped it at the full extent of the chain that had tethered him to the underside of the caravan. If anyone should investigate, it would seem as though the dog had slipped his collar, straining after something or trying to get away.

The heeler pressed against her leg, shivered slightly, and stuck to her side as she moved off, keeping to the hard-packed earth, leaving no record of her final departure from the camp. She stayed off the track, walking back through the scrub to the Land Cruiser, relieved to see it was still there, to see Olivia crouched in the shade of a tea-tree.

Their eyes locked, and Katy nodded. "It's done."

Olivia's hand went to her mouth, but she arrested the gesture, instead pushing back the hair that fell across the side of her face. "Katy!" Her gaze dropped to the dog.

"Better come up with a name and get him used to it. If we're going to pass him off as ours, he has to at least lift his ears when you call. And we should get him some water—I didn't see any there."

Olivia nodded, overenthusiastic, and hurried to the Land Cruiser. Katy took the dog into the shade while she waited. She tried to analyse her feelings and was surprised to find she felt nothing except a desire to hit the road. She was silent as Olivia offered the dog a bowl of water, the desperate animal quickly lapping it dry. Bastard of a man, couldn't even give a dog water. And with that thought came a surge of satisfaction at what she had done.

Katy swallowed. She had expected some guilt, shock, even revulsion at her actions—not pure satisfaction.

"Billy," Olivia said. "We'll call him Billy." The dog wagged his tail.

"Works for me." Katy's voice sounded normal to her ears. "We should go, get right away from Lightning Ridge. I'll clean myself up somewhere else." She gave the rope a gentle tug and crossed to the Land Cruiser. Olivia had left the back open, and the dog jumped straight in, settling next to their camping gear. "Smart boy," Katy said as she stowed her equipment and removed the rope from Billy's neck. "We'll need to get you a new collar." She closed the back and moved around to the driver's door.

Olivia said gently, "You must be exhausted after last night and…everything. Do you want me to drive, darl?"

"Thanks, but the adrenaline is making me buzz like an electric fence, and I think I'll do better keeping my mind on the road."

With a nod, Olivia picked up a fallen eucalyptus branch. "I'll handle the tyre tracks in this spot, then. Just drive out, and I'll brush it down."

Katy climbed into the driver's seat, this time slamming her door—there was no one to hear them now. She turned to the dog. "Billy, huh? Are you a good boy, Billy?"

He responded with a proper bark and more tail thumping. Grinning, she leaned back and slapped her hand on the rear seat, inviting him to move closer. He sailed over the backrest and positioned himself in the middle. Katy placed a hand on his shoulder, and for a moment the two of them just sat. Then she straightened up, pulled on her sunglasses, and twisted the key in the ignition.

Ten minutes after they'd driven beyond the edge of town, Katy let out a long, slow breath. "Was it me or did you feel like there was a target on the car as we went down the main street?"

"I felt like everyone was staring, but when I risked a look, nobody could have given a stuff. Of course, I was busy keeping Billy out of sight."

Katy licked her lips and swallowed, suddenly feeling the dryness of her throat. "Could you pass me some water?"

"Oh, my God! Sorry, darl!" Olivia pulled a sports bottle from the passenger door pocket. "You must be parched."

"I'm only just starting to realise how freaked out I actually was—am." Katy took the bottle in one hand and pulled the spigot up with her teeth. After a glance at the road, straight and empty ahead of them, she took a long draught.

"I also have a stash of lollies here if you need sugar. And do you want to talk?"

Katy wedged the bottle between her thighs. "Thanks. I'm okay. I mean, maybe shock is going to set in later. But right now…" She shook her head. "Perhaps it was the way it happened. If there had been blood or even a confrontation, I might be feeling more…more of something. I don't really understand it. At the moment I can't talk about it. Although, there is one thing you could do for me."

"Anything you need, darl."

"I know it's your stress reliever, and I love you, Liv, I really do, so don't take this the wrong way. But if you start bloody humming right now, I'm gonna lose it. So put a sock in it, please."

Olivia stared at her, eyes wide. Then she snorted, made an exaggerated show of stifling her laugh, and nodded. "I think I can manage that, darl."

They stopped for petrol in Collarenebri, then blasted down the Gwydir Highway. The Land Cruiser ate up the kilometres, running from its ever-diminishing shadow as they travelled east. With nothing but low yellow plains stretched out on either side and a vast sky overhead, it was a good time for meditation and introspection. Yet as Katy drove, she thought only of the road ahead. She slowed as required when they passed through Moree, accelerating again on the other side, pushing the limit until they hit Biniguy, Gravesend, Warialda, tiny towns, some barely more than blips on the map.

Finally they rolled into Inverell, where it didn't take long to find a dog-friendly caravan park and arrange another unpowered campsite. Tomorrow they would have another three and a bit hours to Coffs Harbour, and from there they'd take a leisurely drive down the Pacific Highway back to Sydney. Once they were on the coast, everything would start to feel closer to normal, and they would be able to relax a bit—at least, that was what Katy hoped.

Shower, set up camp, wash dog, buy dog food, feed dog. The light was fading by the time Katy and Olivia were done. They grabbed some fish and chips from one of the local takeaways. Probably not the wisest choice for a town three hundred kilometres from the ocean, but Katy had found herself with a hankering for salt and grease.

Billy had settled in remarkably well, even responding to his name in exchange for the occasional chip. Cleaned up, he looked like a different dog, and the way he curled up next to Olivia suggested a long and happy companionship. Given the scars they had found across his body, many from cigarette burns, it was impossible not to believe the dog was grateful.

Only when night was fully upon them did Katy stir and stand. Olivia looked up, her eyebrows raised in silent question.

"I need to call," Katy said. From the glove box she retrieved a burner phone, along with a SIM card. "Won't be long." Walking away from their camp, she headed into the darkness, staring up at the sky, its star-studded brilliance like a negative image of the sapphire fields that ran through the surrounding country.

After inserting the SIM card, she punched in a number she'd committed to memory, then pressed the receiver to her ear, hiding the dull glow of the screen. She listened as somewhere a phone rang. Once, twice. A click.

"This is Mia."

At the sound of Mia's voice, Katy felt as though she'd stepped onto firmer ground.

"It's me," Katy said. "The trip has been going really well. A couple of surprises, but that's what travel is about! And the dog is loving every minute."

A short silence, a breath. "Well, of course. Did you find those sights you wanted to see?"

"Yes! We've knocked that off the bucket list. We're going to spend a few days on the coast before we head home."

"Sounds lovely. I'd kill to be there with you."

"No need." Katy ended the call.

THIRTEEN

Mia prised off the back of the phone, extracted the SIM card, and carried the tiny piece of circuitry into the bathroom. After dropping it onto the tiles, she ground it under her heel then flushed the misshapen remains down the toilet. She would get rid of the cheap phone tomorrow.

Returning to her office, she unlocked the top desk drawer and pulled out another phone, this one with a dot of blue nail polish on its back. Katy's shade had been frosted pink. There were four more burners in the drawer, all identifiable by small blobs of polish. As the women were also using disposable mobiles, there would be no matching numbers, no pattern of calls to trace, but the more layers of security, the better.

Mia pocketed the blue-dot phone and scooped up her keys. Fifteen minutes later, she swung into the drive-through lane of a 24-hour fast-food restaurant, ordered a coffee, and made her first call on the burner, this one to a normal phone number.

It was picked up immediately. "Gabrielle speaking."

"Call me in twenty on this number." Mia disconnected, switched the phone off, and pulled up to the second window to collect her order.

Eighteen minutes later she was in a large car park near a suburban football ground. She could see a dog walker in the distance, torch in hand and a red light on the canine's collar, but otherwise Mia was alone. She had a sip of coffee, wrinkled her nose at the taste, then turned the phone on. At precisely the twenty-minute mark, the screen lit up, no caller ID. It rang once before Mia answered.

"Sorry. I'm out on my bike. Can you hang on a sec?" Gabrielle sounded slightly winded, and in the background Mia could hear the swoosh of passing cars.

"Of course."

The traffic sounds receded. Mia heard the *tick-tick-tick* of a riderless bicycle, and some unidentifiable scrapes and rustling, before Gabrielle was back on the line.

"Sorted. I'm good now. I think. Depends on why you're calling."

"I heard from Katy."

Gabrielle sucked in her breath. "I don't… I don't know what I should say or ask. I don't know if I even want to be having this conversation."

"That's fair enough. Would you rather not do this now?"

"No, yes. Ah, crap. Tell me."

"He's gone."

"Katy really did it? She really…"

"She didn't say much, but it was very clear that the man who murdered your sister won't ever hurt another woman."

"Is Katy alright?"

"As I said, it was a very brief conversation. I assume she didn't encounter any problems with the plan." Mia moved the phone away, checking the duration of the call.

"Good, that's good. But I mean, is she okay given that she… you know."

"From the sound of her voice, I think it hasn't really sunk in yet. It could hit her in the coming days, but she and Olivia are travelling slowly now, which may give her some space to process. In any case, I plan to see her as soon as they get back." Mia stared out at nothing, the glow of lights from a distant suburban street emphasising the yawning darkness of the open ground in front of her. "Are you okay, Gabrielle?" She kept her voice soft.

"My alibi is solid. I've been at work during the day and catching up with friends at night. And I'm relieved Katy is alright, but as for the rest of it, I don't really know. It doesn't seem real. Are you sure he's dead? Is Katy sure? I wish she'd been able to take a picture. Oh God, that makes me sound like a sicko, doesn't it? But I've spent so long loathing that man, wanting him dead, and I don't know if I can let go of that without proof. And—wow—I actually feel a bit cheated that Katy did it and I didn't. That's awful, isn't it? Sorry, I can't seem to stop talking."

"Don't say sorry. And you're not awful, and you're not a sicko. Everything you've said makes sense. You may not be able to truly understand all your emotions at the moment, but that will come. Just be aware of it, and when it happens—whenever that is—take stock, don't judge yourself, remember that it's okay to cry, and, above all, I am here for you."

"Thanks, Mia. Hearing you say that makes me realise I can identify one changed feeling."

Mia nodded, even though the other woman couldn't see her. "Tell me."

"I've grown so used to the pressure in my chest, I don't really notice it anymore. But hearing the news, hearing what Katy did for my sister—it's as though someone has been squeezing my heart for so long, crushing it, and now their grip has loosened."

Mia smiled. "Message this phone if you need me, or catch me on the Bradleys Head walking track on any Monday."

"Tell Katy thank you."

"I will."

Mia cut the call and switched off the phone. She was reaching for the ignition when she realised her hand was trembling. Holding it up in front of her face, she studied the subtle quiver in the faint light: she had been so busy thinking about Katy and Gabrielle that she had failed to consider her own emotions. She ran her internal therapist's eye over them, drilling down until she could pinpoint the moment that had caused this physical reaction.

There: when Gabrielle had asked, *Are you sure he's dead?*

The question was not surprising. People often had a hard time accepting death, regardless of whether the deceased was loved or loathed, and Mia doubted that even a photograph of the man at the bottom of a mine shaft would have been enough for Gabrielle at this stage. Memory remained, whether as the echoing call of a beloved voice now silenced, or the gut-clenching fear and involuntary flinch away from a hand raised, however innocently. And sometimes, even incontrovertible proof was still not enough.

So Mia understood why Gabrielle couldn't believe. Besides, in every horror movie Mia had ever seen, the monster was never dead when you thought it was. In her experience, a human monster could be like that too—and when he returned, the consequences were devastating. Luckily for Gab, she would get her proof one day.

———

Mia could remember exactly when her sister first told her about Travis. It was a Sunday afternoon, the lazy coda to their regular family lunch. The two sisters were sitting in their parents' garden, half-heartedly batting insects away from drinks, catching up with each other's lives. Of course Mia had already known her sister was seeing someone new; she had an aura about her that Mia had seen before, something that made her seem both softer yet paradoxically brighter, more vivid. When she said his name, told Mia how they had met, her voice was rich with things unsaid. This relationship, Mia could see, was different.

She was introduced to Travis a couple of weeks later. In the years since, she had thought about that meeting obsessively, along with their subsequent interactions in those first few months, looking for something, a warning sign, a wrong note. But there was nothing. He had been charming, attentive to her sister, courteous to their parents. He'd told them he was an only child, and his mother and father were back in the UK. It was not until after, that Mia discovered those were just two of the smaller lies he had told.

One of the things that tormented her the most was Travis's frequent, apparently self-deprecating remark, the words that had made him seem like a regular, upstanding, hardworking guy: *I may not be the smartest bloke, but I'm good with my hands.*

Mia had been wrapped up in her own life, busy with her growing practice, and she'd known her sister was occupied with her work and relationship. So at first she hadn't noticed the growing distance, and when she did, she assumed her sister was simply caught up in the intensity of a heady romance. Calls were less frequent, and if Mia phoned her sister in the evenings or on weekends, their conversations were brief. As the months passed, get-togethers became almost nonexistent; her sister always had plans with Travis. The couple still came to family lunch on Sunday, but there was never a chance for Mia to catch her sister alone. Mia spoke about it with their mother, who was mildly put out but of the opinion that once she and Travis had settled into their relationship, Mia's sister would come up for air.

One Sunday, Mia's sister was wearing a loose sundress, and a gesture sent the full-length sleeve back to her elbow. Five angry blotches, fingermarks, encircled her forearm. Mia grabbed her sister by the hand and turned the arm over, examining the damage. But before she could ask, her sister—with a flick of her eyes towards Travis—was laughing even as she pulled her hand away and readjusted the sleeve. "So clumsy! I slipped on wet tiles and nearly fell, but luckily Trav was there to grab me!"

Mia looked at her sister's smiling face, hesitated, then smiled back. She could hardly push the issue with Travis sitting right there, and it might have happened that way. Mia let it go, but a kernel of doubt lodged deep in her gut. On subsequent Sundays she scanned her sister's face and watched the way she moved, looking for any sign of injury, any indication something wasn't right. But there was nothing to see. Perhaps it had just been a slip.

A new year and the couple moved in together: Travis's place, on the other side of the city. Mia's sister was constantly working, exhausted, or had other plans, and now she lived too far away for Mia to drop in under the pretext of being in the neighbourhood. Mia tried to see it the way their mother saw it, but she was hurt by the constant rebuffing—and worried.

Then came the day when Mia called her sister's mobile, and Travis answered. He was warm and civil, but Mia did not get to speak to her sister at all.

And suddenly she knew. Whether her sister realised it or not, she had been gradually, systematically isolated.

FOURTEEN

The drive down the coast was uneventful. Katy and Olivia spent a lot of time at the beach, swimming in the ocean, throwing sticks for Billy and laughing at his hit-and-miss attitude to retrieving, waiting for the pretence of a holiday to feel real. Waiting, also, for a news bulletin, a hue and cry, some indication that a man had been found dead at a remote opal mine and police suspected foul play. But there was nothing.

Katy didn't actively search for such a news story because the idea of leaving a digital trail was always lurking in the back of her mind. That didn't stop her from paying attention though; she bought the major papers whenever they passed through a town and regularly tuned in to the radio news. Had the body been found and the scene ruled an accident, or was it still down there, in the heat and darkness at the bottom of a mine shaft?

For days after the events at Lightning Ridge, Katy had been surprised that her sleep was deep and untroubled. Then, in Port Macquarie, Billy vanished. Finally, in response to the women's frantic calls, he emerged from a dense tangle of undergrowth looking immensely pleased, with a dark, viscous material smeared across his shoulders. Katy bent towards him, then recoiled, gagging. The dog had rolled in something; the stench of death and decay welled up to meet her. A maggot dropped from his fur, squirming in the dirt before it was crushed under Olivia's boot. It took a while to wash the smell from his coat.

That night, Katy had dreamed of a rotting human corpse, oozing green and yellow, teeming with bugs and worms, all writhing as they reduced it to bones, a time-lapse sequence that ended with a grinning skull. Katy woke with a shout, sweat beading her forehead, realisation settling heavily in her gut. Olivia was quickly there, calming, supportive, but it was the dog who truly reassured Katy, who made her remember why she had done what she'd done—an innocent creature, abused and scarred but still alive. Not Katy's sister, nor Gabrielle's, but still one less victim.

On the last day, as they neared the northern outskirts of Sydney, their conversations became increasingly superficial. They discussed Billy's immediate future—Olivia would take him—then lapsed into observations on city traffic and returning to work. Katy had enjoyed Olivia's company and been exceedingly grateful for it over the past several days. But after dropping woman and dog in a leafy street close to Olivia's lower North Shore home, Katy embraced the solitude as she drove to her house in the Inner West.

At the outset of the journey she had kept herself tightly under control, pushing away fears and doubts so she could not only carry out the job but also spare Olivia from the psychological backwash: she didn't want the woman to have any second thoughts about the task that lay ahead of her. Katy had expected to be working harder to suppress the feelings that arose after she killed a man; instead she found that her emotions seemed to have died back in Lightning Ridge. Strangely, the fact she felt nothing was causing her more anxiety than the act of homicide.

She was aware that by going first, she'd taken an enormous risk. What if none of the others went through with it? Until the second target had been dealt with, she would be especially vulnerable, and given their decision to avoid contact with one another, the only person she could talk to was Mia.

Katy pulled into her driveway, the sight of post sticking out of the letterbox a jarring reminder of normal life. When she stepped onto the pebbled paving, her legs felt shaky, and her body was light with fatigue, hunger, and the odd sensation of movement that follows a sustained period of travel. She stumbled slightly, almost collapsing, but caught herself, tensing tired muscles and holding on to her fence. As soon as she felt steady enough, she grabbed the mail and flipped through the small pile. Among the bills and letters from charities, one item stood out: a jaunty postcard with a photo of Bronte Beach, circa 1950. A message was scrawled on the back.

Fancy a dip? Saturday at 8 am, south end. M

Katy closed her eyes with relief.

She hauled her stuff inside and dropped everything in the laundry. A hot shower and soft slippers beckoned, but she headed to the kitchen first. Standing over the sink, she touched a match to the corner of the postcard, watching as it flared, curled, and blackened, before she turned on the tap and washed the remnants away.

When Katy found Mia, she was standing with her face turned to the ocean and the morning sun. "Nice place for a catch-up," Katy said. She bent down to pull off her sneakers, letting her toes sink into the sand.

"There's plenty of ambient noise from the surf to cover

conversation, and everyone is busy with their morning routines." Mia placed her hands on Katy's upper arms, staring intently at her. "I can see the strain you're under."

"Strain?" Katy laughed, hearing the brittleness in her own voice.

Mia tilted her head. "You clearly haven't been sleeping well. And as for the rest..." Her hand sketched a shape in the air between them, taking in Katy's body from her drawn face to her tightly bunched toes. "What about work?"

"Work was fine these last couple of days. I chatted about my road trip, colleagues admired my tan, and otherwise it was business as usual, dispensing drugs. I double-checked every order in the same way I always do, and other than you, everyone has been saying how refreshed I look."

Mia nodded. "You've always been good at putting up a front, but how many years have you been seeing me now? I know all your tricks. Shall we walk?"

They turned and headed north along the beach, keeping to the firmer sand near the water's edge. Katy, wearing running shorts, moved into the cold shallows, enjoying the ebb and flow of the water as it foamed around her ankles.

After a short distance, Mia half turned towards her. "So, how are you really feeling?"

Katy stopped, looked down, then faced Mia fully. She raised a hand, pushing her wind-blown hair from her face. "That's just it. I keep expecting to feel something—fear, guilt, remorse... something. But I don't. And it bothers me, a lot. How is it possible that I could...do that, and be completely immune to it? What does that make me?" Katy let the hand that had been holding her hair in check fall to her side. "I've always considered myself a good person. Well, at least an okay person."

Mia nodded, then began to walk again. She waited until

Katy drew level before she said, “What happened to your sister changed you, fundamentally. And this does too. You are a different version of yourself. But”—she held up a hand—“it does not change the fact that you are a good person. What you have done rights a wrong, and you have potentially saved others.” Katy began to speak, but Mia’s hand came up again, forestalling further comment. “Think of it this way, Katy. You told me once that your grandfather fought in World War Two, correct?”

“That’s right. Grandad was in the Pacific.”

“Was he a good person?”

“He could be cranky and strict, but, yes, he was a good bloke.” Katy smiled as she remembered time spent with the spirited old man.

“What do you think he did in the Pacific, again and again?”

Katy watched her feet pushing through the shallow water as she thought about her grandfather’s medals and what they meant.

“And why did he do it? To protect others. To make the world a better place. No one wants to go to war, but sometimes fighting is the only option left. If all other avenues have failed…” Mia shrugged.

Katy remained silent as they continued to walk. Around them, the beach was getting busier. She looked at the happy families and chatting couples and thought about her grandad: this was what he and his mates had fought to protect, why they had sacrificed so much. When she finally spoke, her voice was tight. “You cannot, for one minute, liken what I did to fighting a war for your country. That is just wrong.”

“I didn’t mean to, and I’m sorry for not making myself clear.” Mia’s tone was contrite. “What I meant was that I’m sure your grandfather was a changed man in many ways when he came back from the war, but it sounds as though the essence of his character didn't alter." Mia put a hand on Katy's arm, bringing her to a stop, and waited until she looked her in the eye. "He was still a good man."

Katy forced a smile. It flashed briefly across her lips, like a ripple in the water, before her face reestablished its lines of tension.

"Somebody once said something along the lines of, *evil people win when good people stand back and do nothing*. Which means that, whether calling out abusive or aggressive behaviour, agitating for legal reform, or taking more drastic action when everything else fails, sometimes someone needs to act. This time it's you—it's us."

As they stood there, a group of children raced past. Katy and Mia watched as they splashed in and out of the shallows, shrieking and laughing with delight. "I wish I could remember being that carefree and happy," Katy said, turning to follow their progress. "I need a swim."

"Katy—"

Katy waved her off. "I heard what you said. I've taken it on board, and I'll think it over. But right now, I have to deal with the fact that emotionally, I'm dead. Maybe down the track, when my sister's killer is gone, when the others have... Well, when they get to this point and we can all talk about it, that'll help. But for now, I just want to put my head underwater and swim. I love how the water makes the world seem softer. I want my eyes to sting and my throat to catch, and I want goosebumps. I want my arms and legs to get tired. I want to make myself feel something—anything that isn't this numbness."

Mia inclined her head. "I understand. And I agree that the other women will help sustain you, in time. It might also help you to know that Gabrielle says thank you."

Katy nodded, surprised at the short burst of happiness Gab's gratitude gave her.

"I'll get a new burner phone and text you the number. Send a message if you need me." Mia waved and turned to leave, edging back from the lapping waves.

Katy followed her up onto the drier sand, then dropped her sneakers and stepped out of her shorts. She was wearing bathers underneath, a bold tropical print at odds with her current grey mood. Still, talking to Mia had helped; Katy could see that in time, things would get better. For a moment she stood there, breathing deeply, bracing herself for the shock of cold water. Then she turned and ran into the ocean, diving under a wave and swimming, straight and strong, away from Mia, away from the safety of the shore.

FIFTEEN

A fortnight went past in which there was still no alarming news from Lightning Ridge. Perhaps Shane had been found, perhaps not. Either way, the man was dead; either way, there was no going back. Mia realised it was time to set the second operation in motion—time to contact Naomi.

The following Saturday, Mia was up early. She made her way across Sydney to a sportsground in West Pymble, where she found a good place on the grass and sat down with her coffee to wait for Naomi. Today she was wearing a Laura Ashley duffel coat and a fisherman's cap; they had the vintage feel she liked and were warm enough for a cold May morning, and they were also appropriate camouflage.

A number of people were already dotted on the slope around her, and more continued to arrive: a steady stream of parents, the occasional grandparent and, of course, the kids, ready for another round of Saturday morning sport. Mia scanned the arrivals for Naomi's face, waving occasionally to no one in particular, holding up a muesli bar and shaking it in the direction of the teams, checking her phone—in short, acting like every other parent who had given over a quarter of the weekend to their children's pursuits.

"This is unexpected."

The voice came from behind Mia, and she jumped.

"Sorry," Naomi said, dropping to the ground beside her. "I couldn't find anywhere to park! The place is crawling with Double Bay tractors, and I ended up having to leave the car a couple of streets away and hike in."

"One of the disadvantages." Mia smiled. "Good to see you."

Naomi was dressed in black jeans and a fitted black jacket, and her body was toned in a way that looked natural and effortless. It was enough to earn her envious glances from a few of the nearby mothers, and assessing stares from a father or two. She seemed to ignore them all as she inclined her head towards the field, where play was just getting underway. "I didn't know you had kids," she said.

Mia let her smile widen into one of genuine amusement. "I don't. But these events are a great place to hold a clandestine meeting. Everyone is so absorbed in their own child or in making sure they're one-upping the other parents in some way that they completely ignore you. No record we met—because there are all sorts of rules about filming and photographing children now—and it doesn't cost anything, so no financial trail."

Naomi screwed up her face. "Shit. I don't know whether to be impressed or concerned."

Mia sat up straighter and began to clap. "Oh, well done!" she called, as around her a few parents applauded something that had taken place on the field. "Got to at least seem to have a passing interest," she said quietly to Naomi.

Naomi frowned, clearly struggling with her emotions. "My husband, Rich, and I—shit, I don't want to say it because it's such a cliché… We're 'trying.'" She made air quotes. "Which I think is just a polite euphemism for having lots of sex. So I guess I should say we hope to have a baby in the not-too-distant future." Naomi looked down and adjusted her sunglasses, which didn't need adjusting. "Even when we were little, my sister and I always talked about what we'd name our kids, how they'd play together, grow up close to each other... One big lovely extended family. Funny, we didn't talk much about the sort of men we'd choose to be the fathers of our children."

Mia watched her but didn't speak. Naomi didn't often volunteer information, and Mia knew better than to interrupt.

"After Jo was killed, it took me a while to get back to the place where I want to have children." She glanced at Mia. "One therapist told me how life-affirming it would be." Naomi sniffed. "But all I could think of was, how could I go there without Jo? How could my children grow up without cousins or their Aunty Jo? Who could I talk to, laugh, and commiserate with about the milestones or the disasters? Who would also be awake for midnight feeds? My whole idea of parenthood was one where Jo was front and centre."

"And now?"

"Now I feel like it wouldn't be fair to Jo to let those dreams die with her. And I also think telling my children about their Aunty Jo is a good way to remember her." Naomi's voice cracked.

"So this is for Jo?"

"Not just for Jo."

"Okay then."

"Sorry, Mia, this wasn't meant to be a free bloody therapy session! It's just, I hadn't expected to see all these kids." Naomi waved her hand at the match. "Didn't have my happy-family persona in place."

"Never apologise for telling me what's on your mind. You're still technically my client, even if our professional relationship has taken a different form. Besides, I'd be pretty lousy at my job if I didn't anticipate that the approach we've taken would cause some psychological turmoil. My role in this is to give you all the support you need, whether that's logistical or emotional."

Around them another cheer went up.

"How does that work, though?" Naomi asked. "We agreed to keep apart as much as possible."

"And that's what we have to do. But we're all in this, and I'm certainly not going to abandon anyone. So if you need something or there's an emergency, text the number I gave you, and I will call back. If we can't sort things out on the phone, we can arrange to meet somewhere like this. I'll also be discreetly checking on the others to make sure they're okay."

"Speaking of..."

"Indeed. Katy has been back for a few weeks."

"I haven't heard anything."

"A job well done then, wouldn't you say?"

One corner of Naomi's mouth curled, a small sign of approval on her otherwise impassive face. "Is it wrong that as a mining engineer I'm immensely proud?"

"Job satisfaction is important," said Mia. "Although I don't think I'd put that one on your CV."

Naomi swung her legs around on the grass so she was facing Mia properly. "So, you've arranged this meeting to get stage two underway. My turn."

"Are you okay with that?"

"I think so. I don't know. Katy told me about her sister back in February."

Mia leaned back on her elbows, tilting her face to the sky.

"I remembered the case straight away," Naomi said softly. "Pip, Katy's sister, finally felt able to leave the abusive relationship, and Daniel Pavic ran her down. At least the police charged the slimeball with murder! Just typical that he did a deal and pleaded guilty to dangerous driving causing death and a couple of other driving-related offences."

"Yes." Mia's jaw clenched. "Instead of a possible life sentence, he could only get a maximum of ten years for each charge. And then, as the judge said, he had no prior criminal history, impressive character references, and an excellent work record. Which apparently justifies the pathetically inadequate sentence he got."

"When Katy told me he'd been given a non-parole period of only two and a half years, I wanted to scream."

"Did you know that was all he served? He's been out for over a year now."

"Are you kidding me?" Naomi's raised voice caused one or two mothers, their boho-chic attire screaming North Shore, to shoot her reproving looks. She met their censure with a face of stone, and they quickly turned back to the match.

Mia patted Naomi's hand. "Sadly not."

"Shit, as if it wasn't bad enough…" Naomi groaned. "If I had any doubts about this, I think that revelation has just put them to bed." She shook her head. "Katy gave me his address and said he's a heavy drinker. I plan to use that if I can, but I'll need to watch the slimeball for a bit to make sure."

Mia nodded. "Of course. And I don't need to remind you not to use a navigation system when you go there."

"No worries, I like maps and plans! I still have a Gregory's street directory in the car."

"Perfect. The timeline is entirely up to you, but when you've picked your moment, message me so I can let Katy know for her alibi. Other than that, take as long as you need to do what you have to do, as there's no firm deadline. When you're done, get in touch, and I'll notify the phase three ladies."

"Good to know." The corner of Naomi's mouth twitched. "Have you ever wondered about the origin of the word *deadline*?

Because it seems entirely appropriate—only not for us, for them."

Mia shook her head, intrigued. It was a curious word, but she was more interested in what underpinned Naomi's thinking.

"I looked it up ages ago, after a particularly difficult boss threatened me with all sorts of repercussions if I missed the deadline. Of course, the bastard was setting me up to fail so he could get me fired. He couldn't handle working with a female mining engineer—having a woman tell him where and how to dig—so he set an impossible deadline."

"What did you do?"

Naomi smiled with deep satisfaction. "Delivered the project a week early at a meeting that included his superiors—right after he'd told them to expect cost blowouts due to delays. Anyway, I looked up the origin of *deadline,* and it was a line drawn around a prison, or even just a group of prisoners out in the open. Any man who put a toe across the deadline was shot."

"Huh," said Mia, her eyebrows arching. "I presume we're talking about male prisoners? Men who—in the context of what you're saying—deserved to die for crossing a line?"

"Yep, exactly."

"I shall think about deadlines completely differently now." Mia adjusted the angle of her fisherman's cap, shading her eyes. Naomi was a woman after her own heart.

From the playing field there came a shrill blast of the referee's whistle. A moment's hush, then around Mia and Naomi the crowd rose to its feet, cheering. It was all over.

SIXTEEN

As she left the Saturday sports and walked to her car, Naomi was surprised by her tumult of emotions. Fear. The Pleiades women had whipped themselves into a frenzy with their talk of justice and righting wrongs, and now the baton had been passed to her. But feeling afraid of the consequences wasn't going to hold her back—was it?

Grief. Talking about Jo, remembering their childhood dreams, Jo's beautiful personality and her aspirations, always, always caused Naomi's heart to ache. It was something she had come to expect, that twisting, knotting sensation in her chest, the spasm in her gut that ran through to her spine, the pressure in her throat and behind her eyes.

Longing. If Naomi was honest with herself, it was this feeling that threatened to overwhelm her emotional defences. Since Jo's murder, not once had she acknowledged how much she really wanted children; she had buried her desire for a family when she buried her sister. But unexpectedly finding herself at a sports event—surrounded by smiling, supportive families, seeing healthy kids laugh and play—had almost been her undoing. She'd tried to block it out, to focus on Mia, but the air seemed to be saturated with oxytocin. There was a sense of belonging, a completeness she hadn't realised was missing from her life. She and Rich may have decided to try for a baby, but it had been a long, long, time since Naomi knew with certainty that she wanted to be a mother.

She sat in her Jeep Grand Cherokee, eyes closed, letting the emotions wash through her, sorting them into bundles she could deal with, then considering how she was going to achieve the task she had set herself, given she was pregnant. She had planned to tell Rich this weekend over a special dinner, but now…

Obviously, he still didn't know about The Pleiades. A support group-turned-murder society wasn't something Naomi planned to mention over dessert. This, she realised, was at the heart of her turmoil: she couldn't share the happy, momentous news of her pregnancy while a part of her brain was working on despatch plans for one Daniel Pavic aka The Slimeball. She would do the job, then tell her husband he was going to be a father. Besides, the pregnancy was in its early days—better to wait a few more weeks to be sure than to get Rich's hopes up too soon.

"Who are you kidding?" Naomi asked herself. "If you don't tell Rich, it seems less real, and if it seems less real, you won't be afraid to do the job, afraid of being injured."

Jo's death had taught Naomi a lot of things about herself. It had taught her how to pick apart her own defences, but she had also learned to confront her fears and self-doubts and turn them to her advantage. Now she forced herself to flip the inner narrative. Being pregnant wasn't an impediment to the plan, but instead another reason to go ahead. Every parent wanted to protect their child—how could she make the world safer for hers?

Easy.

Naomi pulled the burner phone from her bag, powered it up, and tapped out a message to Brooke. She still had concerns about Brooke's resolve and worried the younger woman might be more of a hindrance than a help. Although Naomi hadn't yet seen where or how her target lived, she had a rough plan in mind, and there was a part for Brooke to play. Naomi would have to be careful to explain everything and watch for signs of weakness. And it would be wise to think of an option B, a way to get out and away if things went pear-shaped and Brooke lost her shit.

After reading through the message once, Naomi hit send. She would meet with Brooke, but she had to be prepared to go it alone.

It took Naomi a while to find Brooke in the heaving throng of women, but that, she reflected as she made her way down another narrow aisle, was an endorsement for the anonymity of the meeting place she had suggested: the preloved and vintage fashion market in the Marrickville Town Hall. Naomi hadn't been anywhere like it for years, but she knew what she'd find: two dollars to get in, communal changing rooms, and a big crowd hellbent on making a fashion find. The noise and confusion meant she could talk to Brooke while they ostensibly rummaged through racks and tables.

She elbowed her way to the next stall, smiled at the two women behind the trestle table, and spent a few seconds watching a girl flick through a rack of dresses with practised fingers. Then Naomi cast her gaze around the hall again and caught sight of Brooke. The waifish blond woman was at the top of the next aisle, in front of a mirror, checking out a bag that hung from her shoulder. As Naomi approached and caught her eye, she pulled it off and returned it to the trader with a quick thanks.

They moved a bit farther down the aisle until they reached one of the busier clothing stalls. Naomi rummaged for a moment, selecting five dresses and a blouse. "Can I try these on?" she asked the vendor.

"Of course. Twenty dollars deposit." She scribbled something on a notepad. "What's your name?"

"Susan," said Naomi, handing over a twenty.

"Know where to go?"

Naomi nodded and led Brooke back the way they'd come. The changing room had been set up on the stage behind heavy velvet theatre curtains, and Brooke and Naomi found themselves a corner at the back. As Naomi slowly undressed, she outlined her plan to Brooke. She timed her words to match the ebb and flow around them, loudly commenting on the clothes she was trying on when people were close, then reverting to the business at hand when she and Brooke had more space or the volume of chatter rose. In this way, as Naomi took her time exchanging one dress for the next, tugged at shoulders and waists, and turned slow circles while Brooke looked on, she explained how she hoped to achieve her goal, what she still had to check and organise, and what Brooke's role in the proceedings would be. All the time Naomi kept a watchful eye on the younger woman's face, looking for any sign she wasn't ready to take the next step.

But Brooke listened closely, nodded, asked pertinent questions, and spoke with an unwavering voice. Despite her misgivings, Naomi could find nothing to fault in Brooke's response. Finally, she changed back into her own clothes, pulling on a T-shirt and jeans soft and pale with years of wear.

"Are you going to buy that last dress?" Brooke was

clutching the hangers, and now she held one forward for Naomi's consideration.

"What? No. I never meant to buy anything." Naomi fluffed out her hair.

With a shrug, Brooke said, "It looked pretty good. But also, we've been quite a while, and I thought if you told the stallholder you couldn't make up your mind and had to try it on a couple of times…"

Naomi glanced at the dress again, a chic number by Altuzarra, classy enough for a wedding, powerful enough to wear to a company meeting when she wanted to kick arse. Brooke was right about the dress, but more importantly, she was right about giving the stallholder a reason for the delay; it showed she was thinking about the broader plan and not just going through the motions.

"You're right on both counts," Naomi said. She took the hangers from Brooke, and they wove their way back through the thickening crowd. Naomi didn't miss the stallholder's relieved expression at the sight of her returning merchandise. "Sorry I took so long," Naomi gushed as she handed back the rejects. "I had to try this one on a couple of times. I hadn't planned on blowing my entire market budget on one dress, but it's just amazing."

"One of my favourites! Lucky you!" The vendor eyed Naomi. "And lucky dress."

When the deal was done, Naomi and Brooke slipped away. They left the hall together, passing out into the late autumn afternoon and descending the broad steps as people came and went around them.

"Give me a couple of weeks to get things in place," Naomi said. "I'm hoping to arrange it for a Saturday night, but until I've spent some time observing I won't know for sure."

Brooke nodded as she pulled sunglasses from her handbag. “Put something in your diary—spa weekend with the girls, antiquing, whatever.”

“I understand, don’t worry.”

Brooke’s thin arms looked even paler out here amid the salon tans of Sydney’s fashionistas, and Naomi paused. “Are you okay?”

The younger woman tipped her head from side to side. “Umm, getting there, I think.”

“No, I mean—sorry, this probably isn’t my business—but are you well?”

Brooke nodded briskly. “I…had a lot of trouble eating after my sister was killed. But like I said, getting there.”

“Okay. I’ll call you.”

“I’ll be ready. I promise.”

They walked away from each other, and Naomi didn’t look back.

SEVENTEEN

It was months ago when Naomi first envisioned how she, with a bit of help from Brooke, would do it.

Immediately after the meeting in Centennial Park, she had gone home and made straight for the bathroom. She'd shed her clothes as she hurried down the hall, calling out to Rich that she was sweaty after her run and needed to shower. He would usually have seen a late afternoon shower as an opportunity for wet, slippery sex, and Naomi had an excuse ready in case he appeared. But he was in their home office, presumably wrestling with the details of a forthcoming merger, so instead of urgent footsteps tracing her own down the parquetry, all she got in response was a preoccupied, "Okay, honey."

Relieved, she took a short, perfunctory shower. Then, with the door locked and the water still flowing, she reached into the back of the vanity and pulled out her pills. She had forgotten how many there were. All the mood-altering, sleep-inducing, memory-numbing things she'd been prescribed after Jo's murder were there, each packet with one or two empty blisters in the foil, all thrown to the back of the cupboard when Naomi had acknowledged once more that, for her, stopping the pain felt wrong—she needed to care.

"Of course you still care about Jo," her then-therapist had counselled. "The medication just helps you to cope and not be in so much mental anguish."

Naomi had argued that caring, by its very nature, implied a certain depth of feeling, but her arguments had made little impact. They had kept talking in circles, she and Doctor Pill-popper, until Naomi had walked. After that she'd battled along, alone, until the day a discreet business card was pressed into her hand, and Naomi ended up on Mia's doorstep.

But she'd kept the drugs, just in case it got too much: the grief of losing her sister, the guilt of living. She'd come close on several occasions, but something had always held her back. And now she had another use for her stash—or, at least, the Valium. Without knowing anything about the man she would target, Naomi had thought about spiking his food or drink with crushed-up Valium. There was no way to ensure he would consume enough, but all she needed was to get him to the drowsy and compliant stage. Then she would helpfully assist him to his car, wait for him to drop off completely, then set him up with the engine running and a length of hose. The scene would appear to be the suicide of a man riddled with guilt at his murderous actions. Any Valium found in his system would be assumed to be self-administered.

When she'd got some details about the slimeball who'd murdered Katy's sister, it gave her a much clearer picture of who she was dealing with. But it had also shown up some flaws in her plan.

Outside of work, the slimeball kept to himself. He was a drinker, but rather than propping up a bar somewhere, he would buy a couple of slabs, park himself in front of his flat screen, and neck stubbies. He lived on a few acres south-west of the city, the house and assorted sheds sitting back from the road at the end of a pitted gravel drive, with dense forest butting up to the eastern and northern boundaries.

Naomi had originally thought she would contrive an encounter in a bar or pub, spike his drink—perhaps with Brooke creating a distraction—then wait for him to leave, trail him home, and finish the job. But there was no pub in the equation, and any public encounter in such a sparsely populated area would be noticed and remembered. It had become clear that Naomi would need to get onto his property. Since she didn't want to be seen on the narrow road that led to his driveway, she would need to hike in through the scrub from a more remote starting point. She had no knowledge of the layout of the land or house beyond what could be seen on Google Maps, which meant she'd be going in blind, hoping to find something she could doctor with Valium. If she could add the drug to a half-eaten meal or an open beer, he'd be highly likely to consume it all immediately, but that meant Naomi needed a dinnertime diversion. A power outage would be ideal, forcing him to abandon his plate in front of the TV, giving Naomi a brief opportunity to act. All she had to do was get Brooke to access the fuse box and trip the main switch.

It was a highly imperfect plan, and Naomi didn't like it. But it was all she had.

She was faced with two big problems when it came to scoping out the slimeball and his property. The first was the need to spend a lot of time in the area, repeatedly passing through nearby towns without being noticed. The second was Rich.

After some consideration, she thought she'd be okay on the first point, provided she didn't take the same route from the city every time and didn't show her face anywhere unless it was absolutely unavoidable. If she was careful to fill up with petrol before leaving Sydney, there would be no reason to stop other than when she was actively engaged in her reconnaissance and planning.

The second point could not be so easily managed. Rich worked hard, but on weekends he was a homebody. That meant all Naomi's legwork would have to be done during weekday working hours—and that meant somehow fitting it around her own work schedule. She briefly considered telling her boss about the pregnancy, using the excuse of additional tests and doctor's appointments to account for time away from the office. But she couldn't drag her unborn child into this, couldn't use a developing new life as part of a cover for homicide. It would taint everything. In the end, her boss didn't mind when Naomi said she planned to work from home for a couple of days here and there over the coming weeks. Avoiding the disruptions of company HQ in favour of the home office was something she'd done sporadically when analysing raw data or working on an implementation strategy, and fortunately there had been recent test drills, giving her just the excuse she needed. When it was time for her to tackle Project Slimeball, working remotely two days a week was an established part of her routine.

Naomi told Rich that from the following week she'd be back in the office every day. She didn't want him popping home for a surprise lunch-slash-sex, calling on the landline, or arranging for deliveries that required a signature, like additions to his wine collection. At least they never travelled in to work together.

Planning and logistics were part of Naomi's DNA, and she found comfort in her system: strategise, analyse, identify potential risks, allow for contingencies.

Implement.

EIGHTEEN

When Monday morning arrived, Naomi was in her black SUV by seven, tinted windows closed. She visualised the route she would take as she drove south, avoiding the toll roads and their pesky record of her passage. She'd packed her work satchel with casual clothes—the sort of things a hiker might wear—and made note of two or three places where she could pull over to change. Naomi had also chosen her corporate attire carefully: a skirt that was easy to strip off, a blouse that never wrinkled no matter what she did to it, and a jacket that would spend the entire trip folded neatly on the back seat.

It took her an hour and a half to reach her destination—or rather, the rural road that ran through bushland to the east of her target's land. Naomi's assessment of satellite maps indicated it was only a kilometre to the slimeball's boundary fence as the crow flew, but the terrain was hilly and densely forested. She was pinning her hopes on bush tracks, barely more than indistinct smudges when seen from the air but reportedly scattered across the region, frequented by mountain bikers and bushwalkers as well as the occasional group of twitchers hoping to add to their tally of sightings. With that in mind, she'd thrown a bird book into her bag, giving her a plausible excuse not only to be where she was, but also to point her high-powered binoculars in the direction of the slimeball's house.

As a mining engineer, Naomi was used to roughing it. She'd often walked over harsh terrain to get to a test site so newly identified the company hadn't invested time or money into clearing a road. She was fit, her sense of direction was good, and on the first couple of forays all she intended to do was work out if she could reach the target this way. There was a chance that when it came time to act, she might have to cover ground in the dark, so if the topography was problematic, she would have to find an alternative approach; she couldn't afford to get lost or injure herself as she fled the scene.

For three days over two weeks, she followed the pattern of dressing for work then heading for the bush: three days of occasionally glimpsing her goal through the trees but always being thwarted by dense undergrowth, a trail that dwindled to nothing, or harsh terrain, unsafe at night. On the Friday of the second week, Naomi finally found what she was looking for.

After moving her start position to approach from the north instead of the east, she had come across the track almost immediately. It wasn't marked on any maps, and it was so overgrown she was only game to take the Jeep in a couple of hundred metres before worrying about damage she could not explain. But it was definitely a track. She left the SUV and continued on foot, confident no one else was likely to pass that way.

Twenty minutes later she came to a gate set in a sagging five-strand wire fence: a property boundary—*the* property boundary. The track she had been following turned parallel to the fence line and continued to meander along, appearing and disappearing in the undergrowth.

Naomi took a moment to double-check her location and

orientation, but she knew exactly where she was: at the back of the slimeball's land. Which meant his house and sheds were across a couple of paddocks and just over the rise, crouching in that scarred depression in the earth she had studied on Google Maps.

It was still early in the day, hours before she would need to head back to the city. She looked again at the gate: wired, padlocked, and seemingly rusted shut. She considered her options. The information she'd received was that the slimeball was a contract worker with steady employment; she could assume he would be off the property from early morning until early evening on most days. She decided to get closer, to cross the wintery paddocks and see what she could see. The more she learned now, the smoother things would go when the time came, and she could always pretend to be lost if she encountered anyone.

Folding herself through the fence, she struck out straight across the stubbly ground. Only someone up to no good would creep around the edges, so she brazened her way directly towards where she knew the house was located. Despite the bravado, she could feel her heart beating and had the sensation of being watched, but she kept her pace steady and didn't falter.

Cresting the hill, she paused. The house and sheds were below her. No smoke curled from the chimney, despite the chill of the day. She took a dozen more steps then stopped, her heart pounding—near the house, something had moved.

Naomi narrowed her eyes, straining to see, then let out a long breath. Washing on the line, caught by the cold breeze that chased across the hills and around the buildings. She stood there for minutes that felt like an eternity, waiting and watching, but nothing else stirred.

Her senses expanded, seeming to stretch out across the landscape, as she tried to feel what might lie ahead. She registered a faint rustle at her feet as a mouse darted between dry tussocks, the distant rumble of a passenger jet, and the call and response of a pair of currawongs back among the trees she had left behind. The collection of buildings remained quiet. Forcing herself to move forward, she ducked through the next fence and across the home paddock. She cut a curving path that would bring her in behind the large machinery shed, out of direct sight of the slightly shabby weatherboard house.

Every step she took without seeing or hearing anything alarming made her feel slightly braver and more in control. She was mindful of the time, directing part of her attention to the driveway, the possibility that a car would appear, but so far, all indications were that she was alone.

She didn't have the Valium, or Brooke.

"Shit," she muttered. Maybe she could have done it today.

Seconds later she was horrified to realise she was annoyed because she wouldn't be killing anyone just yet. She felt a stirring in her abdomen—surely nerves, far too early to be anything to do with her pregnancy, but a reminder, nonetheless. None of this was just about her.

She headed around the far side of the machinery shed, wary of getting cocky, content to take her time and figure out the best approach for when she came back. The closer she got to the house, the more she felt an oppressive atmosphere, as though the memory of violence and death clung to the place. It was here the slimeball had abused Katy's sister, and down that driveway she had fled, trying to reach the road. And it was to this house that he had returned immediately after running her down. He'd sat there drinking while Pip lay dying, less than a kilometre away.

Part of Naomi wanted to bolt off this land and never set foot here again. But a bigger part of her wanted to make him pay for what he had done.

Her feet took her down the side of the shed. She was about to round the corner, step past the blank steel wall and in front of the open end, when there was a sharp clang, metal on concrete.

"Fuck!" A man's voice, harsh with anger.

NINETEEN

Naomi pulled back and flattened herself against the side of the shed, feeling the corrugations press into her spine, ready to run if she had to. All thoughts of pretending to be a disorientated hiker had gone.

Inside the shed, something scraped across concrete. There was another expletive but no footsteps, nothing to suggest anyone was coming. Naomi waited, listening, feeling the dryness of her throat. The man—it could only be him—was silent now, but she could hear the clink of metal on metal, a clatter that made her think of the junk drawer at home, of Rich and one of his infrequent handyman projects.

She exhaled a slow, quiet breath. She'd convinced herself he'd be off the property, and with that assumption she'd almost screwed up everything. The house, which moments ago had felt within her reach, now seemed to have receded. There was too much open space between the shed and house. Even if he was bent beneath the hood of a car or tractor, his back to the open side of the shed, the risk of being seen was too great. Naomi needed to go back the way she'd come and regroup. She'd been pushing her luck.

After two cautious steps, she stopped. Her rational side was urging her to keep moving, but... She wanted to get a look at him. She knew it was stupid. She risked exposure and was in danger of undermining her own resolve, of turning the theoretical notion of dealing with the slimeball into an acknowledgement that he was a real person—a person she was planning to kill.

But Naomi wanted to see this man, and she realised it was because of Jo. Would there be something about him, something that marked him as a violent, abusive man? Probably not. But in looking at the slimeball, she knew she would see Malik and remember the knife he had used.

She returned to the corner of the shed and crouched down, hoping a lower perspective would reduce her visibility. It would just be a quick look, nothing more. She eased forward, stretching her shoulders, craning her neck. The edge of a workbench came into view, a pegboard behind it arrayed with tools and the shadows where tools could hang. Then the back of a ute, tailgate open, tonneau cover drawn back.

Her skin was crawling. What if he was standing just around the corner, watching her appear inch by inch? She gritted her teeth and kept going.

Then she saw him, or at least part of him. He was under the ute, which she now realised was jacked up. All she could see were a pair of thick, denim-clad legs, a large pair of cracked Blundstones, and the hem of a checked flannel shirt.

Without taking her eyes from him, she slowly straightened up, confident that his view of her would be blocked. Now she was standing properly, she had a better line of sight and took her time scanning the area, eyeing the equipment, taking note of any places she could hide when she returned.

A grunt came from beneath the car, pulling her attention back. And she noticed something.

Naomi had spent years working around vehicles and other machinery at remote mine sites, long enough to pick up a few mechanical skills—nothing flash, but enough to handle minor problems. One of the things she had been taught was how to safely jack up a car when you were planning to work on it.

The slimeball wasn't using a jack stand. In fact, the slimeball, big bastard that he was, had positioned the fully extended scissor jack on a cinder block to give himself more room to work.

Naomi stared at the jack, an idea rapidly forming. This wasn't the approach to the problem she had planned. But…maybe it was even better. She would have to enter the shed and walk past him to reach the jack, meaning he'd be able to see her feet. But if she was quiet, and he was concentrating, it would surely be possible, and even if he noticed her before she'd got far, she had her lost hiker story to fall back on.

Naomi's mind raced. The Valium plan was flawed, and if she was honest with herself, probably impossible to pull off cleanly, especially if Brooke dithered. But this… She had to take the chance. After hesitating a moment longer, she stepped around the corner and onto the concrete floor of the shed. She moved quickly, trying to make as little sound as possible but knowing that speed was better than a creeping approach. She passed level with the back end of the ute, eyes and ears focused on the form beneath the vehicle, adrenaline driving her towards her objective.

Four steps away.

"Who's that? What are you doing out here, bitch?" A smoker's growl that became a roar of anger.

He started to slide out from under the car just as Naomi reached the jack. She reared back and kicked the cinder block, hard, with the heel of her boot.

"Hey!"

The block shifted. The jack wobbled. And the car fell with a crash.

Silence.

Breathing heavily, Naomi took several slow steps back, all her attention focused on his legs, watching for a twitch. *Shit, fuck, shit.* What had she done? Bile rose up in her throat, a hot sour rush that she forced down with a hard swallow. She had to get out.

She made for the front of the shed, but instead of going around the side again, she veered the other way. The shortest path to the back of the property and the overgrown track was between the house and the shed, and she didn't want to waste another second. She cut across the open space, hurrying but not running; she didn't want to roll an ankle.

She was only two strides from the first paddock when she heard a hollow crash: the unmistakable sound of a screen door slamming closed.

Horrified, Naomi spun around. She took a couple of faltering steps towards the house. A person was standing on the sagging verandah, just in front of the back door.

TWENTY

It wasn't him. It was a woman, and even from this distance Naomi could see the dark purple bloom of a bruise spreading around her left eye and across her cheek. Her arms were folded over her abdomen, her posture slightly hunched as though standing straight was too painful, her expression one of fear. And she was staring straight at Naomi. For a moment their eyes locked, then the woman slowly shifted her gaze to the shed.

Naomi didn't think; she turned, pushed her way through the wires of the fence, and bolted. In a few steps she would be out of sight, but what if the woman had already called the police? She must have heard the slimeball's yell, realised something was wrong.

Naomi tried to take care over the uneven ground while her brain was screaming at her to run, run fast. She stumbled, regained her balance, and reached the next paddock. Could she hear sirens? No—blood pounding in her ears, the shrill whistle of the rising wind, but not sirens, not yet. She ducked through the five-strand fence and kept going towards the line of trees, moving a bit slower now that her immediate panic was settling to cold dread.

Within minutes she was under the cover of sheltering branches, safe from sight—even that of a helicopter. But of course the woman knew which way she had gone, and presumably knew about the old track. If the police were waiting at her car, there was nowhere else to go.

She'd stick to a version of her original story: she was looking for birds, got lost, found the farm, came across the accident and panicked. It was flimsy, hard to believe she wouldn't have called for help, but if she stuck to that account…

Naomi kept moving down the track, walking now, feeling the chill as sweat dried on her back and chest. The Jeep seemed farther away than she remembered, but finally there it was—unattended, just as she'd left it, innocuous in the dappled light. Safely inside, cocooned in the driver's seat, she realised she was shaking: a physical aftershock, the spasming tremor rippling through her body, beyond her control. Her limbs felt as though she'd run a marathon. Her mouth was dry but she didn't know if she had the strength to hold her drink bottle. She needed to get the car off the track, back to the more populated, less suspicious rural roads. If police stopped her then, she wouldn't need a story; she'd just be another person out for a drive in the country, taking a bit of a mental health trip to clear her mind.

Naomi concentrated on the familiar sequence that preceded driving: press ignition button, release brake, select gear. Grip steering wheel. She hoped to find somewhere to turn the car around, but the narrow track defeated her, and she had to reverse almost all the way to the main road.

There were no police cars waiting for her—in fact, no one was there to witness the moment the Jeep emerged from the bush, indicator flashing, and pulled onto the road.

She chose a longer route back to Sydney, one that wouldn't take her past the front gate of the slimeball's property. After the first twenty or so kilometres, she turned on the radio, punching buttons until she landed on talkback. Usually she couldn't stand all the idiots ringing in, but the one thing this station had was regular, comprehensive news; if shit was hitting the fan back at the slimeball's property, she would hear about it very soon. If police were looking for a tall woman, medium build, long brown ponytail, dressed in outdoor clothing, this station would broadcast the alert.

Her hair—maybe she could colour or cut it. But that wouldn't fool anyone for long.

Don't do anything wildly different, she thought. *Keep it normal.* There was nothing to connect her to the slimeball, and nothing distinctive about her appearance. She just needed to get to the city and slip back into her life as though nothing had happened.

She realised she was freezing and cranked on the heating. Moments later, she was too hot, her face flushed and burning. Long-discarded self-help habits kicked in, and she started breathing in a 4-7-8 pattern, pushing back against her rising panic. Inhale, hold, exhale. The road unfolded in front of her. Gradually, she began to feel calmer.

Then music blasted from the car's speakers: the distinctive, urgent tones of a news bulletin. Her anxiety ratcheted back up a notch. She listened to every story, then through sports, weather, and finance in case there was a newsflash, but it was just another day in Australia, with no manhunts underway, no homicides in regional New South Wales. The pattern repeated every half-hour.

By the time she reached the city's fringe, Naomi was convinced there was some sort of media embargo in place. Tomorrow morning the story would break, and she would open the door to a grim-faced detective with handcuffs dangling from one finger and a search warrant in his other hand.

The tail end of after-school traffic slowed her progress, but she was home well before five. She hadn't stopped to change her clothes. It didn't matter; Rich wouldn't get in until nearly six, which gave her plenty of time to wipe any obvious dirt off the car, shower, and run a load of washing. She studiously avoided turning on the radio or television while she moved around the house, ticking the tasks off her mental list.

When she went to start dinner, she couldn't think what to cook so decided to order takeaway later. At one point she found herself in the kitchen, a bottle of crisp fiano in one hand, a wine-glass on the benchtop. Then she remembered: she was pregnant. How had she forgotten? It frightened her. She needed to get herself under control before Rich got home. In the home office, Naomi pulled the burner phone from the back of the filing cabinet where she'd hidden it among old tax returns. Once the SIM was back in, she sent a text to Brooke.

> Sorry gorgeous—have to cancel our upcoming girls' weekend! All okay but something came up unexpectedly. Will fill you in when I see you. xx

Brooke would be confused, but Naomi couldn't help that, and the less the other woman knew, the better off she'd be. Next she messaged the emergency number Mia had given her.

> Please call.

She stared at the cheap mobile phone, willing it to ring, even though she knew it might be hours before Mia checked her own burner. But perhaps Mia would find out before too long anyway; once the story broke, she would know what Naomi had done. Then a thought hit her.

Katy.

She was supposed to advise Mia when things were going to happen, so Katy could be notified and plan her alibi accordingly.

What if she wasn't at work today? What if she couldn't account for her movements? This was a disaster.

Naomi paced back and forth, clutching the burner, her thoughts spiralling out of control. It was too late. If Katy didn't have an alibi, there was nothing she could do now.

She made herself sit down at her desk, pull up some files on the computer, run through figures. She knew she couldn't trust the work she was doing now and would have to do it all again, but the familiarity of the material, the normality of her actions, helped to settle and ground her. By the time Rich's key turned in the lock, Naomi had her shit together. At least on the outside.

She checked the burner was set to silent and slid it into a drawer. Seconds later, Rich came in, eased her freshly washed hair to one side, and kissed the back of her neck, sending a tingle down her spine. "Hello, sweetheart," he murmured.

"Hey, babe." Naomi leaned into him, feeling herself relax a bit more.

"Tough day?" His hands found her shoulders, thumbs pressing into knotted muscles.

"A bit. Better now, though." She closed her eyes and rolled her head forward, and for a few blessed minutes she thought of nothing.

They ordered Vietnamese takeaway and ate in the lounge with the television on, its volume turned down to a low murmur. It was tuned to a travel show featuring remote places of spectacular beauty, a show that required no intellectual engagement, only appreciation. Naomi was acutely aware of Rich sitting on the couch beside her. She wanted to say something. She could feel the secret bubbling inside her, picture herself blurting it out,

Rich's shocked expression. Instead she focused on her chicken and rice, suddenly both ravenous and exhausted, the exertion and adrenaline of the day catching up with her.

"Are you okay?"

She flinched at the suddenness of his question. "Just bloody tired."

"It's just that you seem tense. I mean, you jumped when I spoke."

Naomi hesitated. She could tell him she was pregnant. It would explain her mood and distract him from scrutinising her. But once again she mentally recoiled from the thought—bad enough to do what she had done and have secrets from Rich without using their unborn child as cover. "I know," she said. "Sorry. I was miles away."

"Thinking about your sister?"

She smiled ruefully and grabbed his hand, bringing it up to kiss, even though he was still clutching his fork. "You know me."

"I also know it can't be easy doing the whole healthy-body-nothing-but-vitamins thing."

She gave his hand an extra squeeze before she released it. "It's okay, and it's what I want to do. We can't wait forever if we're going to be parents."

He set his food aside, twisted on the couch and stared at her face, his probing gaze lingering on her eyes and the spot between her brows that always furrowed when she was most troubled. "Is that new therapist any good?"

"Umm, her approach is very different." Naomi shrugged, trying for casual even though her heart rate had shot up. "I've stopped going, actually. I decided I needed a break."

Rich frowned. "Isn't the whole idea of having a therapist that you keep going?"

"Yeah, but I thought I needed to take a break from the

introspection. You know, stop analysing how I feel all the time and just be. I mean, we've talked about this. Is therapy just a self-perpetuating cycle? You go because you feel crap, then spend an hour talking about how crap you're feeling, thereby cementing the crap in your psyche." She tried to keep her tone light.

"You've talked about it, and I've respectfully disagreed. Besides, I've noticed a change in you these past few months."

"Really?" Naomi carefully placed her empty plate on the coffee table next to Rich's half-eaten pho.

"How?"

He shook his head slowly. His eyes were unfocused as he thought it through, then they snapped back to her. "Hard to define. More centred? No, that sounds wanky—just more at peace with things."

She tilted her head, considering, then placed her hands on Rich's cheeks, pulling him in and planting a kiss on his lips. "You know what? I think you're right."

She'd eased back a tiny bit to speak. Over his shoulder, she caught sight of the television.

The travel program had been replaced by a late news update. Behind the newsreader's back Naomi could see the words, Man killed. Pushing away from her husband, she grabbed the remote.

"Hey! What—?"

"Shh, hang on." Naomi aimed the control and thumbed the volume button. The sound came up just as the newsreader cut to a reporter on scene, a sharp-looking young man in a pale blue shirt and tie.

"Thanks, Ed," the reporter began. "Police and ambulance were called to this remote property today and arrived to find the victim pinned beneath his ute. It appears he was working on the car when it slipped from the jack and fell on him. He sustained severe injuries to his head and chest and was already deceased when help arrived. Police say this sort of tragic accident is all too common and have urged people thinking about any sort of DIY work to make sure they're using the correct equipment or leave it to the professionals. Back to you in the studio."

Naomi stared at the screen, unable for a moment to process what she'd just heard.

"Naomi? Naomi?" Rich was shaking her arm gently. "What is it?"

"Nothing. I thought it… Oh!"

Hit by a wave of nausea, she got to her feet and ran for the bathroom, reaching the toilet just in time to throw back the lid and vomit. Her stomach clenched again and again, long after there was nothing left to bring up.

She was vaguely aware of Rich coming into the room. After a few moments she heard water running, then felt the coolness of a damp face washer on her forehead.

As the nausea subsided, all Naomi could think about was the woman with the bruised face. Had she really said nothing, or were the police playing some sort of game? No, that only happened in fiction. If the police suspected foul play, they would have said so and issued a description of Naomi. But why hadn't the woman told them?

And then Naomi realised something. She'd got away with it.

"Babe, are you okay?" Rich put a gentle hand on her back.

"I think so." Her voice was shaky as she turned to the basin, keeping her back to her husband while she gargled mouthwash. After a minute he left her alone, but she knew he'd be waiting for an explanation and hoping that fatigue plus odd behaviour and nausea equalled pregnant.

Slowly, Naomi wiped a towel across her face. The bruised woman had certainly seen her. Could the woman have found the Jeep earlier in the day, noted down the licence plate? Was she, even now, working out how to track Naomi down and blackmail her?

Another wave of nausea washed over Naomi, and she gripped the edge of the vanity until it passed. Then she turned to the bathroom door. She would tell Rich she was pregnant. This wasn't how she'd wanted to do it, but the more she thought about it, the more she realised that actually, now was a very good time. She had done the job, and even though the man under the car wasn't Malik, something in Naomi felt lighter, as though her sister's death was at least partly avenged.

But first, she wanted to check the burner—surely Mia would have seen the news and messaged her by now? Naomi eased open the door and tiptoed down the hall to the office. She pulled the burner from the back of her desk drawer, thumbed a button, and the screen lit up with a recent text notification.

Will call tomorrow, 9 am.

Tomorrow seemed a lifetime away and Naomi felt a wave of panic. Why tomorrow, why not now?

"Honey? Where are you? Are you okay?" Rich's concerned voice echoed down the hallway, coming closer.

That was why.

She threw the phone back in the drawer and took a couple of deep, steadying breaths.

"Coming."

Tomorrow, hopefully, Mia would tell her Katy was in the clear and help Naomi unravel her thoughts. She had achieved what she'd set out to do, but Naomi needed Mia to tell her if she could call it a success.

Sensing Rich behind her, Naomi turned and held out her arms.

TWENTY-ONE

Detective Senior Sergeant Fiona Ulbrick leaned forward on her couch, firing the remote control at the television, skipping through channels as she tried to find another news update.

That house. That driveway.

She had been on her way to the kitchen when the item flashed up. The volume was off, and she'd only caught a glimpse of the scene behind the earnest young reporter, but it was enough. Some years ago, Ulbrick had spent hours, days, at that property.

Daniel Pavic.

She could feel the tension across her shoulders, the strain of her neck muscles as she searched.

What had he done now?

How bad?

Who?

"Shit," she swore at the television, dragging a hand through her short grey hair.

Ulbrick knew he'd been out for a few years. She made it her business to know these things. When you file charges of murder against a perpetrator of domestic violence and they're pleaded down to nothing, as a cop, you don't forget.

There. She cranked up the volume.

A different reporter was standing in a slightly different spot, blue and red lights flickering behind her. The footage had clearly been recorded earlier in the evening, as there was still enough ambient light to make out the scene.

Ulbrick listened—surprised, then disbelieving. "Tragic accident, my arse," she muttered, leaning even closer to the screen.

But from what she could see of the officers moving about in the background, there was no urgency; no sign of floodlights or forensics. Which was not to say it wasn't all happening off camera, but after nearly thirty years, Ulbrick could read the body language.

The reporter didn't name any names. Maybe it wasn't Pavic under the car. He could've sold the place. Ulbrick shuddered at the thought of living somewhere like that.

Just as the reporter was wrapping up, Ulbrick saw a face she recognised. Detective Nevitt had caught the call. He was walking left to right across the scene, pointing at something only he could see.

Ulbrick reached for her mobile. Gordon Nevitt was a colleague and a good copper. It was late, but depending on what was what, Gordo might still be up. If not, her message would be waiting for him first thing.

Her thumbs hammered the screen.

> Gordo, what's the story with your man under the car?
> Have you ID'd? Is it Pavic?

Pavic had already been in prison when Nevitt joined the homicide squad, but the case had received huge attention both within the force and in the media. If Gordo didn't remember the name Daniel Pavic—and more importantly, the name Pip

McKenzie—one of the other officers on scene would soon fill him in.

Ulbrick hit send then stared at the display, hoping to see the bouncing dots of a reply.

Nothing. The phone slipped back into standby, and she set it on the arm of her chair, ready to grab if Gordo called.

She had been winding down, thinking about bed when the news item appeared, but now... The fingers of one hand drummed, staccato on her knee, then she was on her feet and across the room, dragging open the bottom drawer of her filing cabinet. She pulled out a ringbinder and returned to her chair. Fi Ulbrick had known when she first arrested Pavic that the case against him was solid: the evidence was there, the history of domestic violence was there, and the sequence of events her team had pieced together was like an arrow of neon lights that pointed to his killing of Pip McKenzie. So Ulbrick had been furious when prosecutors cut Pavic a deal, because to her and to everyone else, it was a clear case of murder.

For the first time, Ulbrick had really questioned the system. Not her job—that was part of her DNA—but the lawmakers, defence lawyers, and judicial system that so often failed to help victims of domestic violence and then enabled men to get away with murder.

Back when she was a junior officer, years ago, Ulbrick saw plenty of bruises and bloodied lips, black eyes and broken ribs, but as a homicide detective she was only present when it was too late. So she did the one thing she could think of: she started her own file. Nothing extensive, just name, address, date of release and a few other pertinent facts, enough so that if Pavic's name came up in any context, she'd have a few details to hand without having to resort to the force's Computerised Operational Policing System. Accessing COPS when it wasn't directly relevant to duties was against professional standards. More to the point, if Ulbrick ever got another chance to lock Pavic away for good, she didn't want it compromised by anything, least of all a trail of her digital footprints in the system that a shyster lawyer could twist into evidence of an obsession. Later, when Ulbrick heard about another domestic homicide that ended with a short sentence, then an alleged victim of domestic violence who had died in an apparent accident, it was a logical step to add a couple more names and details to her files—things a homicide detective might want to be wise to from the moment she arrived on scene.

Ulbrick opened the ringbinder and was confronted with a grainy picture of Pavic, part of an article she'd clipped from a newspaper. It made her angry just to look at it.

Her phone buzzed with an incoming message, and she snatched it up, the binder tumbling to the floor. Gordo.

It's your boy. Still looking into things. So far no red flags.

She texted back with a thumbs-up emoji, then let the phone fall into her lap.

Son of a bitch. An accident. Who would have thought?

TWENTY-TWO

At precisely nine a.m. on Saturday morning, the day after Naomi had killed a man, her burner phone buzzed with an incoming call. She hurried into the backyard before answering, then waited, unwilling to speak, unsure what to say.

"Naomi."

Hearing Mia's voice, she felt as though a parachute had opened, arresting her emotional freefall. She closed her eyes. Exhaled.

"Sorry I didn't call sooner," said Mia. "The phone isn't powered up all the time, and of course when it is, I have to be away from the office. Triangulation is unlikely, but I'm not taking any chances."

"That's the thing. I took a chance, and now I'm not sure—"

"I saw the news."

"I assumed you would. I need to see you: there might be a problem."

"Brooke?" Mia asked urgently.

"Not involved. She wasn't there when—"

The back door opened, and Rich stuck his head out, eyebrows raised in a question. Naomi signalled that she'd be just a minute, willing him to retreat, hoping her loose hair was hiding the unfamiliar phone from his sight. But he stepped out into the yard, secateurs in hand, and began to potter about.

"When what? Naomi?" Mia's voice was soft but insistent.

"Sorry, what was I saying?" Naomi turned her back slightly, but Rich was too close.

"Is someone there?"

"That's right!"

"Are you able to keep talking?"

"Oh no, I don't think so. Rich and I are just in the garden."

"I see. Can you hang on till Monday? Bradleys Head walking track?"

"I can make that work." Naomi glanced across at Rich. "Ten?"

"I'll meet you where the track starts at Taronga Zoo Wharf. Message again if things change. I'll check the phone regularly."

"Will do. And thanks. See you then!" Naomi ended the call, plastered a smile on her face, and went to join her husband.

On Monday morning, Naomi was already waiting when Mia came down the sloping path from the road to the start of the walking track. She was standing with her back to the harbour, low cloud and drizzle reducing the city view behind her to grey outlines and shadows. On a wintery day like this, they should have the track largely to themselves.

"Naomi." Mia stopped and Naomi was conscious of the therapist's scrutiny as she went to join her. Today Mia was wearing a crimson waterproof jacket over black leggings, with a red Nordic-style beanie pulled low over her hair. To Naomi she looked powerful, ready for a confrontation rather than a walk through wet bushland.

"Mia, I'm so glad to see you," Naomi felt some of her tension melt away. "Obviously you know things took an unexpected turn last Friday."

They began walking, shoulder to shoulder beneath the dripping trees.

"The man whose car fell on him? Yes. I understand it's not an uncommon occurrence, but certainly not what I was expecting to see when I switched on the news."

Naomi nodded. "Not what I was expecting either, but the situation—"

Mia batted a hand. "Accidents like that happen in the blink of an eye."

"Katy?"

"Was at work until seven, should police have any reason to ask."

Naomi was so relieved she felt faint. She stumbled slightly and came to a halt, bending forward, hands on her knees, head low. Katy had a solid alibi: at least there was that. She could feel the gentle pressure of Mia's hand between her shoulder blades as gradually, the roaring in her ears subsided.

"It's okay, you're okay," Mia murmured.

After a minute or so, Naomi slowly straightened and turned to meet the therapist's worried gaze. "We could have a problem. There was a woman. She saw me."

"Ahh, I see. Are you alright to keep going?" Mia asked, her hand still on Naomi's back.

Naomi nodded. "It overwhelmed me for a minute, but I'm good now. Perhaps if I tell you everything from the beginning?"

They started walking again and Naomi related the whole story, from the moment she'd found the way onto the slimeball's property to when she'd seen the TV news item. Mia probed gently but relentlessly, first about the witness, then about Naomi's emotions and coping mechanisms as the therapist offered suggestions for the weeks ahead.

Their walk had taken them past the Bradleys Head lighthouse and back among the trees when Naomi finally held up a hand, fingers splayed, asking Mia to stop. "I'm here because of the woman who saw me. I wanted to warn you that everything might go to shit, that the police might have my description. Sorry. I know I'm a fucking basket case."

Mia, still walking, shook her head slowly. "No, you're not. Given the situation, you're doing remarkably well. I assume you've been worrying about the woman all weekend?"

"Her and everything else. I've been swinging back and forth between thinking the cops are just gathering evidence before they come for me and deciding the woman said nothing because she was glad." Naomi shrugged and buried her hands in the pockets of her puffer jacket.

Mia glanced at her and smiled. "I don't think you have a thing to worry about, for four reasons. One: the police don't work like that—if they had anything to link you to the accident, they'd already be talking to you. Two: you're right, that woman was clearly his latest victim—who may well have ended up like Katy's sister if you hadn't come along, so she may be grateful. Three: that woman bears clear signs of domestic violence, which means she'd be an obvious suspect."

Naomi gasped, her eyes widening in shock.

"Just think of it from her perspective. She either tells police she was in the house making dinner, vacuuming, whatever—occupied and elsewhere. When he didn't come in at the usual time she went out to check, found him in the shed and immediately called triple zero. Everyone can agree it was a tragic accident." Mia paused mid-step, then half turned, placing a hand on Naomi's arm. "But if she told police she'd seen a strange woman—someone she'd never seen before—come out of the shed and disappear across the paddock, well… Trying to blame a mystery person who left no trace? All that's going to do is make the police look at the scene more closely, to look for malfeasance when they'd been content to see misadventure, and then to look at her, the punching bag who may have snapped. Far better for her to keep quiet." Mia moved her hand away but continued to watch Naomi's face, clearly waiting for her response.

Naomi bit her lip, thinking about what she'd just heard, coming to accept it. For a few moments, there was silence except for the sound of water slapping against an invisible shore.

Then Naomi glanced sharply at Mia. "You said four things. What's the fourth?"

"There's always the possibility that the slimeball had that poor woman so cowed that she did at least try to say something to the police."

"But then—"

"The police know what he was. Don't forget, they actually charged him with murder, but it was all dealt down to nothing." Mia snapped her fingers. "There's a good chance officers have been called out there a few times since he killed Pip, and a good chance they've spoken to that woman before. Maybe they don't want to look too hard. Even if they did, what would they find?"

Naomi inclined her head towards the therapist, a gesture of respect and admiration. "Shit. You've had that in mind all along, haven't you?"

"The police have a job to do, and they're sworn to carry out their duty."

"Except…"

"Except that duty has its foundation in the protection of the wider community. Don't get me wrong; if there is something to investigate, the New South Wales police will do so, and follow through, even if what they're investigating is the death of a scumbag. But if a scumbag has an accident, and society is that little bit safer because of it..." Mia spread her hands, palms up, and Naomi almost expected her to say, "Voilà!" Instead, she folded them across her chest and smiled conspiratorially.

"I never would have thought of that."

"There are no guarantees, of course, and I'd hate for any of the others to tackle their particular task while thinking the authorities won't look too closely. But I've worked in this field for many years—I've seen how it affects police when they attend domestic violence crime scenes. And when the charges against these types of men result in sentences that are either nonexistent or manifestly inadequate, it can make officers question what they do. So, yes, I have been thinking about it for a while, which is how I knew when the right six women were sitting in front of me."

Up ahead, the path forked, one branch continuing to follow the coastline, the other a shortcut back to their starting point.

"This may have been one of the most productive bloody therapy sessions I've ever attended," said Naomi, "but I should be getting back." She gestured towards the left-hand path. "Thank you, Mia."

"You're welcome." Mia smiled. "From what I've seen today, you seem far less angry at the world."

"You're right, I feel less angry—although I did spend a lot of yesterday crying." Naomi raised a hand in farewell, took a couple of steps then stopped, turning to face Mia again. "And there's one more thing that has to happen before I'll really be able to come to terms with my sister's murder."

"Yes. But that's someone else's problem to deal with."

TWENTY-THREE

Mia watched Naomi disappear before striking out once again on her own path. Alone, she lengthened her stride, breathing deeply and relishing the crisp air. It had stopped drizzling and the sky was beginning to lighten. Mia pulled off her beanie and stuffed it in her pocket then fluffed out her hair, ignoring the water still dripping from the trees and ferns that crowded the edges of the trail.

No matter the time of year, Mia loved this walk. Warmer months were far busier, although the increased number of people was offset by the chance to see more birds and animals. But it was this sort of cold, grey day that gave her a real sense of peace and tranquillity. Even though she was still so close to the heart of the city, here there was only bushland and the water, no fences, no boundaries, nothing holding her back.

She veered down some steps, heading for the small, sandy cove that capped Taylors Bay. They had been lucky. She understood why Naomi had seized the moment, taking the chance when it was offered. Mia also admired the woman for doing what she'd done. But…there was an element of rashness Mia hadn't anticipated. If there had been even the slightest hint the death was anything more than an accident, it could have cost them dearly—cost Katy dearly.

Mia stopped at the point where the trail met the beach and nodded slowly to herself. Everything was okay; they could move on to the next job. It was time for her to contact Olivia.

She stared out over the calm bay, contemplating its depth as she assessed her emotions and again felt the rightness of what they were doing. As she watched, the dull, steely blue water began to sparkle with light and colour. Mia looked up, shielding her eyes, just as the fickle sun vanished back into the clouds.

Mia thought of her sister.

When she finally realised the trouble her sister was in, Mia was overcome by guilt and shame. How could she have failed to see? How could she have believed for one second that her own sister would choose to sever contact?

Mia wasted no time. There was no point staging a surprise home visit: even if she got through the door, her sister would be inhibited by Travis's presence, and there was a chance he would be angered by Mia's unannounced arrival, taking it out on her sister later. Instead, Mia waited outside her sister's office building at the end of a weekday, ready to intercept. She stood across the street, glancing between her watch and the revolving door, looking for that familiar figure. Mia's car was nearby, a place to sit and talk. If she couldn't persuade her sister to come away now, Mia could at least drive her home, making sure she arrived at the usual time so as not to arouse his suspicions or spark his anger.

Her sister shuffled outside in time with the slow turn of the door, her left arm in a sling. Mia started across the road, mouth open to call, but the name died in her throat. Travis was already there, walking briskly down the footpath, taking her sister by the elbow, steering her away.

Mia froze, shocked—not only by what had just happened, but also by her sister's appearance. Even from the other side of the street, Mia could see how gaunt and pale she looked, her clothes hanging from thin shoulders, an unfamiliar tension in the way she carried herself.

Mia watched them walk away. To a casual passerby they would have seemed like any other couple, but she saw the firmness of his grip and the way he leaned in to her sister. Any doubts she'd held about her assessment of the relationship were gone; Mia could see no affection in Travis's manner, only possession and control.

The next day, she phoned her sister's work number. As soon as the call went through she started talking. "I don't know what's going on, but clearly there's a problem. Meet me for lunch. I'll be waiting downstairs whenever you get your break, and I'm not going anywhere."

"Mia! I—"

"You don't have to say anything now, except that you'll meet me. Please. Whatever it is, I can help. We can figure it out."

For a moment Mia could hear nothing, then there was a muffled sob. "I don't know what's happened to me." Her sister sounded small and bewildered.

"Twelve-thirty. Let me help you. Please, sis."

"Yes." She cleared her throat, and suddenly there was conviction in her voice. "Yes."

Over a lunch that wasn't eaten, Mia gradually drew details from her sister. How it had begun with little remarks, at first so subtle they seemed the stuff of any new relationship when people move in together and get to see the full picture—small things she did that Travis didn't like. Then came the snide jabs, sapping her confidence, destroying her self-esteem. Even the tiniest error was a chance for Travis to belittle her. Something forgotten in the supermarket? Stupid. Dropped her keys when coming through the door, arms laden? Clumsy. Bruised her ribs on the dresser after tripping on his discarded—and perhaps strategically placed—shoes in the dark? Accident prone. Crying? It made her look ugly. And when he lost his temper and hit her? See what you made me do?

Mia didn't need to ask much about the physical abuse: the answers to those questions were already there in her sister's eyes, the quivering of her lip, the bandaged left arm, and the way she shrunk into herself when talking about Travis's anger.

"I saw Travis pick you up yesterday. Is that every day?"

Her sister nodded.

"Call work, tell them you're sick, and come with me now, back to my place. We can get your things later." Mia spoke quickly, channelling her fury at the man into action.

She was appalled when her sister shook her head. "I can't."

"Of course you can!" Mia smiled encouragingly and reached for her sister's hand across the cafe table.

"No." There was a note of terror in her voice. "You don't understand."

Mia sat back, taking a slow breath. Leaving was always the most dangerous time. She knew it professionally, and now a fraction of it was playing out in front of her. "You'll be safe at my house. Everything locks, and I won't leave you alone." She paused. "Did he threaten you, sis? Have you said you were going to leave before, and he threatened you?"

Her sister looked down and gave a tiny, almost imperceptible nod.

"Is it something he is capable of?"

Another nod. Her sister said something, too soft for Mia to hear.

"I will help you. Mum and Dad will help you too, and there are professionals we can call. The police… We can get some sort of restraining order, an AVO. Sis, you have to leave. I know it's going to be tough and frightening, but you have to get out of there."

Her sister looked up, tears streaming down her face. "He said he'd kill me if I tried to leave, but first he'd deal with you and Mum and Dad. He said he'd destroy everything I love so I'd know what I'd done."

Mia moved her sister into the guest bedroom that day. At four-thirty p.m. she phoned Travis and calmly explained that her sister had already left work and would not be returning to live with him, ever.

He asked where she was.

Mia refused to give her address.

He asked to speak to her.

Mia politely declined, then said she would be round to collect her sister's things on the weekend.

He said there'd been a misunderstanding.

Mia said she disagreed.

Then he started swearing, a vile torrent of abuse. The change was so sudden it took Mia by surprise, and it was several seconds before she terminated the call. She was about to hand the phone back to her sister when it rang, Travis's name flashing up on the screen. Mia hit decline; the phone immediately rang again. This time she blocked the number.

That night, she slept on the floor of the guest room, within arm's reach of her sister.

The next day, Mia took her sister to the police station. Making a detailed statement proved to be a painful experience, and later her sister would say that while the officers were kind, they seemed not to take things too seriously. She felt their doubt. She felt judged. And when the officer in charge explained they would talk to Travis before taking any major steps, she felt afraid.

Mia had already told their parents what was going on, so they were prepared when Travis turned up on their front step. Her father shut the door in his face and told him to clear off, but later, when Mia's father told her what had happened, she could hear the tremor in his voice. "It wasn't anything he said or did, Mia. It was the look on his face. The way he nodded at me, slow. I could see him thinking, You'll keep, you'll regret this. Don't say anything to your mother, though; I don't want to frighten her."

A conversation with her boss reduced Mia's sister to tears; the company valued her and supported her. Receptionists were advised not to put Travis through, the building's security team were alerted, and the company arranged for flexible hours, enabling Mia's sister to come and go at irregular times and to use the secure executive car park.

That weekend, when Mia went to collect her sister's possessions as planned, she arrived to find a neat stack of boxes in the driveway and no sign of Travis. Suspicious, she opened a box, then another. Everything had been destroyed. Clothes were slashed and torn, cups reduced to shards. When she opened a third box, her nostrils were assaulted by the ammonia reek of urine. She left everything where it was and went straight back to the police.

By Monday they had issued a Provisional Apprehended Violence Order, and by the end of the week it had been upgraded to a full AVO that covered not just Mia's sister, but Mia and their parents as well.

Two weeks later, Travis breached the order.

TWENTY-FOUR

Schmoozing and highly effective charm offensives had always been part of Olivia's professional life in talent management. She had spent years cultivating her image as the person you wanted to sit next to at a dinner party, and also the person you didn't want to face off against in contract negotiations. This basically meant everyone in the industry loved her unless they were currently hating her. Her commitment to attending events, flying the flag, and networking as though she was afraid to be alone and disconnected for a single second had now paid off in a way she could never have anticipated.

Because Olivia had already met Rowan Fitzpatrick, the man who had killed Brooke's sister and—with the help of Sydney's most expensive legal team—gotten away with it.

That meeting had taken place several years ago at an exhibition opening, probably at least twelve months before the shooting—or, as Fitzpatrick's media mates had quickly spun it, the tragic accident. Olivia had read about the murder, trying to reconcile the man she'd met with a person others said had an explosive temper, a man who would take his partner out to his country estate and shoot her in the back.

Fitzpatrick was walking behind Gemma and carrying the rifle when it discharged. The bullet hit her below her left shoulder blade, and she died within minutes. He claimed to have tripped and stumbled. Police thought differently.

Fitzpatrick had gone on trial for manslaughter, the police confident of their case. But his legal team had virtually launched an assault on the jury, hammering them with ifs, buts, and maybes. The rifle was an antique from his collection, the barrel rusty, the firing bolt damaged...prone to misfire.

No, he had not pointed it deliberately.

Yes, there had been trouble in their relationship recently—that was why they had gone away, to try to reconnect.

No, he hadn't broken the gun open to carry it: they were only going a few steps, and besides, he hadn't realised it was loaded.

Yes, he had been facing the prospect of a massive financial hit if he and Gemma broke up. They had never married, but she'd lived with him for four years, long enough to be eligible for a de facto settlement.

The jury sat for several days, but the lawyers had done their job: reasonable doubt, and Rowan Fitzpatrick walked free. He made a statement on the steps of the Supreme Court, lamenting Gemma's death. The next week, a gossip mag printed covert pictures of him taken just after the trial. He was on his yacht, partying, laughing, dancing, possibly snorting a white substance, and most definitely groping and kissing a woman who closely resembled Gemma. It was a bad look, but it changed absolutely nothing. Gemma was still dead, and Fitzpatrick was still officially in the clear.

He waited for a few months after the verdict—and the pap shots—before slowly re-emerging on the social and business circuit. It quickly became evident that Rowan Fitzpatrick was not going to fade into the background. He had been found innocent, and, by God, the rest of the world had to come to terms with it, regardless of what they said when his back was turned. A judicious degree of largesse—a few donations here, some company backing there—and the calling in of favours soon had him back where he clearly believed he belonged.

A year or two on, one of Fitzpatrick's exes came forward, ready to tell her story. Rumours flew across social media that she was about to reveal details of his violent and controlling behaviour, and the abuse she'd suffered. Her fear. But no sooner had it begun to trend than it stopped—malicious lies, apparently. The claim was that someone had hacked her accounts. And then she left the country, relocating to LA to pursue a career in film and modelling.

Since then, Olivia had seen Fitzpatrick at several functions and always steered clear, repressing a shudder. Her own sister had been married to a charmer, and she carried the guilt of not seeing beneath that facade, of not recognising Viv's withdrawal and reduced communication for the red flag it was. But Olivia's eyes were wide open now.

From the moment she left The Pleiades meeting in Centennial Park, she had been working on inveigling her way into Rowan Fitzpatrick's wider social circle. She had formulated her plan based on the original post-trial gossip mag article and the continuing rumours of drug use. Her goal was an invitation to attend one of the wild weekend parties held aboard his seventy-five-metre luxury superyacht, where all sorts of things reportedly happened. Not that any of his guests ever said a word—they had their own reputations to consider. Once she was on board, her actions would depend on the level of intoxication and awareness of the other guests, and, of course, access to Fitzpatrick himself.

There had been a lot of variables and unknowns when she

and Katy had gone to Lightning Ridge months ago, but seeing how the other woman had pulled that plan together—even rescuing the dog—had given Olivia courage.

Olivia had been attending every function where there was even a slight chance Fitzpatrick might be on the guest list: taking any invitation that came across her desk, covering for colleagues, and stepping out numerous times as a plus one. When a workmate queried why she was trying to cram even more socialising into her already frenetic schedule, Olivia explained it had been her therapist's idea to put herself out there more, make new connections, talk to people who didn't know about her grief. In a way, it was true.

Her university days—not to mention a number of her clients—had given her a comprehensive education in the behaviour of those under the influence of alcohol and illegal drugs. She'd considered trying to obtain some eye drops to enlarge her pupils but realised that her sight would be compromised. All her faculties would need to be intact to pull this off and get away, so she couldn't have blurred vision and light sensitivity. Instead, she used a computer in the state library to order a pair of black contact lenses from a costume shop.

The other thing she needed was Amy, her backup. If Olivia achieved her goal, she did not want to hang around when the superyacht returned to its berth in Rozelle Bay.

Noise ordinances meant that whenever Fitzpatrick threw a party, his captain had to take the yacht out and anchor offshore. Because of the rules of the high-end marina, that meant casting off before five p.m. and returning after nine a.m. the following day. The marina was naturally very security conscious, so there were guards, gates, and plenty of CCTV cameras for Olivia to worry about. Then there was the yacht itself: she had no idea what she would have to deal with on board.

But all of her strategies, contingency plans, and speculation meant nothing until she scored the coveted invitation—if she scored the invitation.

Olivia almost didn't go to the Goldberg Foundation Gala Spring Ball. Each year her agency, Miller-Simons, supported the cancer charity by buying two tables of ten at five hundred dollars a plate, filling them with upper management, up-and-comers, and maybe an A-lister or two with new projects to push. Occasionally they'd also contribute to the fundraising auction by donating a celebrity experience: a dinner, if the celebrity was particularly erudite, venerable, and charming, or signed memorabilia if the star was a top talent but considerably less personable.

This year, the celeb in question was not one in Olivia's stable, and given she'd been flying the flag at any and every opportunity over the past few months, she'd begged off. But at the last minute a colleague pulled out due to a family emergency, and Olivia's boss asked her to complete the table. She was tired, her face literally ached from all the talking and smiling, and she really wanted a night on the couch with some sushi and a glass of chablis. Instead, she acquiesced and went home early to arrange a babysitter, feed Billy—now an integral part of the family—and change into her trusty sheath dress, steeling herself for a four-course meal and what was promised to be a night of shimmering entertainment. She felt tired just thinking about it.

Nonetheless, two hours later she extended one elegant leg from the back of a Silver Service taxi and eased herself gracefully onto the red carpet. A few photographers from assorted society pages were there, and Olivia smiled dutifully and gave her name when asked, knowing her picture wouldn't make it to the Saturday edition. Inside, bathed in soft artificial light, she immediately felt better. Keeping the lights low was one way organisers tried to make a dinner for six hundred people feel like a more intimate experience, and it made her caramel-brown dress look like a column of burnished gold. After consulting the seating plan, she wove her way through the room to the Miller-Simons tables, close to the front and off to the left of the stage. Finding a place, she switched herself to autopilot.

The first three courses went by in a blur of half-eaten dishes interspersed with air kisses, polite greetings, "call me" hand signals to people on remote tables, a couple of business card exchanges, and the obligatory cabaret numbers and light banter from the emcee. Olivia had glanced through the list of auction offerings, more as a way of disengaging from others than because she actually expected to buy anything, so when Sydney's great and good began raising their bejewelled hands for a series of holidays, spa experiences, a Maserati for a day, and, yes, dinner with a celebrity, Olivia's attention was all for the waitstaff and the dessert. She was just pushing a forkful of mud cake through the berry coulis when something the auctioneer said caught at the edge of her thoughts.

On the stage, a painting sat in an easel and was magnified on the screen behind. The crowd was tittering at something, and the auctioneer was looking at a table on the other side of the room, his eyebrows arched and a wide, cheeky smile on his face.

Whoever he was looking at—Olivia couldn't see from where she was sitting—must have responded, because the auctioneer was laughing and striding back to centre stage.

"Mr. Fitzpatrick tells me it was not an accident—he did mean to bid against himself." The auctioneer waited, teasing his audience. "Because this is for charity, and you're all a bunch of tightwads!"

The crowd roared.

"Actually, I added the last bit," the auctioneer admitted. "So come on, you tightwads—I mean, ladies and gentlemen—who'll give me five thousand for this stunning landscape by Mateja Kaufmann?"

Without stopping to think about what she was doing, Olivia thrust her hand in the air.

"Thank you, madam! Five thousand!"

"Liv! What are you doing?" The PR guy sitting next to her whispered in her ear, his breath heavy with red wine.

"Taking a risk for charity, darl," Olivia said from the corner of her mouth, a serene smile plastered on her face. "Now shh. I can't afford to stuff this up."

"Six from Rowan Fitzpatrick!" The auctioneer swung back to Olivia.

She nodded.

"Seven! Come on, ladies and gentlemen, don't let these two have all the fun!"

"Eight!" a male voice boomed out from the other side of the room.

"Too slow, all of you!" The auctioneer panned his pointed finger in that direction. "It's back with Mr. Fitzpatrick!"

Olivia licked her lips. "Ten!" She pushed her chair back and stood, directing her gaze to where her opponent sat.

"Twelve!" Fitzpatrick stood too and looked back at her, his chin raised defiantly but with a teasing smile on his face.

"Liv!" her colleague hissed, tugging at the seam of her dress.

Olivia ignored him. "Fourteen!" she called, as a bead of sweat trickled down between her shoulder blades. She was in way over her head.

Fitzpatrick locked his gaze with hers, and she tilted her head to the side and slowly shrugged, a gesture that said, *What are you going to do about it?*

He turned to the auctioneer, who was leaning over the edge of the stage, head swivelling back and forth between the two of them.

"Thirty thousand dollars!" Fitzpatrick enunciated each word clearly, his smooth tenor easily making itself heard.

The auctioneer turned back to Olivia, eyebrows arched expectantly. She waited—waited until Fitzpatrick was looking at her again, until most of the room was staring in her direction. Then she raised both hands to chest height, and with slow deliberation in every outsized movement, she dusted them off. The crowd erupted into laughter, cheers, and whistles. She had bluffed Fitzpatrick, lured him into upping his bid, and every person there knew it.

"Boom!" shouted the auctioneer. "And might I add, sold!"

Fitzpatrick was still staring at her. He held both hands out, palms down, and bowed twice. Olivia laughed and took her seat again, and the auction moved on.

Her colleagues were all looking at her, their eyes wide, jaws slack with disbelief. One of them asked, "What in hell's name did you just do?"

Olivia was asking herself exactly the same question, and her nerves were jangling as though she'd just downed several espressos. Even so, she managed to present a serene face to counter their shock. "Raised some money for charity, darlings," she replied coolly, reaching for her wineglass. "That's why we're here, isn't it?"

Now the moment had passed, Olivia was seriously questioning the wisdom of what she'd done. Yes, she'd finally made Fitzpatrick notice her, but she'd made it happen in front of a sea of witnesses. As soon as the auction finished, coffee and tea were served and people began coming up to Olivia—acquaintances and strangers alike—to congratulate her on outwitting Fitzpatrick in the name of charity. The man himself was nowhere to be seen.

A few of the hardier or more inebriated attendees hit the dance floor, but the evening was beginning to wind down. Her plan hadn't worked, and she felt a mixture of disappointment and relief. Maybe at the next function, he'd remember her; or maybe she'd have to come up with another way to get close to him. Tonight, Olivia was done.

She made her excuses, which gave several others on the Miller-Simons tables the chance to stand and bid their own farewells, at which point their entire party decided to call it a night. They headed for the main door, Olivia at the back of the loose group. She was feeling the pull of home and the comfort of bed, determined not to be waylaid.

But when she was halfway across the foyer, a hand clamped around her upper arm. She stopped but didn't turn as she felt him lean in close, his hot breath on her neck. "You're not running out on me, are you? After the stunt you pulled?" His tone was light, teasing: the voice of a man who used charm and a veneer of suavity to bend people easily to his will.

One of the Miller-Simons crew had turned to check on her and was now coming back, his eyes asking a question.

It's okay, she mouthed. *Thank you.*

He tilted his head slightly forward, stretched his eyes wider. *You sure?*

She gave a tiny nod, and her colleague stood down, pivoted smoothly, and headed out into the cool night; she would have to thank him on Monday. Now she refocused her attention on the man behind her. "I could hardly be running out on you when

I don't know you." Turning her head slightly to the side, she pointedly kept her back to him.

"We've met," Fitzpatrick corrected her. "We've spoken on a number of occasions."

She took a step forward, forcing him to release his grip, then she swung around to face him. "Darling," she said in her best North Shore drawl, "we might have met once, eons ago. And even if we have 'spoken on a number of occasions,' in this town that's a far cry from knowing someone. I've probably had more in-depth conversations with my favourite barista. I certainly know who you are, but as for the how, what, or why of it, all I know is what they print in the business and gossip pages." She put her hands on her hips and gave him a slow once-over.

"Well, in that case you owe me the chance to redeem my reputation. How about a nightcap?"

"Thank you, but no. It's getting rather late." Olivia smiled gently, softening the rebuff. She was aware of people flowing past them towards the door, casting sidelong glances, faces alight with curiosity.

"I really can't tempt you?" He pouted, a ridiculously boyish gesture on a man his age, but somehow he could get away with it.

"Perhaps another time," she said, starting to move away.

"Why don't you come and see the painting you were so desperate to buy? Once I have it hung, of course." He shoved his hands into the pockets of his trousers.

"Come and see my etchings?" She arched an eyebrow. "Does that ever work? Besides, I wasn't in it for the painting, darling, I was in it for the sport."

"Oh, now we're getting to it!"

"I really have to go. I'm sure we'll meet again at some party or another."

"Yes! Yes, a party. Would you come to a small party I'm throwing?"

Olivia tilted her head, inviting him to say more. "Saturday week. Rozelle. My yacht."

She met his gaze. "I'll have to check my diary, but send me the details." Then she rattled off her phone number, the legitimate one. "Goodnight, Mr. Fitzpatrick."

"Rowan, please," he said, frantically thumbing her number into his phone. "And sorry, I've forgotten your name..." He drew out the last word, waiting for her to fill in the blank.

Instead she laughed softly. "Darling, let's not kid ourselves. You never knew it." She took a couple of slow backward steps, keeping her eyes on his as she moved closer to the exit. "And perhaps it's better if I don't tell you—more fun." She continued to back away, only turning when she was almost at the door.

"Can I give you a lift?" he called.

Olivia didn't look back; she simply raised a hand and sketched a loose wave over her shoulder as she moved into the dark.

Twenty minutes later, in the back seat of her taxi, she powered up the burner phone. Three messages from Fitzpatrick had already pinged in on her real phone, but she hadn't opened any of them. Now she used the burner to fire off one of her own, sending it to the anonymous number Mia had given her.

Brooke will need an alibi for Saturday week.

She was surprised when the answer came back almost immediately: a row of asterisks. It took Olivia a moment to realise she was looking at seven stars—the Pleiades. She dropped the phone into her lap, ignoring the glow of its screen. She was not bound to these women, not yet, but her own sister... She owed it to her.

Olivia and Vivienne, Liv and Viv—Olivia would do this for her sister. She would go to the party, exchange banter with this man, flatter and flirt in a way that made her skin crawl, and hope her chance came. Tonight she had discovered she'd lost none of the acting skills she'd had as a teenager. Back then, she'd even thought she might apply to NIDA, try to make a career of it. But not even the most talented graduates of the National Institute of the Dramatic Arts ever had the chance to play a part like this, the role of a lifetime. And if Olivia's plan came together, it promised to be a showstopper.

She turned off the burner phone and sat back, closing her eyes as the taxi sped through the sleeping suburbs.

TWENTY-FIVE

Olivia met Amy in the day spa at the Hilton. Olivia had taken time off and booked in for a half day of treatments, while Amy was technically on the clock, doing a bit of secret shopper work to see how the experience compared to what was on offer at the five-star establishment under her control.

Their first encounter, both wrapped in white robes and waiting for their masseuses, was nothing more than a murmur and a nod, the sort of greeting one gave a stranger. They met again a couple of hours later, this time in the shower and change room—where bare boobs and bums made conversation awkward—before they finally arrived, several minutes apart, in the muffled sanctity of the sauna. It was just after noon on a weekday, so the two of them were alone, anonymous in the steam. Olivia filled Amy in on her public duel with Fitzpatrick and the invitation that had arisen from it.

"Was that wise?" Amy's speech was languid in the heat, but there was a hard edge of censure to her tone.

"Maybe not, who knows? But I had to get him to notice me. Even though I've managed to get closer to his circle over the past few months, quite frankly, darl, there are so many people hanging around him that until Friday night, I don't think I'd registered as more than another blond in the crowd."

"For God's sake, Olivia, it made the gossip columns!" Amy tipped a ladle of water over the hot coals and briefly disappeared in a cloud of steam. "All of Sydney is aware that 'Rowan Fitzpatrick met his match in feisty talent maven Olivia Hammond!'" Amy's hands blocked out the headline quote in the hazy air.

"Yeah, my ex-husband even called to make sure he wasn't paying too much child support, given how loaded I appear to be."

"Speaking of your daughter." Amy leaned forward, concern in her eyes.

"Nova's staying with her dad for two weeks to make up for him missing some of his regular time."

"I was wondering how you would arrange that." Amy sat back.

"The timing couldn't be better. God, listen to me! What sort of a mother am I?" Olivia groaned. "I have to go to a debauched party and maybe kill a man this weekend. Good thing my child's at her dad's place and the neighbours agreed to mind the dog!"

"Olivia..." Amy didn't need to say anything more.

The women lapsed into silence, letting the heat and steam do their work. Olivia felt her eyelids drooping; the late nights were catching up with her, and when Amy spoke again it made her jump.

"So, what is it that you want me to do?"

"Darl, all I need is for you to get me out of there after it's done."

"I am assuming you mean pick you up at the marina as opposed to actually getting you off the boat?"

"I did briefly toy with the idea of a Jet Ski getaway, but—"

"But even if I knew anything about Jet Skis—even if we had a Jet Ski—you could not make a more high-profile exit if you tried."

"Pretty much." This time Olivia ladled water over the coals.

She waited for the hissing and spitting to subside before continuing. "The thing is, how can I do that? Just hang around and keep a facade in place for hours after I've—"

"There is no need to engage in polite chitchat, just present an image of being intoxicated and you will be ignored—dismissed. If you feel yourself starting to crack, think of why you are there: Brooke and her murdered sister. Your sister." Amy's voice was calm and emphatic. "Do not think of that time as after, but consider it as the final part of the overall plan, a longer game where his dying is the midpoint. Because whatever happens, you must be on that yacht when it docks, just like all the other guests with nothing to hide. Actually, they probably all have something to hide, so let me rephrase that: just like all the other guests who have not committed homicide."

Olivia's nod was barely visible in the thick atmosphere. "I don't know whether my nerves will be up to driving, but I don't want to hang around for a taxi. And if I have to drink or…take something to keep up appearances, the last thing I need is to get pulled over by police on the way home. So assuming I manage to get off the boat and away from the marina, can you hustle me out of Rozelle?"

"That I can do. The motorbike would be excellent for a speedy getaway, but a bit too noticeable if we're going low-key."

"You said it yourself—things have to look vanilla."

"Okay, normal car pickup." Amy feigned disappointment. "Any idea of the time?"

"The yacht has always docked at nine a.m. after a party, which is when the marina opens. So if I haven't shown up by ten, you should go."

They were silent again. Olivia was contemplating what that might mean, the number of ways everything could go wrong, and she wondered if Amy was doing the same.

Then Amy clapped her hands together, the sound dull in the steamy confines of the sauna. "It sounds like we have ourselves a plan!"

"A half-arsed one, but sure, darl, it's a plan."

"No, it's a good plan. There are variables, that is all. And besides, you have already proven you can act. If the situation goes to shit, feign unconsciousness or at the very least a drug-induced memory loss. All you have to do is follow the steps you've laid out and make sure no one finds you next to a corpse—awake or unconscious, that's always hard to explain."

"Really?"

"When you work in the hotel industry long enough, you see and hear all sorts of things. Olivia…"

"Yes?"

"I believe I'm about to pass out from the heat. Can we get out of here?"

"Christ, yes, darl."

They stumbled into the relative cool of the wet area and back to the showers. By the time Olivia had finished drying her hair, Amy had gone. Olivia took her time dressing, and when she finally pulled on her ballet flats, her left foot met with unexpected resistance. She picked up the shoe and felt inside. A small square of paper had been crammed into the toe. Glancing around to make sure she was still alone, Olivia unfolded it to find a message written in such tiny letters she had to squint to read it.

Do not take unnecessary risks. There will be other times if you don't get the chance. No need to go overboard (literally or figuratively).

Olivia smiled and nodded to herself, reread the message a couple of times, then ripped up the note and flushed the pieces down the nearest toilet.

Amy was right: the plan was basically a good one, but it came with a number of possible scenarios. As long as Olivia thought everything through and had some idea of what to do in any given situation, it should be okay. The worst that could happen would be that she had to make a statement to police, including a fictional account of her attempt to save Fitzpatrick. Actually, no: the worst that could happen would be that the bastard refused to die—that would really make things awkward.

TWENTY-SIX

Olivia wore a Zimmermann silk wrap dress in emerald-green, a touch of boho glamour that advertised its high price with every flutter of the asymmetrical hem. Although it had long, wide sleeves, the tie waist and high slit made it ridiculously sexy, as though it might come undone and fall away at any moment. It was guaranteed to attract his attention. And if things went wrong, well, nothing looked more pathetic than silk stained with salt water. Flat sandals—de rigueur on board a yacht—completed the outfit. Olivia was as ready as she could be for a party with Rowan Fitzpatrick.

They were due to sail at four thirty on Saturday afternoon, and at 3:50 Olivia climbed into a taxi outside the Darling Harbour Sofitel. At 4:12 she paid the fare in cash, including a tip that was generous but not remarkable, and joined several other well-dressed people sauntering towards the luxury marina: a low-key arrival.

But at the gate, she had to give her name to a young woman in a tight nautical-style uniform. A guest list—it was something Olivia should have expected, and she felt a surge of panic as she watched the girl run her pen down a clipboard and make a mark. Olivia's plans to slip away anonymously from the boat were dashed. She hadn't thought like an ultra-rich person. In her world, you invited someone to a party on a Saturday night, and they came or they didn't, but you knew who you'd invited and that was that. In this world a party involved layers of complexity: staff, security, and marking names off a goddamn guest list.

Olivia considered spinning a story about a desire for anonymity and asking the girl about what would happen to the list after the guests were on board—presumably not every A-lister wanted the general public to know about their presence on the *Evanescence*. But then the girl would pay more attention to her and would recall the exchange if the police came calling. Olivia held her tongue, tossed her freshly tinted pale gold hair, and kept her large sunglasses firmly in place as she flashed an insincere smile and sauntered away.

It was okay. She and Amy had agreed she would have to be on the yacht when it docked. There would be witnesses to attest to her presence on board, so her job was to deal with Fitzpatrick and not get caught—simple.

She stepped onto the dock where the *Evanescence* was berthed, then stopped. Fitzpatrick was on the deck, already surrounded by people who seemed to be hanging on his every word. What was she doing? How could she hope to get away with this? Despite the solidity of the dock, the ground seemed to shift beneath her feet, and she swayed.

"Oops!" Someone caught her elbow. "You've started the party early, have you?"

Olivia looked down at the hand on her arm, then up into the face of its owner: a man with the tanned skin and crow's-feet that spoke of a life outdoors. He was dressed in shorts and a monogrammed polo shirt, and it took Olivia a moment to realise that the monogram wasn't some exclusive designer label but the name of the boat she was about to board.

She put a hand to her temple, shaking her head slightly. "Hardly," she said. "It's been a stressful few days and I forgot to eat this morning. I'm okay now, though. Thank you."

She saw him discreetly inhale, probably checking to see if he could smell alcohol. "You're sure?" His grip on her arm loosened.

She nodded. "All good."

A piercing whistle rent the air, and Olivia turned to look at the *Evanescence*. Fitzpatrick was leaning over the stern, glowering in their direction. "Mike!" He made the name sound like a curse as he tapped his wrist meaningfully. "I assumed you'd be at the helm by now and we'd be casting off. Do you mind?"

"My fault!" Olivia called out, smiling and waving, before she turned to the man next to her. "I'm sorry," she said softly.

"Nothing to be sorry about. Mr. Fitzpatrick pays my wages, and he expects his money's worth. So…" Mike tipped his head meaningfully towards the gangway.

"Oh!" Olivia hurried down the dock and onto the yacht, the captain following closely behind.

As soon as they were on board, crew members began to scuttle about. "I need to get us underway, so I'll leave you to it." Mike sketched a mock salute and strode off, leaving Olivia to find the party.

It wasn't hard. She made her way towards the laughter and raised voices, steeling herself for the encounter with Fitzpatrick in his current mood. She wasn't prepared for what she found.

"You made it, you gorgeous thing!" He threw his arms wide the moment he saw her, the drink in his left hand sloshing onto the teak deck and the shoes of the woman standing next to him.

"Of course, darling." Olivia tried to match his smile with one of her own, but she was caught off guard—the man who had been spitting venom moments ago was now charm personified.

She presented her cheek for a double air kiss, but instead he wrapped his arm around her and pulled her in for a strong hug before turning her to face the guests in his immediate vicinity. "Everyone! This is the cunning little creature who set me up at the charity do last week. Whatever you do, don't gamble with this one—you'll lose more than your shirt!"

The crowd laughed dutifully then returned to their own conversations, while Olivia fought back tears of frustration. She had fucked it up. First the guest list, then her encounter with the yacht's captain, who had basically committed her face to memory, for Christ's sake. Now Fitzpatrick had introduced her to half the guests. It wasn't even dark yet, and Olivia was probably the most recognisable person at the party. She should just go now—chalk this up to experience and start planning from scratch.

Then she felt the vibration beneath her feet and heard the throaty growl of the engines. It was too late: she was stuck on this proverbial ship of fools until tomorrow morning. Her thoughts were spinning. She still had to play the game, at least for a few hours. She'd think of it as more research; it might help her come up with a new plan, or even find a chink in Fitzpatrick's armour that she could exploit at a later date. Then, if she was lucky, she could commandeer an empty stateroom with a lockable door, lie down and wait for this whole sorry saga to be over.

"What can I get you to drink, beautiful?"

"Vodka tonic, thanks." She'd swap it out for sparkling water as soon as she could.

As Fitzpatrick snapped his fingers in the direction of the bar, it occurred to Olivia that he hadn't once used her name. Was that just his manner, or had he honestly not even bothered to find out? Her presence on the guest list showed that someone had taken the time to discover who she was, but they might just have been a staff member; Olivia had spoken to an assistant when accepting the invitation.

It also hadn't escaped her how quickly Fitzpatrick's mood had switched between anger and charm, something she recognised all too well from Viv's toxic relationship with Aaron. To Olivia's eternal shame, it had taken her a while to comprehend what her sister was dealing with; to realise the Aaron she knew was a sham, an amiable front hiding a violent man who controlled Viv's every move.

Late one morning, Olivia had just finished a visit with her sister and was getting into her car when she realised she'd left her jacket behind. She let herself back into the garden and was making her way around the side of the house to the kitchen when she heard Aaron's voice. He was pouring forth a litany of abuse: belittling, soul-crushing, confidence-shattering words of contempt, all directed at her sister. Olivia froze for a moment, then did the only thing she could think of doing—she stepped forward and knocked on the back door. The tirade stopped, the door opened, and Aaron was standing in front of her, smiling, seemingly relaxed. He retrieved the forgotten jacket and offered up some banal pleasantry, and Olivia was out in the street again almost before she'd had a chance to think.

That afternoon, thinking was all Olivia did. Suddenly, Viv's sprained wrist and odd bruises made sense. The demure, rather drab way she'd begun to dress and her new habit of wearing scarves—even in the warmest weather—took on a sinister new meaning.

Later, when Olivia had phoned, she'd tried to broach the subject. Viv had shut her down. "Please don't rock the boat, Liv," she'd said. "It will only make things worse. I have a plan, but until I can sort it out, I don't want to give him any reason to be angrier." Olivia had tried to argue, but in the end she'd acquiesced. Viv was smart—Olivia would support her plan. Only Viv never had a chance. Because a few weeks later, Viv was dead.

"Here's your drink, beautiful!"

Olivia snapped back to the present as Fitzpatrick pressed a tall glass into her hand. "Thank you, Rowan." She started to raise her glass, then paused. "I feel like we should be toasting something. What shall we drink to?"

"How about we drink to the start of something big?" He waggled his eyebrows suggestively.

"Are we starting something?" she asked.

"I think it's already started, don't you?"

For the first time that afternoon, her smile was genuine. "I think you're right." She touched her glass to his. "Let's drink to starting things. And to following through."

As she pretended to drink, a lascivious smile crawled across Fitzpatrick's face, revealing the real man behind the cultured mask—the man she was going to kill.

TWENTY-SEVEN

The *Evanescence* didn't travel far. It dropped anchor farther down the harbour, far enough from the shore and other vessels to avoid disturbing anyone, and also beyond the range of any paparazzi with long lenses. Olivia had talked to Fitzpatrick for a while before excusing herself to freshen up. She moved among the guests, most of whom appeared to have left their inhibitions back in Rozelle and were now well on the way to intoxication thanks to one substance or another. Olivia was relieved to find herself universally ignored, despite Fitzpatrick's earlier stunt. To this crowd, she was essentially a nobody; if anyone remembered her at all, they would recall just another blond woman in a cocktail dress, one of several at the party.

Abandoning her still-full glass, Olivia made her way from the yacht's sundeck, the focus of the party, through a vast salon furnished with built-in sofas and a selection of deep lounge chairs. A number of guests were scattered around the space, their talk more muted. Olivia first thought they were simply escaping the noise, looking for a place to enjoy some quiet conversation. Then, from the corner of her eye, she saw a man lean forward to the coffee table, put a silver straw to his nose and inhale deeply—definitely not there for the conversation.

Without breaking stride, she carried on into the interior. It was even quieter here, the party muffled with only the bass notes clearly distinguishable. From the dock she had seen that the *Evanescence* had five decks, two above this one and two below. Presumably the master suite would be on this level, with guest accommodation below and crew at the very bottom. Olivia was surprised that every door opened under her touch; she had expected locks and secrets, but all she got was ostentation. Fitzpatrick liked to flaunt his wealth, and the yacht was a lesson in how the top tier lived. Besides the gym, steam room, lounge, elevator to all decks, bar, and pool, there were seven staterooms, and the master was the last word in luxury: a Bang & Olufsen entertainment system, walk-in wardrobes, his and hers bathrooms with a spa and rainfall shower, and a private office and library, complete with screens and projectors for video conferencing.

Olivia was thorough, exploring as much of the yacht as she could. A couple of times she had to feign disorientation and ask a crew member where the bathroom was or how to get back to the lounge, but for the most part she had the place to herself, and she did her best to commit the deck plan to memory. Finally she was satisfied she'd been through most of the yacht except for the crew area and the bridge. It hadn't given her any ideas. For all she knew, Fitzpatrick would stay up on deck or in the lounge all night, rendered invulnerable by a bunch of drugged-up aristo-brats. This wasn't going to work.

Olivia thought about returning to the party, but instead she made her way back to the guest rooms—opulent, but a definite step down from the main stateroom. They were all empty so she picked one at random, locked the door, and pulled off her sandals. The music wasn't too loud here; she'd try to get some sleep. That way, she'd at least salvage something from the night by wallowing in a little luxury. She lay on the comfortable bed, feeling the crispness of the linen, her head sinking into the softest of pillows. Even the darkness felt opulent on the *Evanescence.* Olivia sighed and closed her eyes, willing herself to relax.

Less than five minutes later, she opened her eyes: this wasn't going to work either. She was here on this yacht with Rowan Fitzpatrick. Even if her immediate plan was in tatters, the bigger scheme was still in play, and she'd need another invitation from him, another chance. Which meant cosying up and consolidating her position.

In the ensuite, Olivia took her time refreshing her makeup then pulled the contact lenses from her purse, thinking she may as well play her part. It only took a few minutes to put them in, and when she looked in the mirror, blackness stared back at her. Shaking out her golden hair, she went in search of the host.

A couple of hours had passed since she'd seen him holding court among the beautiful people; in that time, the mood of the party had changed, and with it the distribution of guests, now more scattered as they entered the endurance phase: the long stretch of time between the excitement of casting off and the harsh return to reality tomorrow morning.

Olivia retraced her steps through the yacht, keeping an eye out for Fitzpatrick. He wasn't among the people in the lounge, or on the sundeck beneath the sparkling fairy lights. The atmosphere out here felt more electric now, perhaps frenetic. To Olivia's eye there was a brittleness to this crowd: their laughter seemed shrill, their movements erratic, as though they were hellbent on forcing themselves to be happy. Perhaps they were afraid of what the next day might bring.

As Olivia moved through the public spaces, she noticed

several small silver dishes: a few in the lounge and another on the sundeck, sitting on a low table between two deckchairs. Each dish contained a selection of coloured pills—greens, blues, and pinks—all stamped with something that looked like the Yin-Yang symbol: ecstasy.

She didn't think Fitzpatrick was the type to retire from his own party—unless of course he was shagging someone. Even without the benefit of drugs and alcohol, there were probably a few women here tonight who'd be up for it.

Olivia moved to the stern and leaned her forearms on the railing, gazing out over the dark water to the shimmering incandescence of the city. She wished she was there, on solid ground.

Then someone coughed. The sound didn't come from behind her, but from the gloom below. Leaning forward, she peered down, and then she spotted him. Fitzpatrick was flat on his back on the bathing platform. She stared, probing the shadows with her eyes as she looked for someone else, because surely he wouldn't be down there by himself.

But he was. He lay near the edge, only a foot or so above the water, a bottle of some sort in his hand. As she watched, he wrestled with the top of it for a moment, then gave up. "Well, fuck." His words fell softly on the night air, lacking their usual clear enunciation.

The only way down to the bathing platform was back through the yacht's interior. Olivia hoped Fitzpatrick was truly on his own, that he wasn't waiting for anyone—and that no one else knew he was there. She turned around and surveyed the crowd; no one was paying her the slightest bit of attention. After she sauntered past them all, she went back through the lounge, this time palming a few of the pills and dropping them into her purse. She made her way to the stairs rather than the elevator, not wanting the ping of its doors to announce her arrival below decks. She was cautious, but there was no one on the stairs, and no one in the corridor.

Opening the door to the bathing deck, she breathed in the salty air, her senses alive to the night, her mind alive to the possibilities. She stepped out and quietly closed the door behind her, cutting off a shaft of light.

"Who's there?" Fitzpatrick demanded. "Whoever you are, I hope you can open this fucking bottle."

"Only me." Olivia's tone was light. "I wondered where you'd got to."

"Me who?"

In the light cast from above, she could see him struggle and fail to sit up, instead rolling onto his side so he could look at her.

"What are you doing out here, darling?" she asked, keeping her voice low, trying to charge her questions with a suggestive undertone. "Waiting for someone?"

"No. Everyone was talking about me. I had to get away."

"Well of course. you're the host of a wonderful party—of course they're talking about you." Olivia took a couple of steps forward then crouched down to his level, leaving a bit of distance between them. He had clearly taken something, and until she had a better idea of what it was and how it was affecting him, she wanted to hang back.

Fitzpatrick shook his head emphatically. "Not good talk," he hissed. He was agitated, talking fast, and beads of sweat stood out on his forehead despite the cool breeze stirring across the water. "What are you doing here, anyway?" His narrowed gaze and accusatory tone made Olivia catch her breath. Had she somehow given herself away? Then he looked up to the deck above, his eyes opening wide at some sound she hadn't heard. In the low light she could see his pupils were dilated, his eyes as black as hers, only she doubted he was wearing contacts. She let out a slow breath—he was just in the grip of drug-induced paranoia.

How to proceed? The concerned friend, the addiction buddy? What would allow her to get close? "I came to see if you were okay," she said. "I wasn't feeling so good. I took something"—she tapped the side of her nose—"and I think it was stronger than I'm used to. I got worried so I came to find you to see if you were okay, sweetie." Moving from her crouched position, Olivia dropped onto her knees.

"I'm really, really thirsty," he said. "And I have a headache, but mostly I'm thirsty and I was going to drink this"—he brandished a champagne bottle then dropped it back to the deck with a clunk—"but then I couldn't open it, and that made me wonder why I couldn't open it, and then I thought, perhaps someone has injected something through the cork—to poison me, you know?—and that had made the cork stick. So then I thought I should probably drink water, but of course the only water here is the harbour water, which you can't drink. Isn't that ironic? I'm dying of thirst, surrounded by water." The words had come out in a torrent, Fitzpatrick barely pausing for breath.

"I think maybe you need to go and lie down properly," Olivia said, then silently swore at herself—she wasn't here to play nursemaid. "Or you could let me open that for you." She gestured to the champagne bottle, unbroken foil still covering the cork.

"Why are you being so nice?" Fitzpatrick asked, suspicion bubbling again.

"Because I'm a nice person. That's why you invited me. Besides, I'm thirsty too, darling." Olivia hoped her matter-of-fact tone might reassure him.

As he stared at her, she kept her features relaxed and neutral, only opening her eyes a bit wider so he could more easily see her dilated pupils. He passed her the bottle. For a moment they each had a hand on it, and he wouldn't relent when she pulled, wouldn't loosen his grip. She half let go, as though she didn't care.

"Alright then," he said. "But you drink first." When he released the bottle, she had to snatch at it to prevent it from falling. He pressed the heel of one hand into his eye socket. "God-awful headache," he moaned.

"Hang on." After setting the bottle to one side, she reached into her purse and pulled out some of the E she'd grabbed. "These'll fix your head." She placed the two pills on the deck between them, then picked up the champagne again and began to peel the foil from the cork. She kept her focus on the bottle but could feel him scrutinising her; from the corner of her eye she saw his head dip towards the pills then back up to face her. As she cast the foil aside and set to work untwisting the wire, she glanced at him. "Found them in the lounge." She shrugged. "Just thought if you're coming down a bit hard, maybe a little something…" Her words trailed away as he picked up the pills, rolling them around in his palm.

Olivia began working the cork with her thumb, turning the bottle, easing it bit by bit. This was the correct way to open champagne, but more importantly she didn't want a loud pop to attract the attention of those on the deck above. When the cork gave, she held on, letting it come free in her hand.

Fitzpatrick was still watching her, still toying with the pills. She flicked the cork into the water then inclined the neck of the bottle towards him. He shook his head, so she shrugged, brought the bottle to her lips, and took a deep swig, spluttering slightly at the end as the bubbles tickled her nose. Pretending to drink was now out of the question, given Fitzpatrick's suspicious mood, and a bit of alcohol in her system might be a good thing, should anyone wish to check later.

She sighed with satisfaction. "You do have good taste," she said, offering Fitzpatrick the bottle again.

He slowly extended his hand and relieved her of the champagne, his eyes never leaving her face as he drew the bottle back and held it against his chest.

"Seriously," she said, with what she hoped was a convincing giggle, "that's divine. If you're not going to actually drink it, pass it back." She leaned towards him, arm outstretched, wiggling her fingers invitingly.

His response was better than she'd dared hope: he shrugged away from her, turning his shoulder and curling defensively around the bottle. "No! It's my turn. You can have it in a minute!" He tipped his head back and poured in a stream of champagne, holding the bottle a few centimetres above his mouth, swallowing steadily.

Keep going, keep going.

Abruptly he stopped, champagne spilling across his chin and chest. He threw the two pills into his mouth and chased them down with another mouthful.

Olivia closed her eyes and sent up a silent prayer—not to God, but to her sister, Vivienne, and to Brooke's sister, Gemma. She was going to do this, and now Olivia knew what her next move would be.

Her eyes snapped open, and she turned her head slightly, staring towards the upper deck. She looked for anyone leaning over the rails, gazing back at her, but no shadowy forms hovered, and the voices from above were muted as though coming from farther away.

"Sit on the edge with me?" she asked Fitzpatrick, before standing and moving to the back of the swim deck. There was no railing here, just a low ledge with a gated ladder in the middle. She sat on the ledge then swung around, presenting her back to

Fitzpatrick, dangling her legs over the water. She heard him stir and leaned backwards, tilting her head so she could look at him and once again sweep her gaze towards the upper deck: still no one. "Bring the champagne," she said, her voice made husky by the angle of her neck.

She waited, forcing herself to breathe.

A shuffle, a scrape, and then he was standing next to her. She put her hand out for the bottle, set it down on the ledge, then patted the space next to it, inviting him to sit. "Look at the lights," she said softly. "How beautiful."

He grunted as he swung first one leg then the other over and around, settling himself back before abruptly leaning forward and peering at the inky water less than a metre below his feet. "I almost fancy a dip," he said.

"In that? At this time of night?" Olivia scoffed. "Don't be silly." She casually reached for the neck of the champagne bottle.

"Why not? That's what the bloody yacht is for! Jump off here, splash about, back up the ladder."

Her hand closed around the cool glass, gripped firmly, lifted the bottle ever so slightly. He hadn't guzzled the lot—it still had plenty of weight. "That might be dangerous," she said.

"Bullshit!" He leaned forward a bit more.

Olivia swung the bottle up and brought it down on the back of his head, hard.

TWENTY-EIGHT

The momentum almost took Olivia over the edge, but she grabbed hold with her free hand and pulled herself back. Fitzpatrick fell straight into the harbour with barely a splash. He landed facedown, his blue shirt ballooning around him, and didn't move.

Olivia stared. Had she killed him? Probably not. Was he unconscious or just stunned? Would the drugs and alcohol do the rest?

She looked over her shoulder. No one was watching. Looked back at Fitzpatrick, who still wasn't moving. His shirt had subsided, weighed down by the water, the captured air gone. Should she go back inside now or pretend to try and rescue him? Fuck.

With a gasp, she remembered the bottle in her hand and dropped it over the edge. It bobbed for a moment then quickly filled with water, sinking from view. If only Fitzpatrick would do the same.

Olivia whimpered. What had she done? She stretched out a hand, but Fitzpatrick was well beyond her grasp. Surely there must be a fucking boat hook or something around here? Some way to drag him back, to drag time back to before she'd...

She leaned forward, head between her knees, and vomited into Sydney Harbour. Her breath was coming in ragged gasps roaring in her ears. Someone must have heard; they must be coming now. She twisted her body, looking for fingers pointing accusingly at her, shocked faces, the glint of phones held up to film, to condemn.

But there was nothing except the steady beat of the music overlaid by a burst of drunken laughter, a dub remix to haunt her nightmares. She stared out at the body again and began to hum "Hey Jude," erratically at first before she captured the melody as her breathing normalised.

Fitzpatrick seemed to be slightly lower in the water, but he was also drifting away from the yacht, increasing the chance that anyone looking from above would see him. Back in control of herself, Olivia made up her mind and scrambled off the ledge. There was a pile of rolled-up towels near the door, and she stumbled across and grabbed one, returning to wipe vigorously where her hands had rested. She'd never get all her prints off the swim deck, but at least if they weren't right near the edge that would help.

After dropping the towel into a hamper, she put the hem of her dress over her fingers before she opened the door. Her hands were shaking so badly that she had to will herself not to let the door slam. Then she was in, hurrying down the corridor to the stairs, getting away.

She just had to hope nobody spotted Fitzpatrick before the water claimed him. And of course, she had to hope he didn't come around and start yelling.

When she emerged from the stairway onto the main deck, she hesitated. Olivia had thought of returning to the stateroom, curling up and feigning a drunken sleep, but—hard as it would be to sustain the pretence—she needed to be seen now. She made for the lounge, forcing herself to move slowly, adding a stumble to her gait as she entered the room. No one looked up when she drifted across to an empty chair and let herself drop messily. The action was only half feigned; there was a tremor in her legs that seemed to be radiating throughout her body.

She closed her eyes, and immediately her mind was flooded with a replay of what she'd just done. She jerked, gasping, her eyes flying open. The noise attracted a member of the crew; a young man who had been passing quietly through the lounge, collecting dirty glasses and topping some up. He looked at her, his shrewd assessment surely taking in her now dishevelled and champagne-stained dress. Then he approached, stepping lightly around sofas and the outstretched legs of guests. Olivia kept her gaze down, focusing on his deeply tanned cyclist's calves, which—by nature of his shorts-and-polo-shirt uniform—were on prominent display. "Water, ma'am?" he murmured, holding out a bottle of still San Pellegrino.

She lifted her head, giving him the full benefit of the contact lenses. "Thank you," she whispered. A few seconds later he placed a glass by her elbow with the bottle, then retreated.

Olivia sipped the water, her mind racing. There was no shouting, so Fitzpatrick hadn't been spotted, and now the crew member had seen her and clearly determined her condition to be just as parlous as that of the other guests. But was he alert enough to realise she'd only just arrived in the lounge, and would that matter? There was nothing remarkable about her. Besides, the crew must be tired. Surely she was safe. She had to be.

Her eyes were gritty. After a quick check of the room, she turned aside and took out the contacts. They could go into the harbour later; for now, she screwed them into a tissue and dropped it in her purse. She didn't want to risk losing them, risk them turning up in the hands of the police.

Letting her eyelids sag again, she forced her shoulders to drop as she sprawled in the chair. The night stretched ahead, filled with empty hours until dawn, and then it would finally be time to head back to Rozelle. All she had to do was sit and wait.

Despite everything, she felt herself beginning to doze. It couldn't really be that easy, could it? Her arm twitched when she remembered the sensation of the bottle connecting with the base of his skull.

Olivia fell asleep thinking about her sister's smiling face.

She woke to light streaming through the lounge's large windows. Other people were still sprawled across couches, chairs, and the floor. The smell of coffee was wafting in from somewhere, and it drew her to her feet. Caffeine—she needed to be sharp. She shuffled to the sundeck where a continental breakfast had been laid out: fruit, pastries, beverages. A few other people were already there, either wolfing down croissants or nursing black coffee, depending on their poison of choice from the night before. Olivia assessed the company as she collected a brioche and espresso. The mood was subdued but not disaster-sombre, just hangover grade. It was a normal morning after on the *Evanescence*.

She felt a surge of relief and satisfaction, followed by guilt. *I've done it! Yes. Oh, God. What have I done?* While it was business as usual now, sooner or later someone would realise Rowan Fitzpatrick was not on his yacht. That was when she would really know if she'd done it right; if she could possibly get away with it.

Despite her churning stomach, Olivia forced herself to eat and drink, watching the harbour slip by as the *Evanescence* slowly motored back towards the marina. The speed slowed even further as they entered Rozelle Bay, giving way to a couple of rowers and smaller vessels. Several more partygoers had emerged, reeling back when the brightness of the September morning hit them, then advancing to the buffet and settling on lounges.

The sun lit up the water with the brilliance of a thousand diamonds, and Olivia pulled out her sunglasses, shielding her eyes from the light—and from close scrutiny. She leaned over the side and pretended to watch the marina attendants as the *Evanescence* bumped gently against the dock. In reality, she was scanning the area for police. She stayed where she was as the yacht was made fast, the gangway put in place, and the guests began to leave. No one seemed unduly troubled that the host wasn't there to farewell them.

A crew member appeared, still immaculate in her uniform, and gave Olivia a practised customer-service smile. "We've docked, madam."

"Thank you," said Olivia, and the girl began to turn away. "Excuse me?"

"Yes, madam?" The girl's tone was perfectly civilised, but Olivia fancied she could hear contempt beneath. Hardly surprising, given the habits of this crowd.

"Is Rowan—Mr. Fitzpatrick—about? I'd like to say goodbye."

"I would think he's in his room, madam. But we have strict orders not to disturb him on Sunday mornings." Although the girl's expression was bland, somehow her words held a world of meaning.

"I see. Thank you." Olivia flashed a brief, insincere smile and turned away, walking with measured steps, desperate to get off the yacht.

Almost at the gangway, she remembered the contacts in her purse. She pulled out the crumpled tissue and half turned, pretending to blow her nose as she let the contacts fall into the water. When she looked up, the crew member stationed at the gangway was facing the shore, studiously staring straight ahead. Nothing like crewing for a cocaine user and his cronies to instill discretion, although she bet Fitzpatrick paid well for their silence.

"Mind your step, madam." The crew member offered her a hand that she declined with a shake of her head and a murmur that might have been thanks but failed to resolve into a word.

Her throat was dry as she stepped from the boat and made her way along the dock. With each step she was aware of the security cameras bristling like tropical weeds from every elevated vantage point. She wanted to duck her head, but she also wanted to glance at them, to see if they were panning as she passed, matching her pace with the slow track of their lenses. Instead she kept her posture loose, her steps steady but not overly energetic. Normal. Heading home after a big party, a bit the worse for wear.

She passed through the marina, nodded to the guard at the main gate without breaking stride, and turned confidently towards the rendezvous point Amy had nominated, a cafe in the shadow of the Anzac Bridge. There was no sign of the woman outside, so Olivia pushed through the glass door. Then she stopped short.

Other than the girl behind the counter and the man she was serving, the place was empty. Olivia pulled out her phone to check the time: 9:35 a.m. Amy shouldn't have left yet.

Unless there was a problem.

Olivia thought she was going to be sick. They must know. They must be watching her, waiting for who knew what before they converged, sirens blaring and guns drawn.

But that was crazy. If anyone knew Fitzpatrick was dead or

missing, police would be everywhere, helicopters overhead. Something else must have happened, but she couldn't think about that now. She had to get away from here without drawing undue attention to herself. Selecting a water from the fridge, she laid the required four dollars on the counter and stepped back out into the bright sun.

On the opposite side of the street, a motorcyclist in full leathers and helmet was standing next to a powerful-looking bike, rummaging through one of the panniers. Olivia looked away. She'd call a taxi; that was what a normal party guest would do.

The bikie whistled at her. She ignored him, focusing on scrolling through her contacts.

He whistled again, and she spun around. The biker had flipped up the helmet visor and was staring at her. Not a he—Amy.

Olivia's mouth fell open, then she walked over. "What happened?"

The woman shrugged. "Problem with the car. Not ideal. I will tell you about it another time. But for now, put these on and let's go." She held up a jacket and pants.

"Just give me a helmet."

Amy shook her head. "A woman in a dress on the back will attract police. Two minutes now, and we will be invisible."

Olivia didn't argue, and while Amy stowed the water bottle and her purse, she yanked on the pants and jacket.

"Pity about the shoes, but you'll do." Amy handed her a black helmet. "Have you ever ridden pillion?"

"Years ago, in Bali."

"So no." Amy swung a leg over the bike and pulled it upright, kicking the stand away. "Get on, hold on, lean forward into my back, and stay there." She flipped her visor down.

Olivia did as she was told. As soon as she was on, Amy

pushed a button on the right handlebar and the machine roared to life. She reached down and gave Olivia's thigh a firm pat, then opened the throttle and they were away, looping round an access road then off towards Drummoyne and the northern suburbs beyond. For a moment, Olivia rested her helmeted forehead on Amy's shoulder. She'd done it. It was over.

But as they weaved through the Sunday morning traffic and flashed past a weekend market, her stomach clenched. It wasn't over, not yet. And what if killing him turned out to be the easy part?

Olivia tightened her grip.

TWENTY-NINE

It didn't happen until Monday.

After Amy dropped her off, Olivia spent the rest of Sunday obsessively watching the news and waiting for a knock at the door. The next morning she went to work as usual, drifting through the day on autopilot. She kept imagining the looming presence of a police officer in reception. The day seemed interminably long.

When she got home that evening and switched on the television, she was greeted by a solemn-faced newsreader. "Fears are held for the safety of Sydney businessman and socialite Rowan Fitzpatrick, after he failed to attend an important board meeting today." The bulletin continued, explaining that his yacht crew assumed he'd left at some point after docking, before it cut from the studio to a glamorous reporter on scene outside the marina.

She nodded self-importantly. "Ed, I can now tell you, police have just confirmed that it is Rowan Fitzpatrick's Maybach in the car park here. At this stage they believe it has been here since Saturday, but of course they're not ruling anything out. CCTV footage has been taken for analysis, and forensics are currently on site, examining both the car and Mr. Fitzpatrick's luxury yacht, the *Evanescence*."

Olivia's mobile began to ring, drowning out whatever else the reporter was going to say. She stared at the phone's screen for a moment—not a number she knew. After muting the television, she took a deep breath and pressed the green icon. "Olivia Hammond."

Police. A man, Detective Something-or-Other: she was too stressed to retain the name.

The first conversation was short. Yes, she had been on the boat. Yes, she had spoken with her host at various points throughout the evening. No, she hadn't seen him after midnight, but she had perhaps drunk a little too much and had fallen asleep in the lounge. Yes, of course she could come in to make a formal statement tomorrow. She didn't have to try to put a quiver in her voice when she asked if they knew anything.

After the call ended, she sat in her kitchen as the house darkened around her, making the silent television seem brighter by degrees. A faint sound roused her, gone almost before she registered it. Billy had been curled up in his dog bed, but now he raised his head, ears cocked, as he decided what, if any, action to take. The noise had come from the front of the house, and Olivia dragged herself upright, using the edge of the kitchen table for support. She felt as though she had aged fifty years.

Switching on lights as she went, she padded through the house in stockinged feet, feeling the warm familiarity of her possessions, missing her daughter but comforted by the clack of claws as Billy followed close behind. A folded piece of paper lay on the polished floor a few centimetres from the front door. Olivia stared for a long moment before stooping to pick it up.

She unfolded the small page: it was printed with a black and white image of seven stars. Beneath that, typed in a generic font, was a message from Mia.

> *Tell them only what you need to. Don't expand. Don't fall for their empathy. Use the truth as much as possible. Don't hesitate before answering. You have already triumphed. M.*

Olivia wandered into the bathroom, reading the note again as she went. Truth in everything, except the main event—it was good advice. She lifted the toilet lid, shredded the note into the water, and flushed.

A few hours of patchy sleep was all Olivia managed, exhaustion warring with flashbacks and anxiety about speaking to detectives. She would need ice in her veins to get through the interview.

Taking the morning off work, she presented herself at the police station precisely on time. The male detective, who identified himself as Bernstein, offered her a cup of tea as he led her to an interview room. "Sorry it's so spartan," he said, gesturing to a chair on one side of the metal and laminate table that dominated the room. "But we're talking to everyone who was on the yacht, so all our rooms are in use and it's much quieter in here than the office. I'll just get my colleague and be back in a jiff."

He let the door close heavily as he went, leaving Olivia alone to count the scuff marks on the antiseptic green walls. Was this a tactic, designed to unsettle? She started to hum but stopped a couple of notes in, as soon as she realised what she was doing—if anyone was listening, she didn't want them to get the wrong idea. Instead, she pulled out a notepad and began to compose a shopping list; the normality of the task would keep her mind occupied.

When Detective Bernstein returned, he trailed in a few steps behind a grey-haired woman with sharp eyes. Olivia made a point of jotting down two more items before tucking the pad back in her purse and folding her hands on the scarred surface of the table. She waited as the detectives sat, fiddled with their notes, clicked pens, exchanged glances and pieces of paper, and generally found ways to stretch the silence. She desperately wanted to break it—to ask if they'd found Fitzpatrick, to comment that she thought he'd have reappeared by now—but she remembered Mia's message and held herself still, a look of what she hoped was polite inquiry mingled with concern plastered on her face.

Finally, Bernstein spoke. "Thanks for coming in, Ms. Hammond. My colleague here is Detective Fiona Ulbrick. You don't mind if we record this, do you? We just need to fill in some of the blanks from what you said on the phone, so let's start with Saturday. Tell us about the party."

Olivia took them through her movements: her arrival at the marina, her unofficial self-guided tour of the boat, her lie-down in a stateroom because she was "feeling a bit woozy," and then how she rounded off the night in a corner of the lounge, woke up for breakfast, and disembarked in Rozelle, where a friend picked her up.

"Why didn't you leave your vehicle in the marina's car park?" Bernstein asked.

"I knew I'd be drinking."

"Why did your friend wait down the street?"

Olivia felt a flash of fear. What if they asked for Amy's name and details? She hadn't planned for this, hadn't even considered that the police might be interested in her friend. She swallowed.

"She's found that when she sits outside expensive venues dressed in full motorbike leathers, it tends to worry security—particularly because she's Asian." Olivia knew it was a cheap trick, but it seemed to do the job as the detectives quickly moved on.

"How do you know Rowan Fitzpatrick?"

"I'm only just getting to know him, really," she said, before she explained her previous encounters with him, keeping the details vague.

Olivia glanced between the two detectives, trying to include both of them as she spoke. Detective Ulbrick's eyes were sharp, but otherwise her face was impassive and she remained silent, leaving all the questioning to Bernstein.

Now he asked, "Why did you wander all through the yacht? Were you looking for something?"

At that, Olivia burst out laughing. "I don't usually travel in those social circles, and I have certainly never set foot on a boat like that. Of course I was going to have a good old snoop! Wouldn't you?"

The detectives glanced at each other, and Ulbrick nodded. "Fair point," she said, her voice low and cool. They were the first words she'd spoken since entering the room.

The detectives asked Olivia about when she'd last seen Fitzpatrick, what she'd been drinking, and if she'd seen him drinking alcohol or taking other substances. She decided to feign embarrassment and stayed silent, staring down at her lap.

"We're not interested in making a drug bust or anything like that." Ulbrick's tone was soft, persuasive. "Detective Bernstein is just trying to build up a picture of Mr. Fitzpatrick's physical and mental state."

Olivia looked up, then down again. "Everyone was drinking and taking things. It was all just...there to be had. Like trays of hors d'oeuvres, really."

"And Mr. Fitzpatrick? Was he...?" Bernstein left the question hanging in the air.

Olivia glanced from one detective to the other, then nodded. "Cocaine, I think, but definitely pills—ecstasy."

"And you?" Bernstein peered at her over the top of his glasses.

"A line or two," she whispered, giving a little shrug.

Ulbrick wrote something in her notebook, while Bernstein sat back, some of the alertness dropping from his posture. *What were they thinking?* Ulbrick's face gave nothing away, and Olivia tried not to stare at the notebook, wondering if the detective's quickly scrawled words were an actual observation or just a ruse to rattle her.

"What's happened to Rowan?" Olivia asked. She didn't know if it was the right moment to ask the question, but surely a lack of curiosity would be just as damning as too much.

The detectives exchanged another look, communicating silently for a moment before turning back to her. Bernstein placed his pen carefully on top of the half-filled page of his notebook, aligning it with the upper edge. "What I'm about to tell you doesn't leave this room," he said.

Olivia nodded and swallowed, even though she knew the detectives wouldn't tell her anything they weren't going to release publicly.

"We don't believe he was on the boat when it docked. There were no sightings of him at the marina, and he's not on any of the CCTV footage. All of the ancillary craft belonging to the *Evanescence*—" Olivia's frown of confusion caused Bernstein to break off. "Apparently that type of yacht has its own tenders—small boats—as well as Jet Skis, paddleboards, kayaks... In other words, lots of ways for someone to leave the boat. But they're all accounted for. No other craft was sighted by the captain or crew anywhere near the *Evanescence*, and they keep a sharp eye out for paparazzi. So we don't believe he was picked up by anyone."

Olivia was thanking God she hadn't tried to get off the boat, while she wondered how the supposedly vigilant crew hadn't seen their boss floating facedown in the water.

"Which means," Bernstein continued, "he may have gone overboard. We're trying to narrow down the time, and Marine Area Command—the water police—are checking tide tables. Unfortunately, none of you party guests were what I'd call... alert."

Olivia's face grew warm, and she hoped they took her blush for shame rather than the weird combination of anxiety and exhilaration she was feeling. "I can't believe it," she said. "I feel awful."

Ulbrick gave a small humph that might have been an expression of sympathy but was more likely contempt.

"Yes, well," said Bernstein, "I think we have all we need for now, Ms. Hammond." He looked at his colleague.

Ulbrick nodded then pushed back her chair, the legs scraping harshly on the worn linoleum. "I'll see you out," she said.

Olivia gave a wan smile. She was desperate to leave, but forced herself to walk calmly, matching her steps with Detective Ulbrick's. As they wove through the corridors, she was conscious of the detective's occasional glances, and kept expecting a comment or question. But when Olivia made eye contact, all she got was the intensity of Ulbrick's direct gaze. It felt like an X-ray of her soul.

At the main exit, Olivia turned and held out her hand. It seemed like the right gesture to make. "I'm sorry I couldn't be of more help," she said.

Detective Ulbrick's grip was firm. "Probably more help than you realise."

Olivia decided to walk straight to her office. After all, there was no reason for her to be too traumatised by Rowan Fitzpatrick's disappearance—he was just an acquaintance. It was a beautiful Sydney morning, warm with a light spring breeze, and everything seemed particularly vibrant, as though the world had been washed clean.

Earlier she'd been too nervous to eat breakfast, and she had strolled less than a block when the scent of coffee and a tempting window display of *pains au chocolat* drew her into a small patisserie, the bell on the door jingling as she entered. Five minutes later she was at a tiny table in the back, sipping a latte, when the bell rang again and Mia walked in. Olivia felt a flash of surprise, quickly followed by relief—she wasn't alone. "Olivia! What a coincidence!" Mia held up a finger, signalling that Olivia should wait while she placed her order.

Moments later, Mia kissed her cheek before pulling out the chair opposite.

"I'm going to go out on a limb and suggest this is no coincidence at all," murmured Olivia as she brought her coffee cup to her lips.

"No such thing." Mia smiled broadly. "I thought they'd have you in this morning and assumed you'd head for the office afterwards, so I waited and watched, and here I am."

"I—"

The waitress arrived with Mia's cappuccino and almond croissant.

When they were alone again, the therapist pulled off the end of her pastry and leaned closer to Olivia. "Tell me."

THIRTY

As Ulbrick watched Olivia Hammond walk down the steps of the police station, she felt vaguely unsettled. Something about the woman was firing a synapse deep in her brain, but she had no idea why.

On impulse, she trailed after Hammond. *Just as far as the corner*, she told herself. When the woman ducked into a cafe, Ulbrick grunted with satisfaction; she would follow, order a couple of takeaways, and try to strike up a casual conversation while they waited in this more relaxed setting.

Ulbrick was metres away when another woman approached from the opposite direction and entered the cafe. She caught the door as it swung closed but quickly decided to let go, instead peering through the display of pastries, hoping not to be noticed. As the newcomer had stepped into the cafe, she'd greeted Olivia Hammond by name.

Ulbrick watched as the woman crossed to Hammond's table: 1950s-style black hair with a white streak, strong jawline, curvy figure, good posture, confident. Ulbrick filed this information away and turned her attention to Hammond, who looked surprised then relieved; this must be a friend, the meeting happenstance. Ulbrick shifted slightly, trying to get a better view of the women; they were now leaning close together, talking intently.

Then Hammond looked up, and Ulbrick pulled back, giving herself a mental shake. What was she doing? Hammond had done nothing unexpected during the interview, and her story of the night on Fitzpatrick's boat was plausible. So what was jarring? Why did Ulbrick feel as though she was watching a foreign movie and someone had messed with the subtitles?

Turning, she slowly made her way back to the station and climbed the stairs to the squad room. Lew Bernstein looked up as she came in, and she paused next to his desk. "Thanks for letting me sit in on a few of these, Lew."

"No sweat. We've got a way to go with the guest list, so you're welcome to join me again."

"Ta. I'll probably pop in on one or two more, or maybe just watch on the video monitor." She shrugged.

"What is it exactly that you're after, F U?" Lew was one of the few colleagues allowed to use Ulbrick's nickname—at least, to her face.

She tapped a finger on his desk, then pulled out the visitor's chair and sat down. "To be honest, I don't know. It's just that Rowan Fitzpatrick is on my list of men who got away with things, and that means I get curious when shit happens." She scratched the back of her head and sighed. "I guess I just wanted to get a feel for the situation, understand what the party was like, that sort of stuff."

Lew nodded. "I know you keep tabs on certain names, but I thought that was only if they came up on the other side of the equation." He tossed his pen lightly onto the desk and leaned back, staring at her over the top of his glasses.

"You're right, Lew. But what's your thinking on Fitzpatrick's disappearance?"

His narrowed eyes and the brief twist of his lips told Ulbrick he'd noticed her deflection, but then he sighed and answered anyway. "We're not quite through the marina's CCTV, so there's still a chance he left with someone and is presently shacked up somewhere, completely oblivious to the current shitstorm."

"But…"

"But that's unlikely. And so far, no one on board the *Evanescence* has reported an argument or anything else out of the ordinary, or what passes for ordinary at a party like that. Every person we've spoken to is telling us basically the same thing."

Ulbrick frowned. "What about the witness we just spoke to? She seemed vaguely familiar. Should I know who she is—an actress or something?"

"Not an actress, but yeah, you might have seen her in the news recently. You remember she mentioned meeting Fitzpatrick at charity events? Made a splash at some fundraiser auction by bidding him up. Everyone—including the man himself—thought it was a riot. Other than that, she's just got a couple of old speeding fines and a low-range DUI to her name." Lew flipped through his notepad as he spoke.

"Did she seem okay to you? It felt a bit off to me—maybe it was when she said she felt awful. Something wasn't right."

"Nah. I know what you mean, but this whole crowd is off. Some of them are coming in with lawyers. None were especially close to their host, hence the lack of sincerity, and all of them are worried about their reputations if it gets out about the drugs on board. I swear, you could almost get a contact high just from stepping onto that boat. Trouble is, that means only the crew were really compos—everyone else was some combination of high, drunk, or passed out. The only thing we're hearing again and again is that Fitzpatrick was drinking and actively partaking of various substances." He shrugged.

"So you're thinking accident or misadventure?"

"Until I have a body." Now Bernstein leaned across the desk. "Unless there's something else I should know, F U. What's going on?"

She held up her hands in surrender. "Nothing, Lew, I swear. You know I'd tell you if I had anything. It's just an itch in my brain."

He sighed. "Yeah, I know. You and your itches." The landline phone on his desk buzzed, and he snagged the receiver, tucking it between ear and shoulder and picking up his pen in a single move. "Bernstein. Yeah, thanks. I'll come down."

Ulbrick jerked her chin at the phone as he hung up. "Developments?"

"Nah. Just the next partygoer and his solicitor. You want in?"

"No thanks, not this time." Ulbrick stood up. "But will you keep me posted?"

Lew was also on his feet, gathering his notebook and mobile. "If anything breaks you'll probably see it on the news first, but yeah, I'll let you know."

Ulbrick nodded her thanks and watched Lew leave the squad room. He was a good detective, and they were friends as well as colleagues. But she hadn't talked to him about Pavic, the name that had recently been struck from her list. She went to sit behind her desk, pondering her motives. She didn't want Lew to think she was losing it. Pavic had been an accident, and the jury was still out on Fitzpatrick. Once they knew the how and why of his disappearance and probable demise, she would tell Lew. It was likely nothing, and Ulbrick and Bernstein would laugh about her list and the crazy coincidence of it all.

Still. Ulbrick scratched the back of her head.

THIRTY-ONE

Trawling the internet for stories about male violence against women had been part of Mia's routine for years, ever since her sister's life had spiralled out of control. Mia had always focused on trauma counselling in her practice, but *afterwards,* working with domestic violence survivors had become her speciality.

So to stop now because she was the linchpin of events that were currently unfolding would be strange. Should authorities ever come calling and wish to check her browser history, it would look significantly more suspicious if the steady stream of articles had stopped just when men began to die.

And of course, there was her sister: always in her thoughts, always urging her to go further, do more, to help other women. So Mia was able—at least to a certain extent—to monitor the progress of the women she had unleashed on an unsuspecting population of murderers. She didn't google specific names but stuck to the key words she habitually used, at times both gratified and slightly put out when those terms resulted in zero hits—at least, zero hits in regard to the recently deceased men—there were always new cases of domestic violence to read about.

Katy had been the most successful so far. Mia had resorted

to visiting the library every week and skimming through copies of the *Dubbo Star*—the only newspaper that covered Lightning Ridge—for any mention of the death. It was four months before Shane was found, and all he got was a generic two inches of column space, a bland piece about a man nobody knew or really cared about: tragic accident, dangers of mining alone. She printed a copy, scrawled, *burn me*, across the bottom, and posted it to Gabrielle.

In Naomi's case, there was little to find beyond the first forty-eight hours after the news broke, only statistics and cautionary tales about the dangers of DIY.

Two problems solved, no suspicious circumstances.

The aftermath of Olivia's job was a different story, but of course the death of Rowan Fitzpatrick was never going to be anything but a media spectacle. Unfortunately, that meant—although they'd deny it—the police were far more persistent. If the average doped-up yob had fallen into the harbour, the investigation would have proceeded diligently, albeit with fewer resources and considerably less fanfare. But the Fitzpatrick name meant headlines, clickbait, and the harsh focus of national and international spotlights. Every move the police made was scrutinised and analysed.

This also meant increased pressure for Olivia, but Mia knew she wouldn't crack. An occasional excess of alcohol was the woman's only vice, and that was more than overcome by her fierce loyalty and protective instincts. Ultimately, she had a backbone of steel.

When Mia had finished her other research, in the dark hours after midnight, she did what she always did when sleep eluded her and googled her sister's case. But the details never changed.

THIRTY-TWO

Amy had been surprised to get Mia's call only days after Rowan Fitzpatrick disappeared from his yacht. With the police actively investigating, she'd thought it would be weeks before the next job.

"Why now?" she had asked, cradling the phone between cheek and shoulder while she straightened the floral arrangement in the foyer of the Sydney Athenaeum Hotel. As the Australian flagship of an international chain, the five-star Athenaeum was a source of personal pride for Amy. Her eye for detail and ability to anticipate what her guests would want or need had made it the place to stay in the Harbour City.

Mia's answer had been at once logical and practical. "You don't have to rush. But current events are going to simmer on for a while, which gives you an opportunity for in-depth research and development of your plan. That way when the time is right, you'll be ready."

That conversation with Mia had taken place three months ago—months in which Fitzpatrick's badly decomposed body had been found. Sydney's glitterati had dutifully attended a service, posted messages on social media, then got on with their lives. A few of the more strident media outlets had been so gauche as to refer to the dead man's murky history; one even contacted Brooke to get her opinion on his demise, given he had been responsible for her sister's. Her response had been brief and dignified: "He's dead. I'm sorry for his family. But it doesn't alter what he did, and it doesn't bring my sister back."

Overall, Amy thought Olivia had done an extremely good job. Her only regret was having to use the motorbike at the last minute. She couldn't risk her green Kawasaki Ninja being seen in the vicinity of another accident, which meant she was now sitting in an anonymous grey Toyota Corolla parked on a twilit suburban street, ready to make her move.

From her position—a few car-lengths away and on the opposite side of the road—Amy watched the flickering of a TV behind the curtains of her target's house. She had disabled the map light, so when the passenger door opened with a soft click, there was no telltale glow as Katy slid into the seat next to her. "The neighbours at the back are still away," Katy said, pulling the door closed without letting it fully catch. "So that only leaves the house on the south side, the old couple."

Amy looked at the house in question, where blinking Christmas lights and open windows behind the security grilles testified to the presence of the homeowners. On the other side of the target's house was a vacant block, covered in thigh-high weeds, a couple of dumped mattresses, and a collapsed and faded sign advertising the sale of the land. Katy would keep an eye out for anyone jogging or driving by. So there was only one set of potential witnesses, then. Good.

The open windows shouldn't be too much of a problem because Amy didn't plan on there being much noise. In case there was, the target had his TV on, and presumably the old couple did too, so that should be enough to mask any sound or provide cover; people in nice middle-class suburbs were far more likely to think yelling and gunshots were part of a movie soundtrack than the real fabric of their lives. Not that Amy was planning on using a gun. Although there might be yelling—she didn't think so, but she couldn't be sure.

She turned to Katy. "May I ask you something?"

"Of course."

"What was the experience like, when you...and afterwards? What did you feel?"

Katy chewed on her lip. "Nothing. Then everything. At first, I was so obsessed with the mechanics of the job, of getting it done, that I wasn't even thinking about what that meant. Besides, it was almost like it never happened: he was there one second and gone the next, and then I was focused on getting out." She paused, drawing in a deep breath. "When it was clear we'd gotten away with it... Well, that came with its own adrenaline rush. And then I just felt numb. I'd killed a man and I didn't feel good, but I didn't feel bad. For a while I didn't feel anything at all, as though the part of my brain that handles emotions had been surgically removed."

"What changed?" Amy asked, redirecting her gaze back to the target's house.

"Thanks to Naomi, the man who murdered my sister had a car fall on him. When that happened, I could feel everyday things again, and the pain of losing my sister..." Katy shook her head. "It was like I'd been buried alive and unexpectedly rescued. The sun hit my face and the pressure was lifted off me. If you're having any doubts—"

"No, I have no doubts. Knowing what the man in that house did to Naomi's sister—remembering what happened to my sister—that's enough for me to be certain." Amy hesitated. "Taking this action means I can at least partly atone for what I did to Sandra."

"You did nothing! It was him."

"But that is precisely it. I could have, should have saved her. And I. Did. Nothing." Amy drew in a ragged breath. "Until I turned off her life support. Our parents are old, frail. When they understood the extent of her brain injury, it broke them; they were unable to face it. So it fell to me. I stood there in my sister's hospital room and instructed them to switch off the machines. Were you aware that when the heart is still beating, a person removed from life support dies from a lack of oxygen? I didn't know. I also didn't know that the person will not necessarily die instantly. I sat on the bed and held Sandra as she slowly turned blue. My sister lasted over an hour. And for every single second, my brain was screaming. Screaming for them to put the tube back in, to reconnect her to the machines. Screaming for Sandra not to go, to fight, to wake up. Tears were pouring down my face, but I did not make a sound, except for once, when I asked the doctor—who had tears on his face—if they were sure, really sure. All he could do was nod. And so I sat there and watched my sister die."

Katy grabbed Amy's hand, holding it tightly, and Amy returned the pressure. She always suppressed the memories and the tumultuous emotions of reliving her sister's death, but tonight Amy let them come, twisting together in her chest, fuelling her will to act. She disengaged her hand.

"A very verbose way to tell you I'm ready. Let's do this." Amy reached into the back seat and collected a pizza box. The contents were almost cold now, but the smell of garlic, tomato, and herbs was still strong when she cracked the lid.

"As soon as you're out, I'll climb into the driver's seat. Don't forget, you'll have to wait at least five minutes." Katy's voice was tense. "And if for some reason I have to shift the car—if you don't see me when you come out—I'll be round in the next street, waiting."

"Don't stay too long. Half an hour at the most." Amy pulled on a baseball cap, the front prominently adorned with the logo on the pizza box. "Can I have it?"

Katy met her gaze. "You're sure about this plan? It's risky."

"No riskier than what you did, or the others."

"It's more direct, much more dicey."

Amy shook her head. "You make it sound like I'm going in with a chainsaw. Perhaps you are just more anxious because you have to sit here. I always find that action is better than waiting. Besides, do you have a different idea?"

She returned Katy's stare until the woman exhaled, puffing out her cheeks. "You're right. I'm more twitchy than when I was in Lightning Ridge." Reaching into her bag, she took out a syringe fully loaded with a clear liquid that glistened when she held it up, caught in the glow of a streetlight. "Remember, thigh is best but upper arm works too."

"It may be a case of wherever I can get it," Amy said coolly.

Katy nodded. "I'm just thinking about a post-mortem—a needle mark in a strange place might raise a red flag."

"Assuming they find the mark."

"They're very good at that sort of thing."

"Mmm-hmm." Amy pulled the stun gun from under the driver's seat. It was a rectangular box about twelve centimetres long, clearly designed to fit in a pocket or handbag. Somewhat incongruously, it was bright pink. At one end were two prongs.

"Are you sure that's going to work?"

Amy shrugged. "I have not yet had the opportunity to try it on anyone, but the hotel guest who left it tucked under her mattress must have thought it worked. And the device took a charge then made a noise when I pressed the button. But I guess we'll know in a couple of minutes." She got out of the car, slipped the syringe into her pants pocket, and arranged herself so she had the stun gun in one hand beneath the pizza box. Its prongs were pointed forward, and she slid the switch to "on." "Wish me luck."

Before Katy could reply, Amy was off across the road and up the front path of the target's house. She kept her head down, conscious of the glowing red dot of a security camera mounted under the eaves, the only one she'd spotted in this part of the street. Behind her, she heard the clunk as Katy closed the car door, not bothering to be quiet this time. If anyone cared enough to look, all they would see was a pizza delivery person at work.

On the porch Amy took a deep breath, made sure she was holding the pizza box low enough to hide the stun gun, then rang the doorbell.

THIRTY-THREE

Amy could hear the television blaring from the room to the left of the front door—some sort of sport, with a crowd that yelled and cheered. It was loud enough to mask other sounds, so when he flung the door open, it caught her off guard. She stared at him, the sheer physical size of him. Naomi had said he was a former rugby player, and Amy had a sudden vision of this man arguing with a thin, fine-boned woman who resembled Naomi. That was all Amy needed: she felt a flash of pure fury, and her resolve hardened.

"What?" His voice was surly, breath reeking of booze even from this distance.

"Pizza delivery." Amy lifted the box slightly, not too high.

"I didn't order a pizza."

"Forty Summerpeak Road?" Amy's voice was steady. The man still had a hand on the door, and she would have to act before he could swing it closed.

"S'right. But I didn't order a—"

She thrust the pizza box forward, and he instinctively grabbed for it. When she let go of the box, her left hand kept moving until the stun gun's prongs made contact with his abdomen. It was louder than she remembered, like a ferocious bug zapper, undercut by his yell.

As he reeled back and fell to the floor, she followed him inside and closed the door with a backward kick. Then she stopped to pull the syringe out with her free hand. It refused to come, caught somehow in her pocket. She let out a snarl of frustration and took her eyes off him for a second, glancing down as she tugged at the fabric.

With a flurry of movement, he was up, rushing at her, slamming her into the closed door. She yelped in pain. Had the stun gun slowed him at all?

Then his hands were around her throat, his thumbs pressing into her windpipe, lifting as well as squeezing, forcing her onto her toes, making it impossible to kick out. Her mouth was open, gasping, as he leaned in close, increasing the pressure. "You fucking little Asian bitch. I'm going to—"

Amy jammed the stun gun into the side of his neck and gave him a blast. She had years of motorcycle riding to thank for not dropping it—when things went to shit, she always hung on for dear life.

He jerked back, releasing his grip on her. Black spots blurred her vision, but she couldn't afford to let the stun gun break contact so quickly. She moved with him, pushing the device in, hard, for as long as she could. This time when he hit the floor, she didn't relent, bending down and giving him another jolt for good measure. She scanned his face: he was dazed but definitely not unconscious. She didn't have long.

Backing away, she tried once again to get the syringe out of her pocket without letting go of the stun gun. With a final twist, the syringe pulled free. She was ripping the cover off the needle with her teeth when he began to move. "Do not even fucking try," she croaked, her teeth still clenched around the plastic cap.

Then she slammed the syringe into his thigh and depressed the plunger, giving him the full dose of fentanyl.

He gurgled something, his eyes wide as he stared up at her. She re-capped the syringe and dropped it in her pocket.

"Relax. It's only fentanyl. Nothing you haven't tried before." She watched him warily, keeping the stun gun ready. "We need to talk. Or rather, I have some things to say that you must hear. Back in there." She gestured towards the front room and the glow and noise of the television.

"Can't…" he wheezed.

"Stand? Then you can crawl. Unless you'd prefer another turn of this." She depressed the button on the stun gun; the burst of staccato noise made him flinch, then start to move.

Casting a lightning glance at her wristwatch, she saw that she had to keep him at bay for at least another couple of minutes. She followed him slowly, close enough to act if necessary, hopefully far enough back that he couldn't surprise her again.

The lounge room was infused with the distinctive funk of a single man on the decline: sweat, fried food, pot, and whisky. She felt a twinge of satisfaction when she saw the smouldering joint on the edge of the coffee table, right next to a bottle of Johnnie Walker Red. "Couch," she said. Her throat felt like she'd swallowed a golf ball, and her head was thumping, but she pushed the pain away.

"Who…?" He inched across the floor and dragged himself onto the three-seater, collapsing along its length.

Amy wasn't sure if the fentanyl was beginning to kick in, or if he was hamming it up, but she didn't think the effects of the stun gun would still be so significant. She gave him another zap to the back of the neck, just to be sure.

"Who am I?" she asked, as he writhed and moaned. "In Shanghai they know me as the Empress of One Thousand Cuts."

His eyes widened, his mind no doubt conjuring imagery to go with the ridiculous title, and Amy curled her lip in disdain.

"Just kidding. The point is, you don't need to know who I am. All you need to know is that I am here on behalf of a friend. I am here for her sister, Jo."

Amy watched his face, seeing the shock of realisation, then the fear.

"Yes. I thought that might assist your understanding of the situation." She scanned the room, looking for a phone or anything he could use as a weapon. With each second the likelihood of that faded, as the fentanyl coursed through his system and flooded his opioid receptors. Tipping her head to one side, Amy regarded the prone man with some curiosity. "You should be feeling the fentanyl a bit now. If you are lucky it will be the pain-free, sense of well-being and sleepiness sort of feelings, as opposed to the cramps, vomiting and nausea."

He blinked heavily. "It was an accident."

"Are you referring to Jo? We both know you stuck that knife between her ribs. Perhaps you should admit it, say you are sorry. Now would be a good time for that, don't you think?" Amy pointed the stun gun at his crotch and let loose a short burst of electricity.

"Sorry! I'm sorry!" Anxiety made his voice loud, but she could also detect a slurring of his words.

"Mmm. I'm really not feeling the sincerity." She shook her head. "And I definitely did not hear an admission. Tell me what you did, then tell me you are sorry." She spat the last word at him.

He blinked again, slower this time, then swallowed.

"You realise you are about to pass out, yes? So it would be prudent—that means wise, in case you are wondering—to sort this out now. Because otherwise I will be unhappy. And when I am unhappy, well… Let's just say I am sure you do not wish to wake up a eunuch. That means without your balls." Amy made a show of looking at her watch this time.

He mumbled something. His eyes were closed and his head was lolling to one side.

"What was that?" she barked.

"I killed her." The words came slowly. "Jo. Sorry." He opened his eyes with some effort, trying to meet Amy's hard stare.

"There. That wasn't so hard, was it?"

She watched impassively as he lapsed into unconsciousness. His breathing became increasingly shallow and less frequent, and after a couple of minutes she pulled a disposable glove from her pocket, snapped it on, then checked his pulse: faint and slow. His lips were starting to look blue.

Time to leave—almost.

Amy retrieved the spent syringe from her pocket and used the hem of her polo shirt to wipe it down. She pressed his thumb against the top of the plunger before letting the syringe fall to the floor. With her gloved hand she picked up the bottle of Scotch and splashed it over his chest and onto the couch and carpet, making sure to include the discarded newspapers and McDonald's wrappers strewn under the coffee table. One of Malik's arms hung over the edge of the couch, and Amy dropped the now empty bottle just in front of his limp hand. She hadn't told Katy, but she'd planned for this. Amy had known the stun gun would leave marks, that she'd have to destroy the scene. But finding the booze right there was a bonus; his filthy habits made it easy.

Amy looked at the man one last time. His breathing was barely perceptible now, the blue tinge more pronounced on his skin.

"Castration is too good for you," she told the inert form. Then she picked up the joint and dropped it on the alcohol-soaked newspaper.

She backed into the hall, watching the tip of the joint.

Nothing was happening. She might have to—

A puff of smoke, quickly followed by a flame. With a soft whump, the newspaper was alight. Fire darted along the trail of Scotch to the couch and its occupant.

Amy pulled the front door closed as she walked out. She headed calmly towards the car and let herself in the passenger side. "Time for us to leave," she said to Katy.

"How did it go?"

Amy fingered her throat. "Well, the stun gun was not as powerful as I had hoped, but the plan proved quite satisfactory."

"Is he—?" Katy asked as she started the car.

"If he's not now, he soon will be," Amy replied, and exploded into laughter.

"Amy? Are you alright?"

Amy, head back and shoulders shaking, could only flap a hand towards Katy, who was staring at her, wide-eyed. Finally, wiping tears from her cheeks, Amy managed to catch her breath. "Sorry, Katy," she said, stifling a couple of snorts.

"It's okay. Just your body's way of dumping stress."

"Precisely. But now we should definitely leave. Besides, my throat—I need a drink."

Katy indicated carefully and pulled away from the kerb. As they turned the corner at the end of the street, Amy looked back. An orange glow danced behind the closed curtains, and her heart danced with it. She smiled.

THIRTY-FOUR

Mia saw the fire on the late-night news, but at first there was nothing about the man. That detail came out the next morning, prefaced by the words "charred remains." Reporters and firefighters were talking about the dangers of falling asleep while smoking.

She went out that afternoon, driving to the mall at Bondi Junction before powering up the burner phone she kept for Amy. It immediately pinged with an incoming message.

Holy crap! I did it!! Better than I imagined! Cannot tell you how elated I feel! Bruce Willis, Chuck Norris, Me. All avengers. You were correct. This is truly JUSTICE.

Mia smiled as she read the message a second time. She'd known Amy would derive the greatest satisfaction from the plan but had not anticipated such an emotional high. After a moment's thought, Mia texted back.

You are a superwoman. The world is a safer place.

She hit send, then deleted the conversation, switched the phone off, and removed the SIM card. The handset went into the nearest bin and five minutes later, in another part of the mall, Mia discreetly ditched the SIM card.

Before leaving, she went to one of her favourite shops and bought a new dress: a 1950s-inspired blue swing dress with a flared skirt, a silent celebration for one. Every time she wore this symbolic purchase, it would help her to recapture the sensation of a righteous victory. Back at home, she hung the dress on the front of her wardrobe, sat on her bed, and thought about her sister. One day, Mia would wear the dress for her.

Mia felt she had failed. She knew her sister would not see it that way, but in her heart, Mia knew she had not done enough to protect her from Travis.

Opening a drawer in the bedside table, Mia drew out a stack of letters and photographs. She and her sister had always written to each other. Even as kids sharing a bedroom, they had always had so much to discuss, so many thoughts and dreams to share. Now she reread the last letter her sister had written, tracing a finger across the loopy letters, feeling the ache of sorrow and regret deep in her gut, remembering.

She drew in a deep breath. Right now she needed to focus on Brooke and Gabrielle.

That's what sisters are for.

THIRTY-FIVE

“How are you going to do it?” Gabrielle’s tone was matter-of-fact. She could have been asking a fellow architect about an elaborate design element: a cantilevered swimming pool or an internal wall that vanished into the floor.

Beside her, Brooke faltered and stopped. Even though they had only been walking, she felt light-headed and a bit wobbly, as though she’d run to the point of exhaustion. She popped the spigot of her water bottle and raised it to her lips, avoiding the question.

“Shall we get off the path,” Gabrielle suggested, “find somewhere to sit for a moment?” She was moving as she spoke, angling towards an empty bench just visible up ahead, strategically placed to optimise the view across the water.

They were on the Manly to Spit Bridge trail somewhere near Forty Baskets Beach, and plenty of other walkers were heading in both directions, making the most of a perfect February afternoon. Brooke had been walking with Gabrielle for nearly half an hour, and after an initial exchange of pleasantries most of that had been in silence. The point of the walk was to talk through the plan, but Brooke kept delaying. Each time Gabrielle tried to ask about it, Brooke deflected her questions. At first she'd mumbled, "Not here, let's walk a bit farther." A couple of times she'd jerked her chin in the direction of passers-by and simply shaken her head. She knew Gabrielle was frustrated; the trouble was, she didn't know what to say.

It wasn't that Brooke hadn't been thinking about it—quite the opposite. Over the past couple of months, the idea of killing someone had been occupying her thoughts to the point that she only found respite in the intense concentration required at work. Each time she'd seen a headline, read an article, or listened to her colleagues exchange gossip from social media about Rowan Fitzpatrick, she'd felt a corresponding change in her body. It was as if her skin was shrinking, growing tighter on her bones, holding everything together while increasing the internal pressure.

And now here she was, dressed—like every woman they'd seen on the trail today—in shorts and a crop top, her ponytail poking out through the hole in her baseball cap, supposedly about to lay out her plan for homicide. Gabrielle had been patient, and Brooke couldn't stall any longer. She dragged the back of a hand across her wet lips and joined her friend on the bench, fussing with the bottle as she set it down, making sure it wasn't going to tip over. When she finally forced herself to meet Gabrielle's eyes, Brooke was surprised by what she saw: compassion. She'd been expecting impatience, and perhaps a flash of Gab's flinty anger, usually in check but occasionally given full flight in their group sessions at The Pleiades, which seemed like several lifetimes ago.

Brooke was even more surprised when Gabrielle patted her leg. "I know," was all the woman said before pulling back.

Brooke scrutinised Gab's face: the set of her mouth, her high, razor-sharp cheekbones, and those dark eyes, soft and liquid instead of their usual piercing and judgemental.

"Do—" Brooke cleared her throat, still dry despite her drink of water. She tried again. "Do you?"

"You're no different from the rest of us." When Brooke started to object, the older woman held up a hand. "You know us. We've spilled our guts, vented, laughed, confessed, and comforted. This isn't easy for any of us." She looked out at the water as she pulled her hair free of its tight bun and shook it out, letting the black-brown curls fall around her face.

Brooke was struck by her strength and composure. "But… everyone seems so…together, so competent."

"Brooke, if there's one thing all of us are good at, it's putting up a facade. None of us ever thought we'd lose someone the way we did. For a while after Evie died, I would start each day by reminding myself to keep breathing. I had to develop a shell, because if I let my emotions show each time someone expressed sympathy, I would have screamed my throat raw a dozen times a day. Hell, I burst into tears when a barista called out my name, because he rolled the *R* just like Evie used to do." She dashed a hand under her eyes, then turned back to Brooke. "And just like we never thought our sisters would die like that, we never, ever could have imagined we'd have to deliver our own justice. I've watched the others get it done, and I've lain awake at night asking myself if I can do it too. And if I go through with it, am I not being like those men? What does it make me?"

She fell silent while a couple with a beagle went past, moving slowly as the dog, nose to the ground, bustled from scent to scent. When they were far enough away, Gabrielle focused on Brooke again.

"Then I asked myself, what would I do if innocent people were being killed in a war, and I was asked to join up, to pick up a gun, and defend those people? Would I do it? Yes! And then, if I had that gun, and the man who killed Evie was there in front of me, his hands raised to grab the throat of another woman, to kill again, would I shoot him? I know I would. So that's how I see it—if I do this, I'm *saving* a life. Do you think you could see it the same way?"

Brooke swallowed. Her chest was tight and she wanted to hug Gabrielle, to tell her she was right, that in many ways her task felt biblical, as though it was her destiny, and yet…

"Maybe," she mumbled. "But I don't—I don't have a plan."

Gabrielle exhaled in a long sigh, not of exasperation but of release, a meditative letting go. "Well, then we have some work to do," she said softly. "What do you know about the man who killed Amy's sister?"

Brooke bit her lip; picked up her water bottle then put it back down. "Umm. The case didn't get a lot of media coverage, and you know Amy has always told us she and her sister, Sandra, lived very, umm…different lives? And they weren't that close? Well anyway, whatever Amy says, she must've been listening to Sandra, because she remembered all the small things her sister told her about, umm, him."

Gabrielle nodded. "So tell me. Let's see what we have to work with."

She sat back and closed her eyes as Brooke related the information she'd received from Amy: address, workplace, car, favourite sports, a minor gambling habit, an obsession with protein shakes, lifting weights, and going to the gym… It all poured out, facts emerging in no particular order, sometimes alone and sometimes with a short story attached.

Gabrielle grabbed Brooke's thigh, startling her. "What was that?"

"He has a bench press set up in the garage?"

"No, before that—something about Indian food."

Brooke frowned. "Umm, yeah. He doesn't eat Indian, Thai, or anything like that."

"Like what?" Gabrielle was leaning forward. "I don't know, spicy foods?"

Gabrielle's phone was strapped to her bicep, and she pulled it free with a rip of Velcro. "I need to call Amy."

"Why? We're not supposed to be in touch with each other." Brooke felt a surge of anxiety.

"I know, but this could be the angle we—you—need. Besides, this is my spare burner; I brought it along just in case. I'll try her at work." Gabrielle was pressing buttons as she spoke, then she lifted the phone to her ear. "Hello? Yes, Ms. Li, please. Is she still in? My name is Ms. Themis. Thank you, I'll hold."

"Themis?" echoed Brooke, puzzled.

Gabrielle lifted a finger to silence her. "She is? Thank you." Covering the receiver, Gabrielle whispered to Brooke, "Goddess of divine law… Amy and I had a conversation about Nemesis and Themis once." Gabrielle straightened up and stopped covering the phone. "Sorry, yes, I know. I have one question—the food aversions. Is he allergic? You might have told a sister. Ahh. Yes, she's here. Thanks." After ending the call, Gabrielle clapped her hands together. "Zac has a peanut allergy, bad enough that he carries an EpiPen."

"So I kill him with peanuts?" Brooke's voice rose, and she glanced around sharply, but they were alone.

"That's the big picture. Now we just have to figure out how to get him to eat them."

"Well, that's not—"

"And how to make sure there's no EpiPen."

A warm breeze sprang up, tickling the back of Brooke's neck. She stared at Gabrielle, then gave a tiny nod. She could do this.

THIRTY-SIX

It was mild for April, but the afternoon buildup of clouds meant there was almost no twilight. Darkness fell within minutes. As Gabrielle pedalled towards the target's house, a smattering of fat raindrops slapped against her shoulders, a foretaste of things to come. The roads were nearly deserted, with just a couple of scurrying pedestrians and only one other cyclist, head down, legs pumping. A few cars flashed past, everyone trying to get home before the storm broke.

While the guts of Gabrielle and Brooke's plan was simple, pulling it off was going to be a formidable challenge. All Brooke had to do was slip some peanut powder into the target's food; the trouble was getting access to his home. It had taken them nearly a month of discreet surveillance and slow drives past his house before they knew enough about the man's routine to finalise their scheme.

Gabrielle had accompanied Brooke on almost all of what they'd termed the study trips. It wasn't that she thought Brooke wouldn't go without her, but rather her own need to control and manage any situation they might face. If Brooke's anxiety caused her to mess things up, Gabrielle wanted to be able to fix it. And if she knew what normal looked like at the South Coogee duplex, it would be far easier to spot the moment things started to go sideways. To Gabrielle's satisfaction, normal included a bike chained up on the tiny porch, and as far as she could tell, no security cameras.

Then, once they'd worked out how to put their plan into action, Brooke and Gabrielle had to wait several more weeks for the right night. They needed a storm, the sort that started to brew late in the day before descending rapidly on the city, bringing thunder, lightning, and torrential rain.

The wind was beginning to howl when, at six p.m. precisely, Gabrielle rang the front doorbell of the duplex. Zac opened the door in his gym gear, frowning as if he was planning to tell her to piss off.

Before that could happen, she smiled apologetically and launched into her spiel. "I'm so sorry to trouble you, but I saw your light—and your bicycle—and I'm in a spot of bother." She tried to sound just the right amount of desperate and pleading; it wasn't a tone that came naturally to her. She gestured towards the driveway, where her bike was lying on its side. "The pedal's working loose. I'm miles from home, and the storm..." A particularly strong gust of wind gave weight to her words. "Anyway, I was wondering if you might by any chance have a thin spanner I could use, please? It will only take a couple of minutes to tighten up the pedal enough to get me home." She smiled and widened her eyes.

Dressed in lycra cycling gear, her body was on display, and the fact that her hair was under a helmet meant her cheekbones were more prominent. She hadn't really thought about her appearance in advance, but seeing the way his eyes crawled over her as she spoke, she felt both sickened and elated.

After a glance at her bike, he checked his watch. "Yeah, okay.

I should have something thin enough. Hang on." He stepped back inside then emerged almost immediately, keys in hand, pointing the fob at the garage; its roller door rumbled to life.

"Oh, my God, thank you so much!" Gab gushed. "You're an absolute lifesaver!"

"No drama. Bring the bike up out of the wind while I see what I've got." He snapped on the garage light and disappeared behind his car.

Gabrielle righted her bike and wheeled it up the drive, the sounds of the impending storm drowning out the familiar click of the chain. Just before stepping into the garage, she cast her gaze across the front yard, towards the side gate, but there was nothing to see except shadows. She realised Brooke must already be through.

"Found it!" He was coming back towards her, a bike spanner in his hand.

She plastered a smile on her face.

In the small courtyard at the back of the house, Brooke was pressed up against the wall next to a sliding glass door. She knew it was unlocked, because moments before the doorbell rang, he had been standing in the doorway, staring out, clearly trying to gauge just how bad the storm would be. He'd sworn when the bell had sounded, slamming the sliding door so it bounced in the track a little. For a minute or two, Brooke hadn't moved, wanting to be sure. If he didn't open the front door or quickly shut it in Gabrielle's face, she would lean on the bell, a signal for Brooke to get out, and an annoyance hopefully too hard for a man with a temper to resist. But the bell didn't ring again.

Brooke eased the sliding door open. The howling wind

covered any noise but gusted into the house, risking currents and banging doors, the sort of thing that might cause a homeowner to hurry through the rooms, securing everything, looking for the source of the disturbance. Brooke stepped inside and quickly pushed the door closed.

The kitchen was a masculine combination of brushed steel and shiny black surfaces, centred around a large island bench. And sitting at one end of the bench was Zac's shaker flask—black lid, clear sides—full of something that reminded her of a vanilla milkshake, white-ish with a head of thick bubbles. Off to one side were various packets and tubs: creatine, whey protein, colostrum, and an assortment of other things with names like Ripped, Maxxx, and Ultimate.

On their stakeouts, Brooke and Gabrielle had learned that he drank the entire shake on his trips to the gym. Five evenings a week, the garage door would slowly roll up at six fifteen p.m. to reveal the man doing squats next to his car. As soon as the door was fully open, he'd grab his drink bottle from the roof of the car and take a few large gulps. Then he'd get behind the wheel and drive to the gym, sipping at his flask all the way. By the time he arrived at Atlas Boxing and Fitness, he was tilting his head back, shaking the last drops down his throat.

Now in his kitchen, Brooke had a moment of panic. She'd expected the shake ingredients to be in a cupboard, somewhere he wouldn't notice the addition of an extra packet. It was just another bodybuilding supplement, one Gab had chosen after extensive research. But buried at the end of the nutritional information were the words, *May contain traces of nuts*. The pack had been opened as if he had tried something new without properly reading the label. And of course, Gab and Brooke had made sure of the nuts. Brooke needed to put the pack with all the other shake ingredients or it would look odd to anyone investigating.

But what if he noticed it and didn't drink? There was no other option—she would have to take the risk.

Breathing fast, she pulled the packet of IntenseDeltz from her pocket and tucked it in among the supplements, trying to adjust them so it wouldn't be obvious.

She couldn't hear anything from the front of the duplex, which presumably meant Gabrielle still had him talking. Even so, Brooke kept glancing towards the nearest door, expecting the man to appear.

Already wearing disposable gloves, she snatched up the drink flask and wrenched the lid free. From her pocket she pulled a plastic bag containing a couple of teaspoons of peanut powder, hopefully enough to do the job. She fumbled with the ziplock, conscious of the time, of the sweat on her forehead, and alert for sounds or a breeze emanating from the entry way, wondering if she would hear him return over the rising wail of the storm.

Finally she got the bag open. Her hands were trembling, but somehow she tipped most of the peanut powder into his shake without spilling anything on the bench. Lid back on, she shook the flask violently then analysed the results: it didn't look any different.

She used the damp ring on the benchtop to replace the flask in the position she'd found it. Then she hurried across to the sliding door. The microwave clock read 18:12.

Just as Brooke eased open the sliding door, she heard something slam at the front of the house.

THIRTY-SEVEN

The wind rushed in as Brooke ducked out and closed the door behind her. She was careful to leave it open by a whisker, just as it had been when he had gone to answer the doorbell. She stood in the shadows, afraid to move in case he looked outside. She was shaking—not with cold, but with an uncontrollable reaction to what she had done.

Suddenly the kitchen light went out. She hadn't heard him close the sliding door, but he had to be leaving. She'd need to wait a few more minutes, give him time to drive off before she could get away.

Gabrielle would be heading back to their rendezvous point by now—assuming her part had gone according to plan. Brooke felt a flicker of fear, saliva welling in her mouth: what if something had gone wrong with Gab? What if he'd killed her? She could be on the floor of the garage or in the boot of his BMW. Brooke's breathing became erratic, control slipping away. Pushing up the sleeve of her black hoodie, she grabbed at the skin near the fold of her elbow and pinched as hard as she could. It made her hiss with pain, but it also brought her back from the edge. Gabrielle was fine; it had gone to plan. All Brooke had to do now was get to her car, which was parked in the next street, then go and pick up Gab. Keeping close to the wall, Brooke moved slowly around the corner of the house and out through the side gate. It slipped from her hand, the wind pushing it closed with a bang that seemed to echo down the street. She froze, but no lights came on, no voices called. It was just one more noise on a cacophonous night, unheard or ignored by everyone. Gabrielle had repeatedly told her to walk normally when she left the property, to look as though she had every right to be there—scuttling and creeping would attract more attention than striding with purpose. Except tonight, as the rain got heavier, a head-down scuttle was normal.

Brooke was almost in the street when she realised the garage's roller door was still up and the BMW hadn't moved. Her first horrified thought was that the man must be sitting behind the wheel, that he would have already spotted her. But the car was dimly illuminated from within by the map lights, and the driver's door was hanging open. There was no sign of his shaker flask. If anyone passed by, it would look suspicious.

Brooke hesitated. They hadn't thought of this possibility. Should she close the garage door, or could he be just inside? Perhaps he'd forgotten the protein shake and was about to come back, in which case she should get away now. Paralysed by indecision, she remained in the shadow of the house, getting wetter by the second.

Then she was hurrying back through the gate—careful this time not to lose her grip on the latch—and around to the rear of the house, where she came to an abrupt stop. Light was blazing from the kitchen once more. He must have forgotten something and come back.

"Stupid, stupid," Brooke muttered. If she had kept her head, she'd have been in her car, heater on, putting this behind her. Now she was stuck in this courtyard again until he left.

The wind had died down as the storm moved in, leaving only the pounding of the rain, so when the crash came from inside the house, it was loud enough to make her jump. Brooke took two quick steps the way she'd come before spinning around. She had to see.

Returning to the edge of the shadows, she pressed her shoulders to the wall. She was soaking wet—hair plastered to the sides of her face, clothes clinging to her body—but all her attention was on what she might see when she eased her head around and peered through the sliding glass door.

The containers of supplements were scattered across the polished surface of the island bench and the floor. One jar had lost its lid, spilling white powder over the black like a vandal's splash of paint. Brooke was so transfixed that it took her a few seconds to notice something else: a sneaker-clad foot poking out from behind the central island. As she stared at the foot, it twitched as though its owner was trying to find purchase, trying to stand.

Before she knew what she was doing, Brooke had yanked open the sliding door and was in the kitchen, water pouring from her, pulse thumping in her throat. She moved forward, one cautious step after another, until she could look around the bench, follow the line from the sneaker up his legs—one bent at an awkward angle—to his broad back…

He was lying on his front, but his head was turned. He was looking straight at her.

She let out a small scream. The man gurgled. His tongue looked swollen, and his chest was heaving as he desperately tried to suck air in through a throat that must have been closing rapidly. In his eyes she could see a plea. His mouth struggled to form words that wouldn't come. He reached a hand towards her and jerked his head up, in the direction of the benchtop, before fixing her again with his imploring gaze.

She wrenched her eyes away and scanned the detritus of his supplements, but all she could see were overturned containers. Stepping away from him, she edged around to look at everything that had spilled on the floor. At first she only saw a mess, then as she moved the angle of the light changed, and something caught her eye. It was across the floor, right up against the cupboards: a small black pouch.

Behind her, the man was wheezing. And there was an odd repetitive thump—slow, getting slower. It took her a moment to realise he must be pounding a fist on the floor, either to get her attention or in sheer desperation as he fought for air. She glanced back, but he was hidden behind the island bench.

Then she was across the kitchen, snatching up the pouch, tugging the zip open. The size and shape of the pouch, his panicked dive that had sent it spinning across the room... She knew what she would find.

She extracted the EpiPen, holding it between her thumb and index finger, turning it back and forth in the bright kitchen light. It didn't look like a syringe, more like a strange makeup device with its orange tip and blue safety cap, and a bright yellow panel down the side. The panel contained simple instructions to remove the cap, hold the pen in your fist, and slam it into the patient's thigh.

On the other side of the kitchen, he gurgled and thumped the floor again, his breathing more laboured by the second. Without thinking, Brooke shoved the pouch into her pocket and retraced her steps until she was standing near his feet once more. His mouth was gaping, swollen lips stretched apart in an agonised rictus.

He thrust a hand towards her, fingers splayed. Then he slapped his leg, hard. She stared into his eyes and realised she was watching a man die.

"I can't." Brooke hadn't realised she was speaking aloud until she registered the sound of her voice. She thought of the other women, of what she would tell them, and of how she would feel tomorrow and the next day. Then she ripped the safety cap away and wrapped her hand around the EpiPen.

THIRTY-EIGHT

Bending forward, Brooke raised her hand—only to feel it caught in a powerful grip.

"No." A woman's voice.

Brooke looked behind her and saw Gabrielle standing there, water streaming off her as though she'd just emerged from a lagoon.

"Let go," Brooke said.

"No." Gabrielle's hold on her bony wrist tightened.

The man was no longer thumping the floor, and although he was looking towards Brooke, his eyes were unfocused.

"Please." Her voice was barely a whisper. "There might still be time…"

"You shouldn't have come back. We need to go." Gabrielle tugged, and Brooke staggered, staring at the man even as she allowed herself to be pulled towards the door.

"He—"

"No. And don't drop the EpiPen—bring it with you."

Brooke didn't know how they got back to her small SUV, but Gabrielle was asking for keys and then Brooke was in the passenger seat, a towel wrapped around her, listening as Gabrielle stowed her bike in the back.

The next minute, Gabrielle was in the driver's seat, pressing the ignition, and they were pulling away. "Put your seat belt on."

Brooke complied then rubbed her wrist where Gabrielle had held it.

"Sorry. I hope I didn't hurt you, but I had to stop you."

"I'm okay." Brooke glanced across at Gabrielle.

In the glow of the dashboard lights, her hands looked relaxed on the wheel, but her face was set, her jaw rigid. Then she let out a long breath and rolled her shoulders. "Why did you go back?" There was no accusation or censure in her tone, only polite inquiry.

"I… The garage door was open, but I couldn't see him. I thought it would look odd, attract attention if anyone went past. I didn't know if he was coming back or if he was there somewhere, and I couldn't go in to check. I was just going to have a quick look."

Brooke's teeth began to chatter, and Gabrielle reached over and cranked the heating up high. "So what happened?"

"I can't—I don't know. One minute I was outside looking in, and the next… Did you shut the sliding door when we left? It was closed when I got there."

Gabrielle shook her head. "No, I left it open. Both of us had dripped all over the place, and the rain had blown in. A closed door would have set off alarm bells—this way it will just seem like he opened it himself."

Brooke nodded. "I didn't think of that. Maybe I wasn't thinking at all. I just…"

"I know."

Pulling the towel more tightly around her shoulders, Brooke realised she was still wearing the disposable gloves. She ripped them off and stuffed them in the bag by her feet. "Where is it? The EpiPen?" Her voice rose in panic. "I had it when we left!"

"I've got it. I took it when I got you into the car. It's fine. I'll take care of it."

They travelled in silence for a few kilometres.

"I don't think I can do it." Brooke had been staring blankly at the rain-streaked windscreen, trying not to think about how the now-intermittent beat of the wipers sounded like a man uselessly banging his hand on the floor. "I don't think I can just go back to my life and act as though this didn't happen, as though I didn't just stand there while—" She broke off with a low moan.

Gabrielle's fingers tapped on the steering wheel as she eased the car to a stop at a red light. "Okay." She kept her eyes forward, watching traffic in the intersection, not even glancing at Brooke, who had slumped against the passenger door. "I'm sorry you went back and saw that; it would have been easier if that hadn't happened. And I knew—we all knew—that you'd struggle the most. But let's look at the situation we're facing now."

Brooke moaned again as the lights changed and the car moved.

"No one can go through this and come out the other side unchanged. This is a different you and a different version of normal life. It's all changed, just like it did when Rowan Fitzpatrick shot your sister."

Brooke sat up a bit straighter. Amid the self-loathing that threatened to crush her, Gabrielle's words were something solid she could hold on to.

"And, hypothetically, if you went to the police, would you feel better? Or would you feel just as guilty? Would anything change except for the fact of your arrest and trial?"

Brooke gasped. She hadn't actually allowed herself to think that far ahead.

"Would you tell the police about the rest of us?"

"No! Never!"

"But how could you tell them only part of the story? What reason would you give them for killing that man?"

"I'd say..." Brooke had no way of finishing the sentence.

"Do you think your admission might then make police look again at Fitzpatrick's death?" Gabrielle's voice was soft but insistent.

This time Brooke stayed silent.

"Think of the reason we began this. Think of your sister—and think of Amy's sister, murdered by the man we dealt with tonight. Then think of all the other people he might have harmed if tonight hadn't happened."

Brooke turned to stare at Gabrielle's profile, watching as successive streetlights fleetingly illuminated her features. She looked calm, in control of the car and the situation; at peace with her place in the world, while Brooke's world was in tatters. "It—it's all very well for you," she said, sobbing. "You haven't killed anyone! You can walk away."

"What's the security code for your building's car park?" Gabrielle flicked on the indicator and turned left. "We're almost there."

Brooke sniffed, rattled off the code, then folded her arms defensively. "You don't have to come in."

"Is someone waiting for you? I won't intrude, as long as you're not alone."

Brooke hesitated. "Umm, I broke up with my boyfriend a while ago. No one lives here but me."

"Sorry, I didn't know."

"That's okay. But really, you don't have to come up. That wasn't... Stop up here, and you can get out. I—I'll be fine."

Gabrielle smiled gently. "You might be fine, but what about me? Or are you giving me the boot? You were going to drop me with my bike a couple of kilometres from my place, but after all that happened I thought we needed a new plan."

"Oh. Sorry. I wasn't thinking. I can take you—"

Gabrielle cut her off. "I'll cycle home tomorrow. Tonight, I'm staying with you." She pulled into the car park entry, rolled the SUV to a stop in front of the gate, then lowered the window to punch in the code. The gate began to rise.

"Th-thank you," Brooke's voice was almost a whisper.

"You don't have to thank me." Gabrielle inched the car forward.

"Yes, I do."

"Where's your spot?"

Brooke gave instructions, and they lapsed into silence as Gabrielle swung the vehicle through a series of turns, headed to the lower levels, and parked in the allotted space.

Gabrielle switched off the engine then turned to face Brooke. "You said that I wouldn't understand, that I could walk away."

"I didn't—"

Gabrielle held up a hand, cutting her off. "First, I made a commitment to you all, and to my sister. That isn't something I could ever walk away from. And I was the one who grabbed your wrist and let that man die tonight. So that's the thought you should hold on to: it was me."

Brooke shook her head dumbly.

"It. Was. Me. Whatever you feel, we're all here for you and for each other. This is the power we give each other—the power to act, and to move on. Never forget that."

Brooke pressed her fingertips against her closed eyes, trying to stem the tears now streaming down her face.

"Come on." Gabrielle passed her a wad of tissues. "Let's go inside and get dry."

"I don't think any of my clothes will fit you." Brooke's voice was thick and phlegmy, but the tears were stopping. She blew her nose.

Gabrielle shrugged and unbuckled her seat belt. "All I need is a dressing-gown...and a drink. I really, really need a drink."

"Well, I do a good hot chocolate," said Brooke, releasing her own seat belt and opening the car door.

"Hot chocolate is...good."

"You can add Kahlúa."

"Now you're talking!"

They rode the lift in silence, Brooke watching the lights jump from floor to floor, avoiding her own reflection in the mirrored panels. Once inside her apartment, she hurried over to the kitchen to retrieve her burner from the top of the fridge. She fumbled with the SIM card, but as soon as the phone powered up, her thumbs flew across the keypad. Brooke hit send, then turned to Gabrielle.

"What did you say to her?" asked Gabrielle.

Brooke checked to make sure the message had sent, then turned the phone off. "I've paraphrased from my CPDV bible: Ecclesiastes Four, verses nine and ten."

Gabrielle frowned. "Refresh my memory?"

"Two women are better than one, because together they can succeed: if either woman falls, the other is there to help her up."

"Says it all."

THIRTY-NINE

It took a large, surreptitious slug of Kahlúa in the cocoa, but Gabrielle eventually got Brooke to bed. She would need to talk to Mia about the woman's fragility, because regardless of their plan to maintain distance from each other, she intended to stick close and support Brooke. Gabrielle's own appointment with a killer was looming, so she needed to focus on that, but she'd been there with Brooke—they were bound by the experience—and Brooke needed her.

These thoughts occupied Gabrielle as she cycled home the next morning, pushing herself hard, enjoying the rare sensation of heading against the flow of the rapidly building traffic. Still several kilometres from her townhouse, she took a detour to a tucked-away corner coffee shop she knew. A short line of walkers and cyclists were ahead of her at the takeaway window, but the barista was fast; soon she was stepping back with her double-shot espresso and a bagged apple-cinnamon muffin. Patrons were using milk crates as seats, and Gabrielle grabbed one, setting herself up in a sunny corner, helmet and open muffin bag at her feet—just another refuelling lycra warrior.

She lingered over the coffee, occasionally reaching into the paper bag to pull off a chunk of muffin. Fifteen minutes later, she put the empty cup down and then stretched, placing her hands on the small of her back and arching her spine. The next time she stuck her hand in the bag, she was clutching the EpiPen and its pouch, retrieved from the rear pocket of her cycling jersey. Moments later she threw her cup and the screwed-up bag into the nearest bin; by lunchtime they would be buried among the discards of dozens of cafe patrons.

After collecting her bike, Gabrielle pedalled away. She was home and showered in less than forty-five minutes, then in the car and on the way to work soon after, making it into her office just before ten. The first thing she did was knock on the boss's door.

"Come!" She stepped into the room as he glanced up from his drafting table. "Ah, Gab. Glad you're in. Still okay for our meeting this afternoon?"

"Of course. I just wanted to let you know I'd made it and apologise for being late. It won't happen again."

He waved away her apology. "Not like you to be late—you're usually the first one in! Everything okay?" He was a good boss, almost a friend, and she could hear the genuine concern in his voice.

"Just women's troubles, but it's all fine now."

"Oh, ah, right. Sorry. I mean…"

"No problem! I'll see you at the meeting." Gabrielle let herself out, closing the door softly behind her. She hated using that excuse, but even in the twenty-first century the phrase "women's troubles" was guaranteed to send most men into an embarrassed retreat. Besides, it wasn't entirely untrue in this context: the violence of men towards women could certainly be classified as trouble, and there was no doubt that after what she and Brooke had done, things were fine. At least, she hoped so.

For the rest of the day, Gabrielle did what she had schooled herself to do in the months after Evie's death: she put on a professional face and got on with it, pushing herself through. She kept it together until a quarter to seven, when she left work and sat in her car, feeling the energy ebb away and fatigue wash in. Her arms were heavy when she lifted them to the steering wheel, and she ached all over, not only with the memory of the past twenty-four hours, but also with a bone-deep pain that felt as if it would never go away. Gabrielle knew it was nothing more than the crash after a sustained adrenaline-fuelled period—still, she felt overwhelmed.

She stayed there for several minutes, wondering if she could even find the strength to go home and fall into bed, let alone get up in the morning. At least she didn't have a partner to consider. Emotional intimacy had been difficult since the death of her sister. After the slow, torturous demise of her twelve-year relationship, Gabrielle had found it far easier to be alone. Beginning something new meant a first date, and every first date included a question about her family. If she avoided the question, she felt angry and guilty; if she answered it, her date either got overly curious or extremely uncomfortable. Either way, she'd never been able to move past that question.

Finally, she started the engine and weaved through the half-empty car park to the boom-gated exit, where she held her key card out of the window. As the gate began to rise, the passenger door opened. Gabrielle felt a surge of fear.

"Sorry, Gab, sorry. Only me." Mia slid into the seat and pulled the door closed.

"Shit, Mia." Gabrielle pressed a hand to her chest.

"I know, but I thought this was the easiest way to catch you. Look, gate's up. Best drive, and we can talk on the way to your place. But I'll be getting out long before then."

Gabrielle filled Mia in on the events of the previous night, and the impact on Brooke. Mia, skewed sideways in her seat, listened without commenting, her shrewd eyes never leaving Gabrielle's face. Finally, Gabrielle fell silent.

Mia exhaled. "I assumed from Brooke's message you'd taken a more active role, but I hadn't imagined that."

"I'm just relieved I went to check on her and got there in time to stop her from…" Gab shook her head, her stomach knotting at the thought.

"He saw her. He saw both of you. If Brooke had used the EpiPen… Well, it would have been hard to explain how she just happened to be passing through his backyard in the middle of a downpour. I'm glad you got there in time too."

Another couple of kilometres passed, then Gabrielle cleared her throat. "Last night I was more visible than I'd planned to be, in South Coogee and then at Brooke's place—I'll be on CCTV there."

"Which is fine because you're going to keep up the contact with Brooke. Any CCTV will show nothing more than two friends."

"I know that, but what I was really getting at—" Gabrielle paused as without warning, a car pulled out in front of her. "Bloody idiot!" she yelled and flashed the car's headlights. Shit. She needed to keep her cool.

"You should definitely wait a bit longer before tackling your own…task."

Gabrielle nodded. "I shouldn't be surprised that you knew what I was going to say, should I? You always seem to know what I'm thinking."

Mia shrugged. "Practice."

"Anyway, you're right. I'm feeling more exposed, so I want to wait. But I'm also the last one, and I feel pressure—to bring this to an end. Then we can all really breathe again."

"Don't rush. Do it when the time is right; when you're ready and the opportunity is there. If you stuff it up because you were in a rush, no one will be breathing easy."

"Thanks very much."

"You know what I mean," said Mia with a quick smile. "Gab, tell me something."

"What?" Gabrielle shot a glance sideways, curious.

"Don't you already find yourself breathing a bit easier now that Evie's killer is dead? Now that the rest of our group have done their work and other women are safe?"

"It's like I've removed a tightly laced corset I didn't know I was wearing." Gabrielle smiled.

"There you are. So take your time. When you're ready, let me know. I have faith in you; we all do. Now, you'd better let me out here."

"But we're miles from your place!" Gabrielle flipped the indicator on and pulled over even while she argued.

"I like the city at night. It speaks to me."

"Are you sure? I can drive you home."

"No. You need to rest."

"I'll phone you," Gabrielle called as the therapist climbed nimbly from the car.

"Only when you're ready to act." Mia shut the door. She stepped away, turned, and began to walk.

Gabrielle watched until Mia vanished around a corner.

The others had all taken time and done their homework. Mia was right—there was no pressure. Besides, Gabrielle had already been researching her target, and if she waited a few extra months, conditions would improve both strategically and meteorologically. And for what she had in mind, the weather would be crucial.

FORTY

Just after seven thirty on Saturday morning, Olivia's phone started ringing. Her head heavy with sleep and alcohol, it took a moment of fumbling before her fingers closed around the handset. She answered without opening her eyes, then was shocked fully awake when the caller spoke.

"Ms. Hammond, it's Detective Bernstein. Sorry to be calling you so early."

Sure you are, Olivia thought. "That's okay," she said.

"It's just that Detective Ulbrick and I are on the road and happen to be heading in your direction. There are a few more things I'd like to go over, and I was wondering if we could stop by? We won't take up much of your time."

"It's not… I mean, it's Saturday, and I have my daughter here. Could this wait?" Olivia hoped she sounded sleepy rather than shifty.

"As I said, it shouldn't take long. We can be at your place in ten minutes and out ten minutes later."

Olivia could hear another voice murmuring something to Bernstein above the swish of traffic. "Sorry. I didn't mean to sound unhelpful. Your call woke me up, and I haven't had my morning coffee yet. Of course you can stop by. Please."

After terminating the call, Olivia spent the next few minutes brushing her teeth, getting rid of an empty wine bottle from last night, firing up the Nespresso machine, and checking on Nova. Her daughter was still buried beneath the doona, but one small hand stretched from under the covers and was tangled in Billy's fur. The heeler was curled up right next to the bed, the place he had chosen as his almost the moment he'd walked through the door and met Nova. Olivia smiled as she looked at her daughter and the dog.

Billy opened his eyes, and his tail wagged the tiniest bit. "Go back to sleep, Billy sweetheart," Olivia whispered, then quietly shut the door.

When the doorbell rang she was still in her dressing-gown, her hair a dishevelled, sleep-mussed tangle, but all traces of her alcohol-induced fog were gone. She was ready.

The front door wasn't visible from the kitchen, and as soon as Olivia rounded the corner into the hall she could see two shadowy figures behind the glass. Walking towards them, she aimed for a measured pace, acutely aware that this morning's visit might be designed to unnerve her, and trying to figure out why. She opened the door wide, a woman with nothing to conceal. "Hi," she said, disengaging the lock on the security screen. "Come in."

The detectives stepped over the threshold, then waited.

Are they hovering politely, or looming? Olivia wondered as she stepped past and started for the kitchen. "Through here. I'm just making coffee. Do you want one?"

"No, thanks," Bernstein replied. He pulled out a chair and sat down at the kitchen table without being asked.

"Detective Ulbrick?" Olivia paused in the act of getting a mug from the cupboard, and looked over her shoulder.

Ulbrick, dressed in jeans, a T-shirt, and a semi-tailored

jacket, was standing in front of the fridge, scrutinising the various notes, photos and other mementos that were stuck to the steel with magnets. It took her a second to respond with a distracted shake of the head. "Trying to cut down, but thanks."

"Sorry for bothering you so early." Bernstein again.

Olivia had to half turn to look at him. Another tactic? She tried to shrug it off. Whatever they were doing here, she was about to find out. "No problem," she said. "I know you have a job to do. You'll just have to excuse my appearance."

"We've seen worse," said Bernstein, then flushed as he realised what he'd said.

Olivia raised her eyebrows but didn't respond, busying herself with adding sweetener to her coffee. She took her first sip with her back to the detectives, then faced them, leaning against the kitchen bench and swallowing another mouthful of coffee, cradling the mug and hoping they couldn't see the tremor in her hands. "So how can I help?" She looked first at Bernstein then at Ulbrick, who remained over by the fridge. "I didn't realise you were still investigating. I thought when the body...when you found..."

There was a pause as the detectives glanced at each other.

Bernstein spoke. "The coroner hasn't delivered his verdict yet, but we're really just tidying things up—"

"You didn't tell us about your sister," said Ulbrick.

Olivia took another sip of coffee before answering. "No. Why would I?" She was pleased to hear herself sounding genuinely puzzled.

Bernstein had placed a notebook on the table in front of him, and now he flipped a couple of pages. "You're Olivia Faulkner, Vivienne Faulkner's sister."

"I was Olivia Faulkner, but I've used my married name for over a decade now."

"But you are Vivienne Faulkner's sister?"

"Yes. I don't see why my sister or my surname matter to you, though." Olivia frowned over the rim of her mug.

Ulbrick tapped a photo on the fridge, a sun-faded picture of Olivia and her sister when they were about fifteen, their heads touching, arms around each other, both smiling. "This the two of you?"

"Yes. Would one of you please explain?"

"I'm sorry," said Ulbrick with no sound of an apology in her voice. "It's just that while we were investigating Rowan Fitzpatrick's unexpected demise, we realised your sister also died in unusual circumstances."

"Unusual circumstances?" Olivia put her mug down on the bench with an audible crack. "My sister was murdered, detectives. I know it, your colleagues who investigated know it, and the witness who suddenly became afraid knows it."

"I couldn't comment on that," Ulbrick said calmly.

"I'm sure you could. You're here, so you must have looked at the case by now." Olivia was furious—of all the things she'd expected to be asked about, Vivienne was not one of them, and she made no effort to hide her feelings.

"It just seems a remarkable coincidence that your sister died the way she did, and Rowan Fitzpatrick was accused and acquitted of being responsible for the death of his partner. You were aware of his history, I assume?"

"Of course. Given the media coverage I'd have had to be living under a rock not to know. I still don't see what that has to do with Viv. She was dead before then, and I'm pretty damn certain she never crossed paths with Rowan. And I'm one hundred percent sure he wasn't the one who pushed my sister off a cliff." Olivia dragged a hand through her hair. Tears were threatening to fall, but she blinked them back. "You started by saying—in a rather accusatory manner, I might add—that I hadn't told you I was Viv's sister. Well, why would I? It's not something I hide, but it's also not something I tend to discuss."

At the table, Bernstein flipped to a clean page and made a small note at the top. "You still felt comfortable associating with Fitzpatrick, given his history? Given your sister's history?"

"No. I felt very uncomfortable. But that's what the business world is like. You make contacts. You use them to make other contacts."

Bernstein nodded, satisfied, but Ulbrick's face was blank.

"Is there something else you want to ask me?" Olivia's tone was sharp.

Silence.

"I can only assume you think I might be some sort of grief-crazed avenger, is that it?"

"No, we don't think that." Ulbrick was still maintaining her cool demeanour. "This is just an anomaly in the case, a loose end we needed to tie up."

Olivia nodded, lips pressed together, remembering Mia's advice once more: volunteer nothing.

Bernstein closed his notebook.

"Is there something you're not telling me?" Olivia asked. "Something about my sister? Did she have a connection to Rowan?" She stared first at Bernstein, then Ulbrick.

"No, nothing we could find," said Bernstein.

Olivia nodded again. So they'd been looking. "I would have been surprised if you said otherwise. Viv and I were very close, she would've told me if she knew him."

The sound of a flushing toilet filtered through from the bathroom.

"My daughter," explained Olivia, trying not to let her anxiety show. She didn't want to have to explain the detectives to Nova. "She'll be out for breakfast in a minute."

"We'll get going," said Ulbrick, clearly taking the hint. "Leave you to it. Thanks for your time."

"And sorry we had to ask about your sister." Bernstein stood and moved towards the doorway, leaving his chair a good metre out from the table.

Olivia pushed the chair back into place as she crossed the kitchen and led the detectives down the hall to the front door, acutely aware of their eyes on her back. They said their goodbyes and offered further apologies, then she watched as they walked down the short front path. She wasn't sure if she should shut the door now or wait until they got into their unmarked car; in the end she closed the door with a quiet click as the detectives opened theirs.

Olivia knew she should talk to Mia, or perhaps directly to Gabrielle, given she was the one charged with taking care of Viv's killer. The detectives already had their antennae up, so if Gabrielle made a move against Aaron in the near future, it could bring them all undone. And besides, now the police were asking about Viv, Olivia wanted plenty of time to book a trip and make sure she was far away and highly visible when whatever happened, happened.

She began to pull her mobile from the pocket of her dressing-gown, already planning how to phrase her words. Then she stopped, letting the phone drop back. Nova was in the hall, running towards her, silky blond hair flying, bare feet slapping on the boards, the dog dancing behind her. "Mum, Mum!"

When Olivia opened her arms, Nova flew into them. Olivia held her daughter as though she would never let go.

FORTY-ONE

"Are you happy now, Fi? Can you let it go?"

They'd found a cafe overlooking a tiny park just down the road from Olivia Hammond-nee-Faulkner's house. Lew had taken off his jacket and was leaning on the bonnet of the car, tie loose, sleeves rolled up.

Ulbrick handed him his flat white with three sugars, then blew out a heavy breath. "I just can't believe it took me this long to realise Olivia Hammond was stuck in my head because of her strong resemblance to her sister." Ulbrick popped the top of her kombucha can and took a swig. "God, that's disgusting! How do people drink that?"

Lew toasted her with his coffee. "Nectar of the gods."

"Hang on." She strode to a nearby bin and dumped her drink. "Remind me of this next time I tell you I'm giving up caffeine."

"Oh, don't worry, I will." Lew eyed her over the top of his cup. "Now stop bloody stalling, F U."

"Lew…" She scratched the back of her head. "It's a big coincidence, and I just don't believe in coincidences." Lew opened his mouth to speak, but Ulbrick held up a hand. "I appreciate you indulging me this morning, but now you've heard what she had to say, what do you think?"

"My turn now?"

Ulbrick snorted and folded her arms. "Go on then, let me have it."

"I get where you're coming from, which is why I'm here."

"Why do I sense a huge 'but' coming?"

"But."

Ulbrick pulled off her sunglasses and pinched the bridge of her nose.

"Using your married name isn't a crime. Yes, she was rattled and defensive when you asked about her sister, but you've read that file. The investigating officers thought the guy did it, and even if her sister's fall was an accident, Ms. Hammond believes the ex was responsible. Of course she's going to be hostile when we—the cops who, in her eyes, let her sister down—start making veiled accusations."

"I wasn't—"

"Of course you bloody were! Otherwise what are we doing here?"

"Okay, except she was socialising with Fitzpatrick, who—"

"Was involved in what appears to be an accident and is definitely a man who'd be a valuable contact for someone in her line of work. I'm sorry, Fi, but it rings true."

"Shit." Ulbrick put her sunglasses back on. She was annoyed—with herself for coming on too strong with Olivia Hammond, with Lew Bernstein for being right but also being logical and nice about it, and with a system that left her like this, chasing shadows. She could feel Lew gauging her reaction. "Shit," she said again, resignation now in her tone.

He nodded and set his coffee cup on the bonnet of the car. "Like I said, I get where you're coming from, but if you take a step back and look at this objectively, why would Vivienne Faulkner's sister kill a random bloke? Why wouldn't she just go after the man she thinks murdered her sister? You may not believe in coincidences, but how often do we chase down clues that lead nowhere? Things that look legit are sometimes nothing more than piss and wind. And you know the Australian stats as well as I do: on average one woman a week dies as a result of domestic violence. Sooner or later random paths are going to cross."

Ulbrick grunted. She wished she still had the kombucha can in her hand so she could crush it. "I'm not trying to fuck up your investigation, Lew."

"I know. And I'm wrapping it up, Fi. We've looked at Fitzpatrick's death six ways from Sunday and spoken to everyone—multiple times in some cases—and the stories all gel. The autopsy didn't reveal anything we weren't expecting other than the blow to the head, which the pathologist determined could've been caused by a number of things, so…" He shrugged. "I've got nothing, Fi—nothing that suggests it was anything other than an accident. Today was a Hail Mary. I've already prepared the brief for the coroner, and I expect the finding will be death by misadventure: drugs, alcohol, and a misstep that saw Fitzpatrick go overboard—hitting his head in the process—and drown."

"Dammit, Lew, I know you're right, but my brain is still itching." Ulbrick laced her fingers behind her head and forced her shoulders back, the tension knotting her spine. "What about—" She snapped her lips shut, biting back the words.

"What about what?"

She hesitated.

"Come on, spit it out."

"Did you see the little movie poster she had stuck to the fridge?"

"A poster? Are you suspicious of Olivia Hammond's decor choices now? I didn't see anything—you were standing in front of the fridge."

"Shit. Look, I know how this is going to sound, but there was a small version of a poster for the Hitchcock film *Strangers on a Train.*"

"Well, heck, let's lock her up!" Bernstein slapped one hand into the other.

"Lew."

"Sorry, but I'm clearly missing something."

"*Strangers on a Train* is the one where two people swap murders. So there's no connection."

"Oh, come the fuck on, Fi! Now you're accusing her of an elaborate plot because of a movie poster? If it had been for *West Side Story*, would you suspect her of gang activity?"

"When you put it like that… Shit, forget I said anything." Ulbrick sighed. Lew was a good detective, a cop's cop, and he'd kept her in the loop right through the Fitzpatrick investigation.

If he said there was nothing, then…

"Fi, I know how much it pisses you off that Daniel Pavic got off so lightly for running that woman down, but he's dead now, and so's Fitzpatrick. Two blokes who are proof that accidents happen, especially when you do stupid things."

Ulbrick nodded. "Yeah, I know. Thanks, Lew." She pushed herself off the car and moved around to the passenger door. "Come on, I'd better let you have the rest of your Saturday."

On the drive back she was quiet, mentally pulling things apart and rearranging them, trying to make the pieces fit. She hadn't talked to Lew about the OD and house-fire death of Malik Spicer, a man previously involved in a fatal domestic violence stabbing. Now that Lew had determined the demise of Rowan Fitzpatrick was nothing more than an accident, what was the point?

Looking on the bright side, she could purge three files from her private records. Except there was something about coincidences she'd once been told by a friend, a medical researcher, and it lodged in her brain: if something happened three times, it was no longer a coincidence... Three times was a trend.

Ulbrick absentmindedly reached behind her ear. And scratched.

FORTY-TWO

The first time Travis breached the Apprehended Violence Order was on a Sunday. Presumably he'd been expecting the family to gather for lunch, as they always had done, at the home of Mia's parents. The family were still together but elsewhere, a restaurant, somewhere very public, unknown to Travis.

Late in the afternoon when the girls' parents pulled into their driveway, he was suddenly there, banging on the car's roof, yelling demands. But just as unexpectedly, police arrived and pulled him away. Mia would later find out that a neighbour had grown suspicious of the man sitting in his vehicle for hours and had already dialled triple zero.

He was arrested and charged.

Less than twenty-four hours later, he was out on bail.

Mia had always been protective of her privacy, cautious to make sure there was a solid divide between her professional and home lives, careful that her address could not be easily obtained should a client—or anyone else—wish to find her. Now her sister was living with her, Mia took additional precautions, checking the cars around her as she drove home from work via different routes, alert to static figures in otherwise moving crowds, always on the lookout for Travis.

Weeks passed, and the sisters began to think that he had decided not to bother, or—awful to contemplate—turned his attention to the next unsuspecting woman. They began to relax. It happened on a Wednesday, the most normal day of the week. Mia was at her office, finishing up with a client, another in the waiting room. On her desk, her mobile lit up with an incoming call. She glanced at it as she ushered the client out: her own home number, the landline.

Mia frowned. Her sister was home alone, moping around with a bad cold; she rarely called Mia at work and never used the landline. A chill ran through Mia, and she snatched up the phone. "Sis? What's wrong?"

"Mia!" Her sister sounded frantic. "He's here! Outside! How did he find me?"

"Sis, Sis! Is everything locked?"

"Yes, no… I don't know. I think so."

"Have you called the police?" Mia snatched her keys from the desk drawer and burst into the waiting room. "Emergency, sorry." She threw the words at the waiting client and didn't stop, breaking into a run as she hit the street.

"I called you." There was a second's pause, then she screamed. "He's at the back door—he's hitting it with something! Mia!"

"Stay on the line. Don't break the call. I'm putting you on hold while I dial triple zero."

"Please, Mia!"

"I'm coming, Sis. I'm getting in the car now. Let me phone the police." Mia punched in the zeroes. She was accelerating out of her parking space by the time the operator connected her to the police despatcher, then yelling the address as she blew through an intersection as the lights changed. "My sister has an AVO against him. I'm on my way there, but please hurry!"

Mia ended the call. A car pulled out from a side street, forcing Mia to brake hard. The phone fell from her grasp. "Shit!" She fumbled around in the footwell for precious seconds until her fingers closed around the handset. The car surged forward again as she lifted the phone to her ear. "Sis? The police are coming. I'm five minutes away. Hang on!"

There was no reply.

"Sis? Talk to me!" Mia shouted.

And then she heard the screaming.

FORTY-THREE

Mia slammed the car to a stop, two wheels up on the nature strip, and left the engine running as she threw open the door and sprinted up the path. No sign of police, no sirens in the distance, and the house seemed quiet. That frightened her more than anything.

The front door was closed. As quickly and quietly as she could, she fitted her key into the lock and let herself in, then stood, feeling the house around her, testing the air.

She took a cautious step forward and then another. "Sis?" She had meant to call loudly, but it came out soft, afraid. She strained her ears for a response.

Silence.

Her sister must have fled. That was it. Hope flared in Mia's chest then died just as quickly. Her sister had been in the house, screaming, just before the connection dropped.

Was he still here? Did he have her sister?

Mia advanced down the hall, glancing through an open doorway into her empty study—tidy, normal. Nowhere to hide. The end of the passage was a few paces away, beyond it an open-plan living area. From where she was, all she could see was the corner of a rug and an expanse of sunlit floorboards.

She took a steadying breath, ready to rush forward, when a ferrous tang hit her nostrils.

Blood.

She noticed a mark on the doorframe: a smeared fingerprint.

Abandoning caution, she burst into the room, spinning to her right the way her sister would have run if she'd been heading for the back door.

Mia's foot slipped. She skidded and almost fell. Blood was splattered over the floor, flecks of it on the walls, an obscenely red handprint on the side of the bookcase. Across the room, beyond the large modular lounge, the back door stood open, the wood around the lock splintered and broken. Mia was aware of her own rasping breath as she slowly moved forward, side-stepping the blood, curving around the end of the lounge.

Slumped against the cushions was a body, with closed eyes, torn shirt, and a single stab wound oozing fresh blood staining the upholstery a deep crimson. And just near Mia's feet, a knife. Without thinking, she picked it up: one of hers, a big carving knife from the second drawer, the handle slippery in her palm. She couldn't tear her gaze away from the body.

Suddenly, his eyes flew open. His chest rose. Blood bubbled at his lips, and he made a wet, sucking sound.

She looked at the knife in her hand, back at the man on her lounge. When he pulled in another breath, she could see the effort it cost him.

Seconds passed, or was it minutes? She became aware of sirens in the distance, getting louder. Leaning close, she watched as he registered her face. Then she raised the knife and plunged it in a second time, feeling it glance off bone before finding the softness between two ribs.

His eyes widened, his body arching. She yanked out the knife and flung it aside.

Behind her, a floorboard creaked.

She spun around, then gasped. "I thought he'd killed you."

"He was going to," said her sister. "If I hadn't hidden that knife under the couch days ago, he would have." She looked over Mia's shoulder. "Is he dead? I just ran, I—"

"He's dead now."

"Mia!" Her sister pushed past. "Where's the knife?"

"I threw it over there... I think it went under that chair. I had to do it. After everything he's done to you, everything you've suffered. It was never going to end until he'd killed you!"

Outside, a siren abruptly cut out, quickly followed by the slamming of car doors.

"Listen!" her sister hissed. "You can't be part of this! We have to say I did it all, stabbed him twice. I have an excuse—I was in fear for my life! They won't charge me."

"My prints are on the knife! Besides, I can't let you—"

"Police!" someone shouted through the still-open front door.

"You came in and took the knife from me. That's all you have to say." Mia's sister turned towards the cautiously approaching footsteps. "Here!" she called. "We're in here!"

FORTY-FOUR

Ulbrick had intended to shred three of her files: Pavic, Fitzpatrick, Spicer. Three men, erased.

Instead, she read through them again and again, until the details of each case were seared into her synapses: what the men had done or been accused of, their victims, the punishment or lack thereof, their sudden ends. But no matter how much she raked through the minutiae and rearranged the facts, there was nothing to link the men to one another, or to suggest they were the victims of anything except their own stupidity.

Slowly, Ulbrick had come to the grudging realisation that maybe she was wrong. More to the point, she knew what a shrink would say about her behaviour. Lew had recognised it and let her run, no doubt hoping the obsession would burn itself out, while ready to give her a dose of reality if needed.

Deep down, Detective Fiona Ulbrick believed that when Daniel Pavic had received a pathetically inadequate sentence for running down Pip McKenzie, she had failed to get justice for a victim. She had therefore failed as a police officer, and being reminded of the perpetrator was like salt in her wound. But if she hadn't been watching TV that night, if she'd never seen the farm or heard the news item, he'd just be another man who ignored basic safety measures and wound up dead. And if her connection to *that* case had never materialised, she wouldn't have thought twice about a drunken playboy falling off his yacht, or a drug-affected man falling asleep and dropping his cigarette.

It seemed the only place where the cases collided was deep in the recesses of Ulbrick's brain.

She didn't shred the files, but after some deliberation she marked them all *NLAP (No Longer A Problem)*—and consigned them to a bottom drawer. Then, just for shits and giggles, she fired up Google and ran one more search for stories about domestic violence perpetrators who had met their maker. Unsurprisingly, the top hits for her key words brought up the reverse: women who'd suffered years of domestic violence before being killed by their partner. Then Ulbrick started to come across stories about women who'd defended themselves against abusive men. She kept scrolling and clicking, dipping in and out of articles and reports with increasing despair. There were no fresh stories of accidental deaths among the men, but the abject failure of the system was writ large not only in the volume of material about abused women, but also the legal penalties they suffered when they fought back.

Ulbrick dragged the cursor across the screen, closing multiple tabs, then pulled her focus back to the room around her: comfortable chair, good lighting, orderly shelves, Mozart's Piano Concerto No. 24 in C minor spilling softly from strategically placed speakers. She was just about to close the browser when an image in an online article snagged on her cop sensors. It showed a group of people protesting against the jailing of a woman who, fearing for her life, had killed her ex.

Ulbrick leaned closer to the screen, unsure what had caught her attention. The case was vaguely familiar, but that wasn't it.

When she tried enlarging the image, the faces lost definition, pixelating and blurring into nothing. Zooming out, she looked again and saw it, or rather, saw her, standing front and centre in the group. The hair was different—long and light brown—but the curvy figure and strong, square jaw were the same. It was the woman who had met Olivia Hammond in the cafe near the police station.

Hardly daring to hope, Ulbrick checked the caption:

A group of supporters led by Mia DeVries, sister of the accused, outside court.

"Hello, Mia," Ulbrick whispered.

It hadn't been hard to find Mia online; a therapist, with a website for her practice.

The next night after work, Ulbrick drove across to the inner west of the city and parked a few doors down and across the road from The Pleiades. It was part of a strip of shops and businesses, the street active without being too busy: local traffic, grocery shoppers, families on the takeaway run, and diners heading to the various restaurants and bistros in the area. Ulbrick spent ten minutes or so taking it all in and getting a feel for the local vibe before she stepped from the car and lined up at the pedestrian crossing. When the lights changed she tucked herself in behind a couple carrying pizzas and beer, veering off once she reached the opposite side.

She sauntered past the solid white door that blocked her access to the world of Mia DeVries. A light glowed above the portal, while next to it was a doorbell, a keypad, and a plaque: The Pleiades, Trauma Counselling and Therapy. Ulbrick clocked the details without breaking stride. She kept walking down the street, bought herself a bundle of hot chips, and circled back to the car, settling in for a stakeout where she didn't know the stakes.

Nothing happened, but Ulbrick wasn't discouraged. The next evening she drove over again, found a convenient parking spot, and sat, her eyes on the white door. Still nothing, but she went ahead and did it again the following night.

Just on seven thirty the street was quiet, a strong wind causing most people to scuttle to and from their cars. Ulbrick was tossing up between pizza or a burger for dinner when the door to The Pleiades swung open, spilling warm light onto the footpath. Two women stepped out. One—haggard, thin, thirty going on seventy—descended the steps before turning for a final word. The one who remained on the threshold, wrapping her cardigan more firmly across her curves, was instantly recognisable: Mia DeVries.

Ulbrick tried to snap a picture with her phone, but the lighting was too poor and she had parked too far away. She would not make that mistake again.

After that, visits became part of her routine, and she began to pick up the patterns of The Pleiades: the evenings and Saturdays when numerous people turned up, presumably for group sessions, and the nights for private consultations. Then there were the occasions when the entry light glowed but no one entered or exited.

Once, just when Ulbrick was thinking of calling it a night, DeVries stepped out alone. The therapist locked the door behind her and set off up the street at a brisk pace, the click of her high heels ringing out. After she rounded the far corner, Ulbrick started her car and took off in pursuit, already arguing with herself. On the one hand she was following her detective's instincts; on the other, her behaviour was verging on that of a stalker.

Just this once, she decided. The chance to see where DeVries went was too good an opportunity to pass up.

But Ulbrick was forced to wait at the corner, and as soon as she entered the stream of traffic on the next street she had to speed up or risk attracting attention. Seconds later, she'd driven past her target.

"Dammit." She smacked her hand on the steering wheel then took the next left, circling around the block, not ready to concede defeat. She felt a thrill of elation when she spotted that straight back again, quickly followed by a wave of disappointment when DeVries entered a railway underpass.

Probably just as well, Ulbrick told herself—watching the consulting rooms was one thing; trailing a woman through the streets of Sydney at night was a whole new level of obsession. She promised herself she'd tone it down, limit herself to watching not trailing, and cut back on the number of evenings she was dedicating to this quest. After all, it made perfect sense that Olivia Hammond would be seeing a therapist like DeVries.

Except Ulbrick's itch didn't go away. She knew the deaths meant something, even though she didn't know what it was. Connecting DeVries to Hammond had been the first step; now if she could just find the next link in the chain, someone else connected to one of the men who had died. If she could place that person here, in this orbit…

Ulbrick continued to watch the solid white door in the leafy suburban street. Not all the time—occasionally a week would pass when every waking hour was consumed by her caseload or the demands of a court appearance, but that was rare.

She hadn't seen anything to raise her suspicions to the next level, and in her self-analytical moments she considered the notion that she never would, that her theory was crazy. But one of the things she had always enjoyed about being a detective was the hunt, however long or relentless. Every time she drove away from The Pleiades, her detective's brain pulsed with the same tantalising words: *Next time.*

FORTY-FIVE

When Mia had told Gabrielle, months ago, that waiting was an imperative, she'd been relieved. Then Mia informed her that Naomi, the woman who was supposed to have her back, had recently given birth to a baby girl.

At first, Gabrielle thought she'd have to revise her arrangements and go it alone. Using the burner, she sent Naomi a message of congratulations, and let her know she could manage by herself. Gab was shocked when the phone rang almost immediately.

"What's the plan?" Naomi asked, sounding tired.

Gabrielle could hear the baby gurgling in the background as she outlined her strategy, and despite Naomi's assurances she ended the call with no expectations. She was pleased for Naomi, but it was a big setback. Still, nothing she couldn't handle.

As the weeks ticked past, she and Naomi communicated sporadically, and every time she waited for the other woman to apologise and bow out. She was surprised when Naomi told her she'd be there, in Thredbo. Gabrielle was even more surprised when Naomi said she was bringing her husband.

The ski season was turning out to be one of the best in years, and Thredbo village was buzzing. Gabrielle had come in on the Thursday Snowex bus, her ticket bought at the departure point that morning. Normally she hated buses, and the thought of a coach tour made her shudder, but the resort was in a national park, which meant every car coming in needed a pass. She'd only driven herself once—an unavoidable but necessary part of her planning. Other than that, Gabrielle didn't want her details recorded anywhere, so she intended to use cash wherever possible, just as she'd done on all her reconnaissance trips over the past two months.

The exception to her cash rule was the hotel. Accommodation in the village was heavily booked during the season, and turning up without a place to stay was unthinkable. So Gabrielle had made a reservation using a fake name and direct debit from an anonymous-sounding account. It wouldn't be hard to trace that back to her if she stuffed up the job and police had a reason to look in her direction, but she'd considered her plan from every angle. As far as she could see, the only consequence if things went wrong would be a man who didn't die when he was supposed to. And if everything went right? The perfect homicide.

Gabrielle hadn't seen Naomi for months when she laid eyes on her friend and the man she assumed was Rich in the reception area of the Triglav Hotel. Designed to look like an upscale yet traditional European establishment, the hotel had a chequerboard floor dotted with several large rugs, each one marking out a cosy seating area of sofas, chairs, and low tables. This welcoming space was flanked by a cedar reception desk and a pair of elevators, while a broad staircase dominated the far end of the room. The Triglav was the most luxurious hotel in the village, far more upmarket than Gabrielle's accommodation, and the fact that it sported a restaurant, casual cafe, nightclub, gift shop, and award-winning day spa meant there was plenty of foot traffic—and plenty of excuses for hanging around.

Bending to tie her shoes, Gabrielle studied Naomi and Rich from the other side of the room. Naomi looked thin in her winter coat, and although she was smiling brightly at her husband, Gabrielle thought there was a certain vulnerability about her. She watched as Rich placed a gentle arm around Naomi's shoulder.

When the women had spoken weeks earlier, Naomi had explained it was Rich's parents who'd suggested a short break and offered to look after their granddaughter. At first Naomi had demurred, not yet ready to leave the baby. Then, acknowledging her own fragile emotional state, she'd bowed to their gentle pressure and nominated Thredbo. Both she and Rich were good skiers and, as she told Gabrielle, he didn't need much convincing. The trip was locked in.

Gabrielle crossed the foyer and entered the gift shop, where she feigned deep interest in the extensive range of hand-carved Swiss music boxes. In less than a minute Naomi was by her side, picking up a souvenir cowbell and giving it an experimental ring. "These must drive the sales assistants insane," she said, by way of greeting.

"That and endless tinkly versions of 'Edelweiss'," replied Gabrielle. She turned her head slightly, looking at Naomi from the corner of her eye. "You're looking—"

"Crap? Yes, I know." Naomi put down the cowbell and moved closer, examining the painted lid of a music box.

"Actually I was going to say, you're looking like a working mother with a new baby who's trying to juggle everything. And your perfume is divine."

"Thanks." Naomi flashed a quick smile. "That's a nice way to say I look bloody crap, but thanks. Anyway, enough about me; we don't have long, so..."

"So tomorrow night, Saturday, is our chef's big night. The Top of The World does a signature dinner, then he likes to get off the mountain and head back to Sydney."

"Not a skier then?"

Gabrielle shook her head.

"How late?"

"It's a reasonably early sitting because most patrons ski back from the restaurant, and night skiing ends at nine. But he leaves about an hour before that—snowmobile down to the village and straight to his car. Which means we need to be in place by seven thirty."

Naomi nodded. "Okay."

"What about your husband?" Gabrielle picked up a snow globe, gave it a shake, then returned it to the shelf.

"All sorted. Rich has always wanted to ski at night, and when he heard they're trialling it at Thredbo, he didn't need much persuading. I told him the only thing I was craving was an early night and at least ten uninterrupted hours of sleep. I'm all yours."

"Make sure you dress warmly, because we're going to be out there for at least an hour." Gabrielle hesitated and shot Naomi a worried glance. "Are you sure you can do this? I don't want—"

"Sweetheart, I have a very cosy snow suit. There's a travel rug in the Jeep, and I can even take a thermos. I'll be fine; just worry about the rest of it."

Gabrielle wanted to hug her, but they were supposed to be strangers.

"Rich will be looking for me in a minute," said Naomi. "The Jeep's in the public car park next to the village green—down the far end. Shall we meet there at seven?"

"Perfect. His car's there too, a RAV4—bright blue with a grey roof and personalised plates. They—"

Naomi abruptly moved away. "Sorry, babe, I couldn't resist a peek!"

Rich, who had appeared at the end of the aisle, said something Gabrielle didn't catch. Then she was alone, the scent of Naomi's perfume lingering in the air.

Gabrielle stayed in the shop a little longer before purchasing an overpriced Toblerone and leaving the Triglav. Dusk was settling over the alpine village, and lights shone warmly from dozens of windows. With no night skiing on Fridays the lifts had stopped for the day, and here and there skiers were straggling back to their accommodation, skis and poles across their shoulders, feet heavy in ungainly boots.

Tucking her chin into her scarf, Gabrielle walked among them, heading for one of the public car parks scattered through the village. Perhaps it was paranoia or too much attention to detail, but she wanted to make sure Aaron's car was still there.

When she'd first discovered he was a chef, she had been stumped. How could she engineer a casual crossing of paths with a man who worked insane hours? She had experimented a couple of times, loitering in the shadows near the inner-Sydney restaurant as she waited for him to appear after last service. But the man emerged as part of the general exodus of chefs and kitchen hands, sometimes laughing and joking, on a high, sometimes subdued, irritable, but always one of the pack. Then a snatch of conversation, overheard on one of those dark vigils, gave Gabrielle a glimmer of hope—and the germ of an idea, far better than anything she had envisaged for the streets of Sydney. "Mate!" From her watching place, she saw the speaker give her target a playful shove. "Winter at Top of the World! That'll look good on your CV! When do you start?"

The rest of their words were lost as the group broke up in a flurry of goodbyes, fist bumps, and backslaps. Gabrielle retreated farther into the gloom, studying her target as he slid into his RAV4 with the MARIN8 vanity plates. She committed his gait to memory and took note of the way he drove off, accelerating and braking hard.

The exchange meant little to Gabrielle until she got home, googled the name, and discovered that Top of the World was the highest-altitude restaurant in the country. Located in the Kosciuszko National Park, up the mountain from Thredbo, it offered breakfast and lunch from June to late September, the height of the ski season. And on Saturday nights, Top of the World served a three-course dinner. She could immediately see the possibilities. There were many environmental advantages: steep mountains, snow, ice, the cold. She thought of all the skiing accidents she'd read about, snowstorms, hypothermia, avalanches, people who were underdressed, ill-prepared, stupid, drunk, cocky—so many ways to die with or without help. A Saturday night would work best, unless the man followed his habit of leaving work with a group. For the rest of the week it would be daylight when he finished, the mountain still busy with skiers and snowboarders, limiting her opportunities.

She decided to wait until he was a month into his Thredbo tenure, giving him time to establish his routine, to get comfortable. And giving her time to watch him, and to pick the moment when she could bring him down.

Throughout July and into August, Gabrielle had taken the bus to the alpine resort on a few occasions, always using the same assumed name. Each time she arrived on Thursday or Friday and stayed for three or four days, always in the same budget hotel; she was just one of thousands of people having a long weekend at the snow. They were familiar with her there now. She was unremarkable, and her current visit would not stand out, especially as she planned to return at least once more before the season drew to a close. On each trip, she took snowboarding lessons and went snowshoeing, dined in various bistros and cafes but never stayed out late, made use of the athletics centre, and, most of all, tracked her target.

His days, at least on the weekends when she was there, had a certain rhythm. He started early for the breakfast service and remained at Top of the World until around four thirty p.m. on Thursdays and Fridays, an hour after the restaurant closed. He'd use a snowmobile to return to the village, hit the gym for a weights-and-cardio session, then head back to his shared lodge, reemerging a couple of hours later to trawl the nightspots.

Gabrielle discovered he had Sundays and Mondays off, and he preferred to spend them in Sydney. So every Saturday, he finished work and hit the road. Despite the darkness. Despite the possibility of icy conditions.

Really, Gabrielle thought, *an accident waiting to happen.*

FORTY-SIX

Saturday—*the* Saturday. Gabrielle hunched into her coat as she hurried across the village green. Rain had begun to fall, still fine enough to swirl in the light of a streetlamp, and she glanced up anxiously as she passed. Deteriorating weather was a bonus—she'd hoped to put her plan into action under poor conditions—but if it started to snow heavily, it wouldn't be long before the roads became impassable. Thredbo could be cut off. And if that happened, everything would fall apart.

She reached the car park and peered into the gloom, confirming MARIN8 was still in the same place. Over to her left, a car's lights flashed: Naomi. With a final glance over her shoulder, Gabrielle hurried forward and let herself into the passenger seat of Naomi's Jeep, dropping her small backpack in the footwell.

"Nice night for it," said Naomi, as Gabrielle slammed the door.

"I hope the snow holds off a bit longer." Gabrielle pulled on her seat belt. "He has to leave the village, and we have to get back."

"Then let's go," said Naomi, pressing the ignition. "Maybe he'll decide to hit the road early."

Gabrielle raised her eyebrows. "Hit the road, huh?" She unzipped her jacket as the Jeep's heating began to blast. "You know where we're going? The Alpine Way?"

Naomi manoeuvred the car onto the road. "Yep. You'll have to tell me exactly where, though."

"I drove up here once so I could check the distances and timing; I know them by heart. We need to travel 16.8 kilometres, but this rain might slow us down a little."

Naomi leaned forward, peering through the windscreen. "Shit. We're now officially talking about snow."

Gabrielle felt apprehensive as she rubbed a hole in the fogged passenger window. "Will the night skiing go ahead? What happens if Rich comes back early and you're not there?"

"They'll call it off if the snow gets too heavy. But Rich's made a couple of friends who he was planning to have a drink with anyway—and if not, I left a note saying I've gone for a walk."

"Seriously, in this?" Gabrielle snorted.

Naomi didn't respond.

"Naomi?"

"It's fine. Rich knows I get restless. He'll assume I'm either on a treadmill or walking the hotel corridors." Naomi's voice cracked on the last word.

"What's going on?" Gabrielle twisted sideways to study Naomi's profile.

"I didn't want to tell you."

Gabrielle waited, concerned.

"I've been struggling with everything. After dropping the car on the slimeball, I just…fell apart. Then, after giving birth, post-natal depression hit me really hard: no appetite, feeling totally incompetent, crying a lot. And when I say a lot, there have been days when I've literally cried myself dry."

"I didn't realise you were having such a hard time. I'm sorry."

Naomi shook her head. "Don't be. I'm getting better, really. Rich and his parents have been amazingly supportive, hence this getaway. Anyway, you don't need to hear this shit—not now."

"You should have said something." Gabrielle felt awful; she should have been more aware, more sensitive. "You don't have to—"

"I bloody well do—I want to finish this." Naomi shot Gabrielle a quick glance. "So, I'm watching the trip meter, but what else do I need to know?"

Gabrielle was silent for a moment. She turned to stare out at the snow, white against the blackness of the night. "Once you drop me off, double back. There's a small track about eight hundred metres away—just past the turn to Lake Crackenback, but I'll point it out to you. Pull in there. If you think you'll get snowed in, move to the lake turnoff. Both places will give you a good view of the road, but you'll be less visible on the track."

"As it happens, I have some experience with driving on shitty bush tracks," said Naomi, a touch of irony in her voice.

"I'd offer you a fist bump, but I'd rather you kept both hands on the wheel."

"Thanks."

"As soon as you're in position, call me on the burner. Timing will be tight, so we'll need to already be on an open line when he appears. You saw his car?"

"Yes. Thank God for personalised plates and huge fucking egos."

"I know. So if any other car comes first, just say, 'no, no, no.' If his car comes but there's another one close behind, do the same—just repeat the word *no*."

"And if it's his car and there's no one else on the road? What do I say then?"

"Action."

Gabrielle watched the taillights of Naomi's Jeep recede, then turned and walked a bit farther around the corner, the softly falling snow immediately blurring her footprints. She wasn't much of a cold-weather person, but she'd used a blog on travel to Antarctica as a guide on what to wear, so she was more than dressed for the conditions.

After finding a spot to hide in case other cars came past, she crouched down, unzipping the backpack. First she grabbed a hand warmer, stripped the packaging and dropped the little charcoal pouch in her right pocket. Then she pulled out the handheld spotlight she'd purchased months ago; it had been expensive, but the small size, gun-style grip, and incredibly bright beam were exactly right for the job.

The wind was picking up, sending the snow in different directions, chilling her face. Stiff-jawed, she used her teeth to pull the glove from her right hand, spitting it into the backpack. The warm gloves were too thick for fast, accurate work, and her timing would need to be perfect. She re-zipped the pack and slung it over her shoulders. Finally, she unrolled the balaclava she'd been wearing as a beanie, blocking out the cold while concealing her features.

How long had it been since Naomi left?

Just as the thought entered her head, the burner phone buzzed inside Gabrielle's jacket. She had her earbuds and mic plugged in, but she fumbled to answer the call.

"I'm on the lake road," said Naomi. "The smaller track didn't look too bad, but with the way it's snowing I didn't want to chance it."

"If he's coming at all, it shouldn't be too long now." Gabrielle straightened up, shaking out her limbs and staring into the night, back towards Thredbo. The fingers of her right hand were now only covered by a thin latex glove, and they already felt numb and stiff. She thrust her hand into her pocket and grabbed at the heat pack. The change in temperature was so abrupt it hurt, but it did the job.

Her plan wasn't sophisticated; even if she pulled this part off, it could all come to nothing, and she would have to try again. But simplicity had always appealed to her. She preferred things to be clean and elegant—functional. So she had pushed ahead, and now she felt a surge of satisfaction as she walked into the middle of the road. She was ready.

Standing on the Alpine Way, she was surrounded by absolute silence. Naomi was still on the phone, and occasionally the women would murmur something to each other, mainly to ensure the connection was live. But Gabrielle had never felt more alone.

It had stopped snowing, and the wind had died back to a gentle zephyr, teasing the newly fallen snow into small flurries. The darkness was almost complete. She had expected there would be at least a sliver of moonlight reflected by the snow, but this was better. She drew in a deep breath, feeling the cold air in her throat, and waited.

"Headlights." Naomi's voice was loud in her ear.

Over her shoulder, Gabrielle saw only blackness. No cars coming up the other way.

"One car."

Gabrielle swallowed.

"Action!"

FORTY-SEVEN

Gabrielle raised the unlit spotlight in front of her. She held it like a gun, double-handed, with one finger on the switch. The sound of an engine reached her ears, faint, growing closer. And then she could see the glow of headlights from beyond the curve in the road.

Suddenly the vehicle was round the bend and bearing down on her. She flicked the switch, spotlighting the RAV4. She saw the licence plate, MARIN8, then shifted her gaze high, above the level of his halogens, and for a split second she was staring at Aaron's face scrunched up against the blinding brilliance of her light.

She heard the squeal of tyres trying to grip, then registered the swing of his headlights as the RAV4 slewed to the left. Lunging in the opposite direction, she threw herself into the snow and undergrowth. She felt the wind of the car as it passed and the shock of cold beneath her, and heard the snap of branches as the RAV4 ploughed off the road and into the scrub.

Gabrielle raised her head.

A crash—grinding metal, breaking glass. Then nothing.

She clambered to her feet, retrieved the spotlight from the

snow where it had fallen, and made her way on unsteady legs back onto the road. Aiming the beam at the road surface, she traced the path of his skid to the point where asphalt met dirt, only centimetres before the start of the wire safety barrier. She released the breath she'd been holding.

At the sound of another car approaching, she snapped off the light. Her earbuds were still secure beneath the balaclava. "Naomi?" she asked.

"It's me. I'm coming around the last bend."

Gabrielle moved to the side, shrugging the backpack from her shoulders, as Naomi's Jeep appeared. Her hand was on the door even before it came to a stop, then she was in, cocooned in warmth, bathed in the glow of the dashboard lights. "Let's go," she said.

Naomi looked at her, eyebrows raised.

Gabrielle smiled grimly. "Well, it happened, but I didn't go to check on him."

Naomi nodded and carefully turned the car around. "Anyway, if things didn't quite work out, hopefully it's nothing a night in the great outdoors won't fix."

Gabrielle sighed with relief as she let herself into her hotel room. She locked the door, turned on the lights, dialled up the thermostat, and finally dragged the curtains shut. She'd ditched the burner phone, but the spotlight would have to wait until morning.

Despite a hot shower and a bed piled with blankets, it took hours before her feet felt warm. Hours of feeling exhausted but unable to sleep, hours of wondering what had happened to the man behind the wheel of MARIN8. The crash had sounded bad—as though the car had rolled, possibly even hit a tree—but what if it wasn't enough? What if the driver was shaken but very much alive? What if the cold actually helped by slowing down bleeding or something like that?

Scenarios ran through her head. She had intended to stay in Thredbo for another night, go snowboarding again, act as if she was just another powder hound determined to make the most of a four-day weekend before reluctantly returning to Sydney.

But now she wanted to get out, get far away. Just in case he came back.

The first bus didn't leave until eight, but as most visitors would at least try to squeeze in a morning of skiing, Gabrielle thought she'd have no trouble getting a ticket. She would check out a day early—stay in her room until the last minute, feign a slight limp when she handed in her key, and head straight to the bus depot, dumping the spotlight on the way.

It was close to three a.m. by the time she settled on her plan and at last felt the heaviness in her limbs that preceded real sleep. She made sure the alarm on her clock was set, then allowed her body to rest.

The half-full bus ended up leaving at twelve minutes past eight. Gabrielle knew, because she had been checking her watch obsessively since the official departure time had come and gone. Ploughs had removed whatever snow was left after the rain, and the road was clear, the remains of last night's dump mounded to the sides and already grey and dirty.

She'd found a double seat for herself halfway down the bus, a place where she could monitor the other passengers, avoid the visibility of the front, and escape the scrutiny of the back, where—in her experience—passengers who were either hungover or still drinking tended to congregate. It would take over seven hours for the bus to get back to Sydney, and Gabrielle was prepared for the first long stretch to Canberra; she had put on a neck pillow and earbuds, spread out her belongings, and set up her iPad to do some work, mindful not to let it connect to the on-board Wi-Fi. As the bus left the village and headed out on the Alpine Way, she positioned herself diagonally across the two seats, back propped in the corner against the window, and cast her eyes over her fellow passengers. They all looked completely normal. Some were already dozing, others were finishing breakfast, and a large proportion were staring at phones or tablets. She knew she was being paranoid, but that didn't stop her from analysing every face. Nobody looked out of place or met her gaze.

It was only when she finally turned to the iPad on the fold-down tray in front of her that she realised it would be impossible to concentrate on work or anything else. At least, not until they reached Jindabyne. Not until they'd passed the spot.

Leaning her head against the cold glass of the window, she pushed her sunglasses more firmly onto her face. She hoped that to anyone who looked her way, it would seem as though she was either asleep or lost in thought. But her stomach was in knots, her mind racing. She was fully awake, oblivious to the passing landscape.

They had been on the road for twenty minutes and were roughly halfway between Thredbo and Jindabyne—about a kilometre from where she'd stood last night—when the bus began to slow, then gradually came to a stop. Around her, people stirred, craning to look through the windows or leaning into the aisle, trying to see what was going on. Gabrielle could see a line of cars up ahead, none of them moving. Her heart began to pound. She knew what the delay was, but what would she see?

"Snow on the road." A man sitting a few rows forward and across the aisle from Gabrielle made the authoritative pronouncement before he pulled his beanie down over his eyes, clearly content to sleep through the hold-up. Others were not so sanguine, already speculating about the potential length of the delay and what it might mean for their arrival in Canberra or Sydney.

And then the news rippled through the bus, travelling from the driver back through the rows until it reached Gabrielle.

An accident, people murmured. There was an accident up ahead.

The bus was still too far away for its occupants to see anything, but after a few more minutes it began inching forward in fits and starts. Gabrielle, along with most of the other passengers, kept her eyes glued to the road in front of them.

For what seemed like an eternity there was nothing but the cars ahead and the occasional vehicle travelling in the opposite direction. Then, as the bus rounded a curve, the vista opened up, and Gabrielle could see flashing lights: an ambulance, at least two police cars, and the pulsing orange glow that signified either a road crew or a tow truck. A police officer was directing traffic, holding up oncoming vehicles to allow a few at a time to ease across from their side of the road and crawl around the cluster of emergency units.

She wanted to look away, to wait until the bus was right at the scene before pressing her face to the glass. But she couldn't. They moved forward at an agonisingly slow pace, and with each metre her tension ratcheted up another notch. She could feel it in her gut, in the clench of her jaw, in the tightness around her wide eyes. At one point she tugged her hair free of its bun, unable to stand the pressure on her scalp.

Then they were there, only one vehicle in front of them. As the bus idled, Gabrielle could see the place where his RAV4 had left the road, just shy of the safety barrier guarding the corner. A tow truck was backed up towards that point, its winch straining, while at the edge of the short drop a police officer waved a hand over his head in a circular motion, encouraging the tow to keep going.

Gabrielle dragged her eyes across the rest of the assembled personnel, focusing in on the ambulance. The crew was standing around with no sign of urgency, no indication that a life hung in the balance. Their arms folded, they watched the edge where the tow's chain continued its inexorable return, quivering under the weight of its still-unseen burden.

Just as the bus began to move, the front of an SUV crested the top of the slope: a crumpled blue bonnet, a shattered headlight, a bumper hanging askew—and beneath that, a bent, mud-smeared numberplate.

MARIN8.

Gabrielle pressed a hand to the window, then pulled back. She didn't want anyone on the bus to notice her voyeuristic fascination with the scene, but then she realised everyone else was doing exactly the same thing. Some had their phones up, capturing the moment for social media. Even the bus driver was watching as the front wheels of the SUV rose slightly into the air, then—with what looked like a surprisingly gentle thump—the rest of the vehicle was dragged up over the edge.

The police officer's lassoing hand switched abruptly to a flat-palmed stop gesture, and the first responders stirred. A group of SES workers hurried forward, unfurling a blue tarp and holding it up to shield the badly damaged vehicle from the sight of passing motorists. At the same moment, the bus started to move again.

But not before Gabrielle had seen the cab of the RAV4, crushed to nothing on the passenger side. Not before she had seen the shattered windscreen, with a shocking smear of crimson forming a grotesque, Nike-like swoosh above the steering wheel. Not before she'd seen the bloodied, lolling head of the driver, the violence and anger forever erased from his sightless eyes.

It was him. She'd done it.

Gabrielle twisted in her seat, trying to take in as much detail as she could before the accident scene slipped from her view. A police officer turned to look at the line of slow-moving traffic, and his eyes locked on to hers. She felt her chest tighten. The eye contact lasted only a second before the bus accelerated. Gabrielle sat back in her seat with a thump. There was no way a policeman could connect a random bus passenger with a random accident. She pushed the thought aside.

It had been over a year since her sister's killer had died in Lightning Ridge, but that had been remote, anonymous. Suddenly it was real. The bloodied corpse in the car could just as easily have been him. She felt sick; the relief was almost too much to bear.

A wave of heat and nausea rushed over her, and she bent forward, head between her knees, swallowing hard. She couldn't afford to make a fuss. Lips pressed firmly together, she forced herself to take deep breaths, tasting bile in the back of her mouth.

A gentle hand on her back made Gabrielle jump. "Sorry," said a woman. "Are you okay? That was pretty full on. Do you need water? Or I have some chocolate."

Gabrielle turned her head slightly. A woman about her own age was crouched in the aisle, one hand holding the seat for balance, the other still a comforting presence between Gabrielle's shoulder blades.

"Thanks," the word came out as a croak. Gabrielle swallowed, tried again. "Thank you. I've never…" She gestured towards the window. "I have my water." Slowly, under the concerned gaze of the stranger, she sat up. She waited a moment, assessing the sensations in her body, then nodded. "I'll be fine."

"Are you sure? You looked like hell… Sorry, that came out wrong."

Gabrielle smiled. "I know what you mean. Thank you. You're very kind."

The woman shrugged and returned the smile as she stood up. "You'd do the same. And I'm right behind you if you need anything."

Once they were through Jindabyne, Gabrielle finally began to relax. The bus was travelling fast now, every kilometre consigning the violence to the past.

She was surprised to find that even after seeing the wrecked car and lifeless body, she felt almost no guilt. Now the shock had passed there was only relief and quiet triumph. At the same time, the rage and emptiness she had felt since her sister's murder were gone. Gabrielle didn't want to analyse her feelings too closely—not yet, anyway—but one thing was already apparent: at least in her case, Mia had been right. Revenge had achieved what no form of therapy had been able to do. For the first time since her sister's murder, Gabrielle could see a future that held a glimmer of promise. She would buy a new burner as soon as possible, call Mia, and tell her it was done. They were *all* done.

FORTY-EIGHT

Mia held the phone to her ear, listening to Gabrielle's carefully chosen words. She was sitting in the shadows of her living room, curled up on one end of the sofa and watching a muted television. The latest news bulletin once again showed images of a crushed RAV4 in a snowy landscape. Pixelation and the tarpaulins placed on scene by SES workers shielded viewers from the gory details, but Mia had no need for them.

"I'm so glad things worked out," Mia said. "I try to give each of my clients a toolkit to achieve success, but it's even more gratifying to me when a woman not only knows which tool to use but also exactly how to use it in a given situation."

With her free hand she reached for the remote control and powered off the TV. It plunged the room into darkness only relieved by the orange glow of a streetlight, leaking around the edges of her curtains. She let Gabrielle talk, contributing just the occasional "hmm" or "ahh" of encouragement.

Only when Gabrielle fell silent did Mia draw breath to speak again. "I mustn't keep you. But if at any point you need to talk..." She let the suggestion hang in the ether between them, then Gabrielle batted it away with an assurance that filled Mia with confidence.

The women exchanged warm but noncommittal farewells, and Mia waited to hear the triple beep of the call's termination before dropping the phone between her thigh and the arm of the sofa. She sat in the near-dark for several minutes, thinking about what her group of women had achieved and analysing her own feelings: satisfaction, and above all, pride. The women of The Pleiades had stepped up where the criminal justice system had failed, and they had triumphed. Even Brooke, with Gabrielle's continued support, had made it through the roughest of times. Mia's chin lifted as she thought of each woman, and then of her own sister.

Since Travis's death, Mia had been carrying a heavy burden of guilt and grief. She felt as though she'd let her sister down not once, but twice. First when Travis had ensnared her, then when Mia had watched her sister being led out of the courtroom, convicted of manslaughter.

Her sister's lawyers had been confident in their approach: a plea of self-defence—given the AVO, the documented history of domestic violence, the recording of the triple zero call—and surely the court couldn't fail to show mercy. But the court had failed.

Mia had felt as though the ground was crumbling beneath her feet as the prosecution relentlessly hammered home their arguments, bringing her sister to tears.

"Why didn't *you* just leave the house?"

"Why didn't *you* call the police?"

"He didn't bring the knife—*you* were the one with a weapon."

"*You* weren't injured in the altercation."

And to Mia's horror: "Your response to the situation was excessive. Once was maybe panic, *but why did you stab him twice?*" The verdict caused a sensation, and an appeal was immediately launched. Meanwhile, bail was refused and Mia's sister was jailed.

When Mia went to visit, she came across others like her sister—women who'd killed to stay alive; women who committed petty crimes to stay in prison, the only place they felt safe. It was then Mia discovered the shocking statistics: only about seven percent of women who killed violently abusive partners successfully argued self-defence. Of the rest, a few were unfit to stand trial, but forty-six percent received manslaughter convictions. And forty-three percent were found guilty of murder.

Mia had been highly visible in court, and she was vocal in the time that followed. It took a number of appeals, but finally the conviction was overturned. Her sister was released: grateful, alive, but profoundly, irrevocably scarred. When the burden of memory became too great, she chose to move to the country, to a place where she could regain her anonymity and begin rebuilding her shattered life.

With nothing to hold her, Mia also moved. A different city in a different state. Somewhere she could also be less visible, somewhere to begin her campaign for justice.

FORTY-NINE

Lew Bernstein leaned one hip against Ulbrick's desk, regarding her with exasperation. "I busted my gut on the Fitzpatrick investigation, and the coroner ruled the death an accident. The guy was a known drug user, he fell off a boat, end of story."

"I—"

"A pact to switch murders? There's a reason Hitchcock made that movie, and it's because shit like that is a Hollywood fantasy, not a bloody how-to guide. So why are you still hung up on this, Fi?"

Ulbrick shook her head. "I'm not. I know how thorough you are, and I know what the coroner said. Hell, he's probably right. And we agree Fitzpatrick was no loss to society! It just bothers me that Olivia Hammond was there, and then the man who pushed her sister, sorry, watched her sister fall off a cliff, dies in a car accident less than a year later."

"Yeah. But Ms. Hammond has an ironclad alibi: we know she was in Byron the week her sister's ex died, with plenty of CCTV to confirm. Plus, don't forget the guy at Thredbo had a bad reputation and a string of driving offences as long as my arm. It's like being surprised when members of a bikie gang get offed. If you live a certain way, sometimes shit happens."

"Still…"

"And you've read the accident report. I'll say it again. Accident. Report."

"Yeah."

"The car was checked. No mechanical issues. Single set of skid marks on the road. Driver error, poor conditions." Lew sighed.

Ulbrick stared at him for a moment, then shook her head. "Intellectually, I get what you're saying, but it still feels too neat."

"You know the saying about bad things happening to good people? Well, sometimes shit things happen to shitheads. You know it as well as I do. Let it go, Fi. I mean, it's not as if we don't have plenty of other cases to be getting on with."

"Quite the philosopher, aren't you, Lew?" Ulbrick flashed a smile and sighed. "Not much I can do about it anyway."

"That's what I'm saying." He straightened up with a groan.

"Getting old?"

"Nah, just been kicking too many heads." He ambled back to his own desk. "Don't mention that to the boys and girls in integrity, though."

"Perish the thought."

Ulbrick stared at the notes on the pad in front of her: attempts to connect accidents, to see crime where none existed. Maybe she needed a holiday.

She dropped the pad in her satchel under the desk. Lew was right—there were plenty of real crimes requiring her attention. A pile of paperwork sat in her in-tray, and she pulled the top file. Elbows on the desk, she began to read, one hand under her chin, the other scratching the back of her head.

Months passed. Despite what she'd said to Lew and the resolution she'd made that day, Ulbrick hadn't been able to let it go. She still had plenty of domestic violence perpetrators in her personal files; it was easy enough to keep tabs on some of them through social media, and she had search alerts set to flag their names if anything happened. Ulbrick also continued to stake out The Pleiades a couple of evenings each week, and she swung past any time she was in the area, although she wasn't sure what she was hoping to see. Common sense told her the connection between Olivia Hammond and the therapist was purely professional, but her instincts whispered of a more complex story. Still, the only information she had uncovered was that Mia DeVries was running a successful trauma counselling practice.

Again and again Ulbrick told herself she'd return her focus to preventing the perpetrators from causing further harm, but her time sitting in the car had taken on an oddly meditative quality. Watching The Pleiades had become a space in her week when she was neither pondering her active cases nor thinking about the men on her list.

Ulbrick had long been aware that her interest in tracking domestic violence perpetrators bordered on obsession, but the knowledge was tempered by the thought her actions might mean saving someone's life. If the courts were failing women, if her powers as a police officer were not enough, she would find other ways to try to keep women safe.

But when some of the men on her list began dying, Ulbrick had been forced to confront her own motives. Why did she care? DIY mishap, drowning, overdose, car crash…all unquestionably accidents, no sign of any third-party involvement, no crimes to investigate. Nothing to connect the deceased except the commonality of their histories and perhaps what could be considered their hubris, patterns of risk-taking behaviour that ultimately contributed to their respective downfalls. So if someone was killing the killers, did it matter? And if she found out the answer was yes, what then?

Ulbrick decided to worry about that later.

She kept updating her records, crosschecking information, and searching for another link in the chain. She found a fifth death purely by chance: a newspaper hit on one of the names, dated months before the Thredbo fatality. From just a few lines in an obituary column, the words "suddenly at home" and "unexpected" leapt out at her. A death at home was always referred to the coroner; as a member of the police force, Ulbrick could request the coroner's report. She agonised for days—with no clear reason to lodge the request, she risked serious departmental blowback if she was accused of improper access and misuse of information.

In the end she decided to cover her arse. She took it to her commanding officer, telling him as little as she could while arguing that given the dead man's history, a routine check was only due diligence.

The CO stared her down, jiggling a pen between the fingers of his right hand. "Got something you'd like to share?"

Ulbrick said no. After a bit more back-and-forth, the request was granted. She knew her CO thought she was up to something, and she left his office unsure if the intention behind his surprise acquiescence was to allow her to play a hunch, or to give her enough rope.

It turned out to be another exercise in futility. The man had died as a result of a severe anaphylactic reaction to nuts in a sports supplement—another accident.

Except...weren't people with life-threatening allergies usually hypervigilant to the point of paranoia? How could the man have failed to see the warning on the packet? Or had he tried some quack remedy and convinced himself he was cured? There were a dozen unremarkable ways it could have happened, but no matter how often Ulbrick told herself, *accidents, no evidence, no crimes,* the situation still made neurones in her grey matter jangle.

All Ulbrick could do was cross another name off her list of domestic violence perpetrators—then add it to her new list, the one of men with fatally bad luck. Those men were gone, but there were plenty of people still at risk of serious injury or death at the hands of an abusive partner. Ulbrick acknowledged her mental itch one last time, then put aside her disquiet to focus on the living.

FIFTY

Nearly a year had passed since the final job, and it seemed strange to Mia that even though the time had been marked by a sense of absence, she hadn't felt the despair that had previously accompanied absence in her life. This one had been borne of necessity, a known quantity, finite, purposeful—and now it was over. Mia knew Gabrielle and Brooke remained close, but otherwise there had been no contact between the women of The Pleiades. Now that could change, because in all those long months, there had been no questions, no inquiry, nothing.

Mia emailed each woman, inviting them to once again attend a Thursday night group. The session, her message explained, would be a chance for them to assess personal progress, champion successes, and discuss any issues that had arisen in the time since they had ceased therapy. Essentially, the equivalent of an oncology checkup after the excision of a cancer. Of course, the session was really a celebration, but Mia felt no need to explain that.

The women all knew the front door's entry code, and now Mia heard the distinct tap of high heels coming down the hall. Olivia entered the room and stopped. She looked around, taking it all in. "It looks exactly the same," she said.

"Those cushion covers are new," Mia replied with a smile.

Olivia laughed. She threw her bag onto a chair then hurried across to Mia, embracing her so tightly she could feel the woman's heart beating. "Thank you, darling Mia," she whispered before letting go.

Gabrielle arrived next, striding through the doorway, head high, loose limbed. She paused to wait for Brooke, still frail and thin but with a broad smile on her face. Gabrielle nodded a greeting to Mia, then linked her arm through Brooke's, drawing her in, settling her in the wingback chair and pulling another chair close. Within twenty minutes they were all there. Mia felt immensely proud as she looked at them: Katy and Olivia in the kitchenette organising drinks, Naomi showing pictures of her baby girl to Brooke and Gab, and Amy, the last to arrive, shedding her motorcycle leathers.

Amy turned from stowing her jacket in the corner and caught Mia's eye. "Did any of you notice that woman hanging about across the street? Short grey hair. Looks a bit like a younger Judi Dench. I thought she was staring at me, but it was possibly just the whole small-Asian-woman-on-a-motorcycle thing." Amy settled herself into the corner of the couch that had been hers in the past.

Katy, navigating the room with a tray laden with water-filled glasses, stopped where she was, a bemused look on her face. "I know just the type you mean," she said, handing Amy a glass. "Reminds me of Fiona Ulbrick, the detective who did a sterling job on my sister's case. Dogged; never gave up. She was ropeable when the court—"

"Wait a minute," Olivia cut in. Her face was white, and her eyes darted between Katy and Amy. "Did you say Detective Ulbrick? That's one of the detectives who questioned me—short grey hair, piercing eyes."

Naomi shook her head. "Can't be the same person. Don't get all bloody worked up just because it's the first time we've been together in ages. How many women with short grey hair are there in Sydney anyway?"

"Naomi's right. Don't panic." Mia's calm voice belied the adrenaline coursing through her system. She looked at the women one by one, meeting their eyes, trying to project confidence. She watched as Gabrielle put a strong arm around Brooke's shoulders, saw Olivia's anxiety in the way she fidgeted with the buttons on her shirt, and felt a thrill of pride when Amy's chin lifted. "It's been almost a year. If the police had anything on any of you—if there was one skerrick of evidence—they would have spoken to you by now. It wouldn't be one woman standing in the street, there'd be officers everywhere, banging on the door and shouting. We'd know." Mia took a deep breath and placed a hand on the back of her chair, waiting. Gradually, the tension in the room began to ease.

The doorbell rang, cutting through the air like a scream.

For a moment no one moved, then Mia stirred. "Talk among yourselves," she said. "And remember—no matter what anyone says or asks—this is a therapy group, nothing more, nothing less. That's all we have to prove." She stepped into the hall, closed the door, and went to find out who was waiting.

FIFTY-ONE

Ulbrick was on her way home from a domestic assault callout. Technically it would only become her case if the victim succumbed to her injuries, but Ulbrick had been put on notice about the assault and had wanted to visit the scene for herself. Two young children had been in the house when the vicious, sustained beating had taken place, and they were now in the care of a caseworker from the Department of Communities and Justice. The eldest, eight years old, had dialled triple zero when their father fled. Both children were scared and anxious about their mother, but from the few pieces of information they'd volunteered, they had seen all this before. The thought tore at Ulbrick's gut.

The man had not yet been apprehended and his victim was currently undergoing emergency surgery to stop internal haemorrhaging. Ulbrick had been advised that it was likely the spleen would have to be removed. Additional surgery—for the fractured cheekbone—wouldn't be possible until the patient was more stable.

Ulbrick was feeling wrung out. Her emotional barrier was a delicate thing, a fine line she walked between the detachment needed to do her job and the empathy she felt for victims and their families. Today, thinking about those children, imagining what they had witnessed before seeing their unconscious mother being stretchered into an ambulance, Ulbrick was almost overwhelmed with despair.

She was looking forward to getting home, decompressing, when without thinking she flipped on the indicator and slowed the car, ready for a turn. It took her a few seconds to disengage her mental autopilot, then she realised what had happened: habit had kicked in, and she was heading for The Pleiades.

"Bugger it," she muttered. "Not tonight."

But she was already in the turning lane, the arrow was green, and she felt she had no choice but to go. She sighed as she followed the familiar backstreets. Now that she was here, she thought she may as well stop briefly, just long enough to check her messages for an update on tonight's victim and the hunt for her abuser.

A couple of minutes later, Ulbrick cruised slowly past the familiar white door, swung the car in a U-turn and pulled into a parking spot. For a moment she sat there, engine idling, arguing with herself about the absurdity of her actions. *Accidents, no evidence, no crimes. Go home, Fiona,* she told herself.

A burst of laughter from the footpath broke into her thoughts. A group of people, rugged up against the winter chill, walked past her car and into a Thai restaurant. She hadn't considered dinner, wasn't actually hungry, but she needed to eat. Now she was here, she decided she may as well grab some takeaway. She killed the engine, unbuckled her seat belt, and reached into the passenger footwell for her bag. Snagging the strap, she sat up and automatically glanced across to The Pleiades—just in time to see a familiar blond woman disappearing through the front door: Olivia Hammond.

"What the fuck?" whispered Ulbrick.

Adrenaline coursed through her system. She told herself once again that the woman had every right to consult a therapist, and the fact that Mia DeVries had a similar past wasn't a crime. Scores of people were inspired by events in their personal lives to follow particular career paths.

Let it go, Fiona.

But now she needed to know, just to satisfy her curious itch. She wouldn't try to follow Hammond in, would refrain from ringing the doorbell. She would get her takeaway, eat it in the car, and then leave. If Hammond reappeared after forty-five minutes, Ulbrick would know she'd been attending a therapy session.

Ulbrick told herself she was only doing this to prove there was nothing untoward going on, like a reformed drinker venturing into a pub. *See? I don't have a problem.*

The return of old suspicions brought with them something new, an uncomfortable question from her subconscious. Maybe it was the juxtaposition of the crime scene she'd just left and the unexpected sight of Olivia Hammond, but suddenly Ulbrick found herself wondering: had her fixation on the accidents been driven by concern that someone was targeting men who had killed their partners, or had she been *cheering the killers on*?

She was about to open the car door when a woman walked past, heading up the street. Ulbrick registered red hair. As the woman prepared to cross the road, she turned her head, checking for traffic. Ulbrick saw her face, and the world seemed to tilt on its axis.

Fiona Ulbrick knew that face. Because she had spoken to that woman, sat with her, comforted her, and ultimately apologised to her again and again. It was Pip McKenzie's sister, Katy. As Ulbrick sat frozen in her car, mouth open in shock, Katy McKenzie let herself into The Pleiades.

"Holy shit!" Ulbrick shouted. She moved to snatch her mobile from its cradle, intending to call Lew Bernstein, then stopped, hand in midair. First she needed to know what this was—or rather, she needed to be sure.

She scrambled out of the car and hurried across the street. The door, when she tried the handle, was firmly locked. Her finger hovered over the doorbell, then she snatched her hand back, balling it into a fist. This was stupid. Why wouldn't the two women attend trauma counselling with a therapist like DeVries? It made perfect sense. If Ulbrick barged in, she'd only make an idiot of herself. She turned away.

Traffic had thinned out, and she meandered back across the road, so deep in thought that she walked past her car. She stopped just as a powerful motorbike roared into the street. It slowed, and the rider lowered his feet, easing the bike up onto the footpath just in front of The Pleiades.

"Huh," Ulbrick murmured and took a step back, pressing herself against the glass shopfront of a darkened boutique. She watched as the rider moved the bike onto its stand, dismounted, then pulled off his helmet.

Except it wasn't a he. It was an Asian woman.

Ulbrick's mind was spinning. Motorbike. Asian woman.

Where had…? "Shit."

When Hammond had left the marina after Fitzpatrick's party, she'd been collected by an Asian woman on a motorbike. Had Bernstein ever asked for the friend's name? Had Ulbrick? Even as she thought it, she knew the answer. She'd been through the file dozens of times, and the name wasn't there; it simply hadn't seemed relevant.

The woman turned to shake out her hair. From the other side of the street, Ulbrick raised her phone, splayed her fingers across the screen to zoom, and snapped a picture. The woman was staring at her now, so Ulbrick bent her head over the phone as she fiddled to get the image as clear as possible. She didn't recognise the woman, but there was a facial recognition website she'd used before. It only took a second to upload the image to EyeTrieve.

Moments later she was scrolling through hits. She clicked on one that looked promising and found herself on the website of a luxury hotel chain. In this corporate picture, the woman from across the road looked very different, but it was definitely her. When Ulbrick read the caption beneath the image, the name jumped out at her: Amy Li. The surname wasn't rare, but Ulbrick knew this wasn't a coincidence. Amy must be related to Sandra Li, another victim of an alleged domestic homicide—with another recently deceased perpetrator, the one allergic to peanuts.

Standing in the shadows, Ulbrick barely moved as her brain sifted details, rapidly clicking everything into place.

Accidents, no evidence, no crimes.

But her scalp was tingling.

She was halfway across the road when her phone pinged with an incoming message: today's victim was out of surgery but still critical, and the perpetrator had not yet been caught.

This time when she stood in front of The Pleiades, Detective Senior Sergeant Fiona Ulbrick pressed the doorbell.

FIFTY-TWO

A minute later Mia DeVries opened the door with one hand on the frame, blocking entry. Her half smile suggested polite inquiry, but Ulbrick could see the rigidity of DeVries's shoulders and the glint of authority in her blue eyes. "Can I help you?"

Ulbrick craned her neck, trying to see past the therapist. "My name is Fiona Ulbrick and—"

"I'm sorry, but office hours are over for today. Please call tomorrow if you'd like to make an appointment."

"I thought I saw someone I knew coming in here just a few minutes ago. Someone I haven't seen for a while."

"Possibly. I'm running a group session. And as I'm sure you'll appreciate, client confidentiality prevents me from confirming if your friend is here."

Ulbrick could tell from the woman's tone and the way she'd paused a fraction before saying the word *friend* that DeVries didn't believe her story.

"I'm sorry," Ulbrick said, trying another tack, "I didn't catch your name."

"That's because I didn't give it. You'll excuse me, but I work with a lot of domestic violence survivors, and I don't know who you are or why you're here. If you'd like to consult me professionally, please call back tomorrow and we can get properly acquainted, otherwise I have clients waiting for me." The therapist moved as though she was about to close the door.

"Wait!"

"Is there a problem?"

"Maybe."

DeVries let out an exasperated sigh. "I really don't have time for this, Ms.–?"

"It's not Ms. It's Detective."

"I apologise, Detective. But if this is a professional matter, you'll still need to come back during business hours."

"It is a professional matter, and it concerns you and the women who are here tonight."

The therapist didn't speak. She still had a hand on the doorframe, and now she twisted her arm, staring pointedly at her wristwatch.

"A number of men are dead—all accidents, it seems."

"How tragic."

"Shall I give you their names?"

"They'd mean nothing to me."

"Oh, I think they would. Because each one of those men was guilty of domestic violence, and each one of those men killed his partner."

"There are a lot of violent men in the world."

"Ah, but here's where it gets really interesting! It turns out their victims were all sisters of women who are here tonight."

DeVries nodded. "In that case, you'd better give me the names so I can break the news. Thank you for drawing this to my attention. It doesn't change the past, but it may bring some consolation to know those men won't be able to harm anyone else."

"Bit of a coincidence that all the sisters are here." Ulbrick returned the woman's cool, unblinking gaze.

DeVries shrugged. "Hardly. I specialise in helping people with that sort of trauma."

"Yes, you do, don't you? And your methods are *highly* specialised. What do you call it? Jungian? Hitchcockian?"

"What is it you're trying to say, Detective?" The therapist arched an eyebrow.

"Have you ever seen *Strangers on a Train*? The Hitchcock movie where two people exchange murders?"

"Actually, my favourite is *The Trouble with Harry,* the one where everybody thought the loathsome man had been murdered, but he died of natural causes and there was no foul play involved," DeVries said lightly.

"I'd forgotten about that one."

"Many people do."

Ulbrick stared, and DeVries stared back.

The therapist gave an exaggerated sigh. "Look, Detective, I don't have time to stand outside discussing classic cinema."

"In that case, could I come in?"

"I have a room full of vulnerable women here."

Ulbrick scratched the back of her head. Unbidden, an image leapt into her mind of today's crime scene. She saw again, filtered through the ceaseless red-and-blue flicker of emergency lights, the overturned furniture, the holes punched in the walls, and the cowering children. She thought of a woman in hospital, hovering on the brink. And she thought of her job. "And I have a city full of them."

DeVries shifted, and for a moment, Ulbrick thought she was going to have the door slammed in her face. But the therapist was studying her, watching her expression, and her eyes narrowed slightly at whatever it was she had just seen.

"In that case..."

DeVries opened the door wide.

READING GROUP GUIDE

1. What is your favorite murder, and why? Which sister does it best?

2. Should Ulbrick have confided more in Lew? If she did, what do you think his response would be?

3. Do you think the women are motivated by a desire for justice, the belief that they are protecting other women, revenge, or all three? What matters most?

4. What do you think about Mia's cure for grief and violence? And what does that say about justice?

5. How does the system still fail victims of domestic violence?

6. How far would you go to protect or avenge a loved one?

7. Do you think Mia returns to normal work, or does she recruit a new group of women?

8. In fiction and film, the idea of a man avenging the deaths of loved ones is nothing new and even considered a natural response. Is it different for women? Why?

9. Why does Mia let Ulbrick in? Is she planning to brazen it out and prove there's nothing to hide, or does she have an ulterior motive?

10. What do you think Ulbrick should do?

ACKNOWLEDGMENTS

The statistics relating to the conviction of women who kill abusive domestic partners is taken from "Women Who Kill: how the state criminalises women we might otherwise be burying," a research report coordinated and written by Sophie Howes, released in February 2021 by the Centre for Women's Justice, UK.

There are a number of people who have been instrumental in bringing this book to life. My heartfelt thanks to: Grace Heifetz, agent extraordinaire; Anna Valdinger, who threw herself into the project and only gave me a tiny bit of concerned side-eye as I outlined the number of ways I could kill people (theoretically, of course); Rachel Cramp, my brilliant editor at HarperCollins who pulled me back into line when I most needed it; Kate Goldsworthy, for so delicately pointing out the bits where my brain had stalled; and Pam Dunne, for such diligent proofreading.

Special thanks also to R. W. R. McDonald, my writing BFF, for reading early drafts, enthusing about my crazy ideas, and listening to me grumble (a lot).

Finally, Mum. There aren't enough words, so simply, thank you.

ABOUT THE AUTHOR

© Rebecca Taylor Photography

Katherine Kovacic is the award-winning author of many short stories and books, including the Alex Clayton Art Mysteries and the TV-to-page adaptation of *Ms Fisher's Modern Murder Mysteries*.

In 2023, *Kill Yours, Kill Mine* was shortlisted for an Australian Crime Writers Award for Best Crime Fiction under its original title, *Seven Sisters*.

Katherine and her hounds live in Melbourne, Australia. You can follow her on Instagram or visit katherinekovacic.com.